THE
GREEN AGE
of
ASHER
WITHEROW

THE
GREEN AGE
of
ASHER
WITHEROW

M. Allen Cunningham

UNBRIDLED
BOOKS

Excerpt from the *Contra Costa Gazette* of 1880, courtesy of Contra Costa Central Library, Pleasant Hill, CA.

The Principal Upanisads. Copyright © 1994 by S. Radhakrishnan. Reprinted by permission of HarperCollins Publishers Ltd. Copyright in the customized version vests in Unbridled Books.

Passage on p. 242 quoted from *The Saviors of God; Spiritual Exercises* by Nikos Kazantzakis, translated by Kimon Friar. Copyright © 1960 by Simon & Schuster.

UNBRIDLED BOOKS,
Denver, Colorado

Copyright 2004 M. Allen Cunningham

Library of Congress Cataloging-in-Publication Data

Cunningham, M. Allen.
The green age of Asher Witherow / M. Allen Cunningham.
p. cm.
ISBN 1-932961-00-3
1. Coal mines and mining—Fiction. 2. California—Fiction.
I. Title.
PS3603.U667G74 2004
813'.6—DC22   2004013507

1   3   5   7   9   10   8   6   4   2

Book Design by SH · CV

For Katie, every day a miracle

The force that through the green fuse drives the flower
Drives my green age; that blasts the roots of trees
Is my destroyer.
And I am dumb to tell the crooked rose
My youth is bent by the same wintry fever.

—DYLAN THOMAS

The supply seems to be inexhaustible. From the figures in my posses-
sion I have reasons to believe that over 2,250,000 tons of coal have
been shipped to the market from the Diablo mines; and considerably
more than half of that immense amount was shipped from the Black
Diamond mines at Nortonville. Where is the mine in the State that
can show a better record in regard to the past, or as bright a prospect
for the future?

—LETTER FROM NORTONVILLE,
CONTRA COSTA GAZETTE, JUNE 28, 1880

On a boggy day in 1806 a detachment of Spanish soldiers apprehended a band of Bay Miwok Indians in a marsh at the foot of a solitary California mountain. Commanded to redeliver the natives to the stern grace of the mission they'd fled, the Spaniards detained them in a nearby thicket as night fell. A dun darkness came on, browning out the stars. The night grew quiet but for the din of crickets. Then at some deep and slippery hour the Miwoks vanished, turned to vapor and floated away in the mist, dematerialized as demons were known to do. The next morning the soldiers woke in a dawn steam thick enough to blank the big mountain from sight. They found themselves bereft of their errant mission-folk and turned round on their heels till their heads swam. Bedeviled as they were, they forswore the place Monte del Diablo, Thicket of the Devil, and for years the name lingered like a fog over that marsh. When at length the English-speaking settlers arrived, the Spanish Monte was taken for Mountain and was believed to refer to the twin-shouldered mass looming nearby. So the mountain became Mount Diablo, made to bear an unholy namesake.

EARTH

IT IS A TUESDAY IN THE EARLY SPRING OF 1950 AS I WRITE THIS. I AM no longer young, to say the least, and these recollections have come whistling through my ancient brain like wind-wraiths. Even these early years, though I thought I'd get them down without much trouble, perturb me in some faint manner. Might it be that even back then we should have caught the malignant whiff in that valley air? But if so, how? Ah, I mustn't get started on that—that's idle thinking. There's no rearranging things now. Though the slightest recollection stirs up a terrific haunting, I know one can't expect much of memory, whose utility is limited. In my old hands I turn the pages of a book where a Greek poet writes that every day on this earth begins and ends in the mind, the dawn occurring on one side of your head, dusk on the other. And I think it must be a good thing that I've read this only toward the end of my life, for how lost it might have made me in my years of learning.

My earliest Nortonville memory is father's smell as he entered the house at night, an odor like wet burlap and dead animal. I remember the grind of his washing barrel as it scudded across our floor: wood against wood; his naked perch on the barrel's rim, black above his neckline, white beneath, scooping water from between his knees; the plashing as mother washed his back.

I remember the growl of the breaker. I woke each morning to its wheel-and-shaft clamor, like a terrible grinding of teeth. I remember the gray smell as mother shoveled the coal in our stove. And I remember the culm banks, steaming in the June sun, slothing from here to there. They rose on the edge of town like charred monuments: black lopsided pyramids. Mother loved the shimmer-sound those banks made when they moved. She said it reminded her of the beaches in Wales, the seawater ebbing back from the rocky shore. She closed her eyes sometimes and listened to it, muted as it was beyond the squawk of chickens.

Early one April morning, 1863, father had awakened to find mother standing at the window in her peach chemise, shuddering with a horror she couldn't name. He coaxed her back to bed and bore her convulsions the whole night through. The next evening when he returned from the works he found her seated on the stoop. She was pawing her belly and weeping tearlessly but with abandon. Believing it to be a spiritual ailment, he read to her from the letters of the Apostle: *"But though our outward man perish, yet the inward man is renewed day by day,"* and she strained to find comfort in the old cadences. But her melancholy was incurable and the paranoiac fits bulged in time with her growing belly. She had believed herself fruitless. The new roundness of her stomach could barely convince her that this *haunting,* as she called it, was maternal and not demonic. For the next seven months mother quavered, soothed only by readings from the New Testament. Her torment would not fully subside till I was delivered from her womb.

Under the shadow of Mount Diablo, with a terrible warble which filled the little company house, Abicca Witherow squeezed me into the world. The labor began one indigo morning when she spasmed awake in tears. Then she struggled an entire day and night, clear to the following afternoon. The midwife, Sarah Norton, darkened my parents' door as a bulk of shadow. She had the stout hands and mannish arms of one who pried at wombs for hours on end, and wore a string slung crosswise on her breast, dangling with pouches of fresh and dried herbs. Tisanes, roborants, analeptics, caustics, tonics, and salves—all of old-world or Indian concoction. She put her mouth to mother's twitching ear.

"First thing is to calm those nerves, dearie." She gave four pouches to father. "Each in a separate pot. Boiled." And as he dashed out, she stood smiling down upon her tremulous patient. "We're bursting, aren't we, dearie? The little thing's eager for air. Here's a comfort for you."

Her black hair stranded downward as she bent and slipped hooks from eyes, spread open the belly of her own blouse, bunched the undershirt clear. She moved into the light and showed mother the long blue scar running from her navel to the dark pubic swatch.

"And still the child was lost," she said. "But yours won't be anything as bad as that. Yours wants to come, so don't shudder, sweet."

Mother's head thrashed on the damp pillow. Years later she told me: "I just had to give myself up to her, shadowy though she was. And she delivered me well, but I was happy to have her gone."

Finally at dusk I was born. Father—who knelt by the bed with his left hand cracking in mother's grasp till the knuckles nearly broke, and with his right hand wiping her nose, which bled as eagerly as her womb—he said the room seemed to tremble at my coming. But both my parents assured me that once I kicked free of the belly I glowed with a healthy infant-light which healed the nine-month malaise.

They named me Asher. I never learned why, but now I think it a good name for someone born in the night amid culm banks and black-water drainage bogs.

It means much that Sarah Norton delivered me. With her callused pagan hands, she gripped my knuckly arms, yanked me from blue amniotic to gray November night, lifted me wailing, slashed my cord, swaddled me, and imparted to me something unreckonable. I still do not understand it fully, but I've always listened to its reverberations. They say the woman delivered six hundred infants in her lifetime, and in a quiet ritual of hers she planted a cottonwood tree for every one of those babies. Dreaded apothecary of secret medicine, maven of birthing and its converse—even now I often have visions of her: hunched in hillside greenery, breaking up the moist earth to set my own cottonwood seeds in place, then patting the soil firm with extra care.

A S SOON AS I WAS OLD ENOUGH TO WALK AND TALK, MOTHER SENT ME out by morning to climb the banks and pick the shards of coal from the slate and shale. I would sometimes get up with father and go with him and the men just as far as the banks, then watch them shamble on toward the works, dark shapes before the dawn. The squeak and thud of boots, the rattle of lamps, the glassy shake of the mule riggings, voices murmuring in Welsh. The men spoke of adits and pillars and collars and goaf, talked of the fire-boss, who seemed to me a kind of magician. Boys not much older than I tromped along the road with them, their mouths thick with tobacco. One day I would walk to the pits myself. Patience was hard. I could barely muster disinterest in the face of marvelous words like *fire-boss*.

The culm banks were known to shift without warning. A child

picking coal always hazarded stumbling into some disguised cavity, unsettling the whole mound, and ending up entombed under the chunks of slag, all air squeezed off overhead. The company had issued plenty of warnings to this effect—tales of boys gobbled up in the dumps for their thievery, as if by the unforgiving mouth of justice. But always leery of the company's tight-fistedness, mother saw straight through the moralistic pretext of such warnings and relished the subversion of sending me out with an empty pail.

So I scurried up the jagged banks and combed the lumped tops for the chunks with the dull sheen. Those were the coal. The slag gave rise to a blackish dust that caked my shins and fogged my mouth. Shadowy taste. From atop the banks I could see over most of the buildings along Main Street, gossamered with dark smoke. And almost parallel to Main Street: the railroad, car after car jittering up and down its incline.

Now and then I ducked over the backside as a brakeman rode by, or I lay flat on the rubble when a watchman patrolled below. Spread there with my chin chafing on slate, I watched the sun splinter atop the hills and pour its first light into our valley.

Father, for the trouble these culm pickings posed him should the bosses learn of them, opposed them with a stance of high ethics. But mother knew her husband feared the company, and worse— was willing to bow to its stinginess. She sent me out despite him. Like Elidyr of the Welsh legend, who stole the gold from the Little Folk, I only sought to do my mother's bidding.

In all my mornings at the dark banks I was collared only half a dozen times, but always by the same captor: an irascible watchman named Boggs. The mottled Irishman was arrogantly alert at his post. I believe it delighted him in some sadistic way to ensnare me and other coal pickers—and he had a brutal grip. "Witherow!" he would bellow. And if he had not yet locked my eyes, I would try to

9

creep down the back of the bank and come running out the side opposite him. But flight was futile, for not long after I'd reached home and ditched what little coal I'd found, Boggs would come swaggering up to our stoop. Finding mother at work in the yard, he would proclaim in his curious official manner: "Abicca Witherow, your young Asher has pilfered sellable goods from the Black Diamond Company, the return of which I herewith demand."

Then the charade would begin, variations on a scene familiar enough to seem scripted.

"Mr. Boggs," mother might say, smoothing out her apron or pressing a forearm to her brow—tired gestures intended to show that the watchman was interrupting something important, "my husband, as you well know, is a miner in one of your shafts. He tells me the Black Diamond Coal Company conducts its business with the utmost care. He's right in this, isn't he? And he tells me that when the cars are lifted from the shaft their coal is sifted and sorted to determine waste as waste and goods as goods. That's what that god-awful breaker house is for, isn't it? Now, as long as the company knows waste for waste well enough to litter our town with big black dumps of it, then we folks who have to live next to the ugliness should be entitled to use what the company cannot."

"But Mrs. Witherow, your son has trespassed—"

"And as far as I can tell, Mr. Boggs, you're trespassing now: coming uninvited onto my property to point your finger at my son."

However many times Boggs came up against it, mother's iron will never failed to stun him. And though in all legality our house and the land it stood on was the company's property, not ours, invariably he'd be too rattled to recall this fact, let alone address it.

"Now if you'll let pass Asher's infraction," mother would say, "I'll let pass yours, so long as you make haste at once."

And away along the railroad Boggs would go, as soon as he'd made an awkward bow.

After such a scene, word of mother's brusqueness would travel all along the circuit of company employees. From the mouth of Boggs it would pass down to the floor of the shaft within the afternoon, finally reaching father's ears in mutated form. The events having swollen to the level of hyperbole, he would come home at night ready to admonish her.

The other workmen chided father for his wife's distemper. He confessed his predicament to mother, begged her to allay her eccentricity a little. To this she always listened quietly, her jaw locked, and father never knew whether she meant to take his dilemma to heart.

David Witherow was a young man when he came to Nortonville. Narrow-chested and wiry, he worked with a gritted nerve at the longest and deepest of rooms in the vein. He wore a mustache and long beard and spoke in a hushed, bearded voice, peering through eyes the jade hue of polished quartz. His hands were wide and tough as paws, the skin flecked black on the fingers and wrists, tiny flakes of coal spotting the knuckles. Coal followed the sweat furrows in his brow too, streaking beneath the skin in faint lines like letter paper. Beside mother he cut the figure of an unlikely mate. She was a thin woman, but big-boned and hardy. She wore by habit a vague scowl which spread clear in the most luminous smile when he spoke kindly to her.

My parents had come from Monmouthshire, Wales, to the Diablo hills with all the high ideals of people in exodus. Jolting in the westbound stage from Stockton, they watched the mountain swell upon the horizon—the sun cresting the peaks like a burning bush. In the Carbondale valley they found a ragtag township. A new railroad snaked through high grasses, the tracks trestling up to a humpbacked bunker house. A few wood-and-nail structures leaned along the main street amongst a few fine brick ones. Noah Norton's house towered on a hillside beyond the smokestack, and a number of miners' cottages dotted the edges of the valley.

Mr. Norton himself secured my parents a room in George Scammon's lodging house, and the next morning father went to work as a haulier on the Mount Hope Slope. Within the year, as the mines proved stalwart and Nortonville's population flourished, hammers set to ringing on the skeleton of the new Exchange Hotel. Father moved to the Black Diamond shaft to work laborer on the Clark Vein. Six months later he made miner there. This was his job when I was born. By that time he and mother had befriended a number of other Welsh. They attended weekly Bible readings in a neighbor's house and father frequented the small saloon, to the protests of his wife.

They secured a wooden company house, a sturdy place with a broad front stoop and six narrow windows. It stood at the northern end of the valley, at the head of Main Street and below School House Hill. Fifty feet east of the front door, the Black Diamond Railroad ran north through the cleavage of two camelback hills to slither six miles down to New York Slough. Otherwise, the house was surrounded by a clutch of company homes, which all stood mutely amid lisping grasses. A wide fur of chaparral spread up the hills on the west, and down among the shops and meeting houses stood a few eucalyptus trees.

MEMORY IS A NIGHT LANDSCAPE. SHADOWS OF HILLS AGAINST SHAdow of sky. I walk into myself when I travel back through my memory, and I find a dark world, streaked with intermittent lamplight. Yet some deep place within me, some smooth-worn reservoir, contains all the unbroken images of my past—people and moments long gone. Somewhere in the body we carry even the humblest moment we've lived. So maybe I can behold the intuitions that were already flitting through that valley eighty years ago, but I can't blame any of us for failing to notice them. I was a little boy, not the wizened and brittle-boned thing I am now, sitting here enjoying the privilege of remembrance and poised to damn myself for all I couldn't have known. The price of memory is a certain profound impotence. One can do nothing but observe, collect, revise this impression and then that one, and enjoy the pure futility of illumination.

Slinking into focus now is the Diablo of my youth. You could see it from the ridge just above Nortonville. As a boy I went up there to find a great canyon gashed between the peaks, as though some blast had cored the mountain. The twin summits gazed across the hollowness at each other, awaiting a massive earth-lunge that might one day unite them again.

In those days I was a mess of legend, and that Diablo was like my Sinai. I dreamt of William Israel, gangly farmer who hunched at a wound of earth on a day in '59, a stained hat pushed back on his head, his fingers poking at the black ground. Israel's pastures six miles south, where coal first showed itself, seemed to me as distant and wondrous as the Egyptian desert. I thought Mr. Israel the heroic figure from the Book of Exodus which mother read to me: *"And there Israel camped before the mount."* I dreamt of Francis Somers and Cruikshank unearthing the great Black Diamond Vein. I saw the black deposit worked with sack and shovel, the paltry yield packed out load by load on the backs of mules. These early men labored away at something momentous, like the minions who hauled those great stones to the pyramids. And Noah Norton was the new pharaoh in these daydreams of mine. Not long after his arrival he had linked the meager operation to shareholders in Martinez fifteen miles west. In '61 he raised his hands and decreed that railroad tracks be laid to the docks on the slough, a move that roused the works to a monumental standing, so that by the time I was born our company steamers had sewn the waters countless times to Stockton, San Francisco, and Sacramento.

In my boyhood the Welsh folk were entranced by all sorts of quasi-historic and fairy tale beliefs. And so in addition to Bible stories and the ancient yarns of the old country, mother and father taught me all about the Welsh Prince Madoc and his heroic escapades. Most impressive was his discovery of America in the twelfth century. I learned of our fierce brethren, the Welsh-speaking Padouca Indians, natives of our region whom we'd surely encounter one day. I learned of the adventurer John Evans, the Welsh Methodist minister who prefigured Lewis and Clark in his exploration of the northern Missouri while searching for the ancestors of Madoc.

Though fictitious, all these legends were harmless—especially harmless when compared with that larger fiction by which I was nursed for my first twenty years: that our town was an empire in its own and would thrive till time ran off its spool.

BLOOD

BEING AS OLD AS I AM NOW AND SITTING AT THIS DESK ON THIS spring morning, thinking back through all the trouble and the mystery—it's a bit like trying to find something precious in a cluttered drawer, something I would give to my kin when I am gone. It would be simple to stop the search. But somehow, someplace, all the debris from the earliest years has accreted and begun to make a kind of sense. If I'm now powerless to change or correct, at least I'm able to comprehend. True, I'm walking in the dark, but beneath my blind feet there's a clear path, and often enough paths go places—even when it's late and hard to see.

Before me on the desk, in a hot glint of window light, is the dancing Hindu figure of Shiva, god of destruction and death. Fashioned of heavy bronze, he is ringed in flame, with wild hair fanned out, a bare skull ensconced upon his brow, his four spidery arms akimbo. He holds in this hand a drum, in that hand a ball of fire, one foot lifted in his apocalyptic dance. He is worshipped, even for all his wrath. Maybe I ought to start here, because this I can understand: the adulation of death, the plain reckoning with impermanence. For on a frosted morning when I was five years old, watching a small coffin slide roughly into its raw grave, a number of blue flowers at my feet opened their blossoms in silence.

Nortonville's Protestant cemetery stood on Rose Hill, a mile over the eastern rise, on that tilting shelf of earth above Somersville. The folks of the town went up there to crowd about open graves and feed the hungry earth her lot of bodies. It was a frequent ritual. We climbed the steep Somersville Road with a casket borne before us on the shoulders of our men. From the high windy graveyard, the neighboring town was just a smatter of slant-roofed buildings squatting below. On a frigid January morning in 1869 we buried Edward Leam—nine years old.

Mother gripped my right hand and father my left as we trudged through seething mud toward the crest of the hill.

"Where's Edward gone to?" I asked, squinting at the sting of my sinuses. Edward walked to the works every day with father and the men. He'd once given me a thumb's worth from his tobacco pouch.

"He's gone away, Ash," said father.

Looking up, I saw the underside of his beard, the white throat afuzz with dark whiskers. "But *where's* he gone, father?"

Mother squeezed my hand. "To heaven, Asher."

"How's a boy get to heaven?"

"He works good and hard," mother said. "Enough questions."

"Wait," said father, halting.

Mother took two steps more till my body twisted between them, my arms flung wide. She stopped and turned to father, who was squinting down upon me.

"He ought to know, Abicca," he said.

"David—"

"Hush. I can't let him wonder." Father stood before me, enormous against the gray sky. His jaw looked heavy and thick. He said nothing as some townsfolk lumbered by us up the hill. His breath plumed white, paisleys somersaulting from his face, vanishing. At last he spoke low. "Edward was a breaker boy," he said. "He climbed up to the breaker's gears because he wanted to clog em. The boys do it now and then to choke the machine a while. But the grinders took his scrap of wood and his arm too and pulled him in."

"Pulled him in?"

"Crushed him." Father laid a hand at my cap. "A boy's bones are like driftwood to a machine of that size."

"David," said mother, "please."

That morning I stood on Rose Hill, encompassed by a solemn party of townsfolk, and felt death draw close quietly, like a cat at my legs. I watched nine blue flowers unfurl just above the icy grass, watched the frozen blades themselves grow warm, a deep green circle expanding about my feet.

No one seemed to notice it but me. The several adults around me stared grayly at their knees and mouthed silent prayers for the dead. A few children dawdled among the headstones, lunging and clutching at their own fuming breath.

So here is death, I thought. *It's a place where we stand.* And I thought I must have died. But all those folk about me—they hadn't died yet themselves. The grass remained frosted at their feet. I didn't understand that. But I had died, that was clear.

Reverend Parry stood at the head of the grave, bundled to his chin in a frock coat, his hat squashed under one arm. His baldpate steamed as he read aloud from his little book. He spoke to the infinite charity of the Lord's embrace. At Parry's side stood his protégé of the time. A seminary scholar of about seventeen, he had a peaked look like a revenant: dark hair and pale eyes and a face of angular, jittering features. He bowed his head, his two sinewy hands folded before him. After a moment Parry turned and passed his small book to the apprentice, whispered something near his ear, and drew back.

The apprentice stepped to the lip of the grave. He knelt and scooped up a handful of dirt and sprinkled the coffin. Then he smiled broadly. "Whether we live, we live unto the Lord, and whether we die, we die unto the Lord: whether we live therefore, or die, we are the Lord's."

After the funeral the mourners mingled a few minutes, then dispersed and started drifting over the ridge toward Nortonville. I stayed with father and some other men who had volunteered to fill the grave, wandering among the white headstones while they set to work. Mother walked back to town with a number of women.

The sun had not yet appeared. The sky was a slate of cloud above our hills. I went up to the ridge-top and looked down over Nortonville. Houses breathed in that darkness below, thin chimneys respiring smoke. A few silhouettes of persons moved in the streets. The works stood very still.

From the Somersville valley at my back, a freezing wind barreled past me down the hill. Then a dark figure moved through the headstones, opened and shut the cemetery gate, and I saw Reverend Parry's apprentice coming up the road. He had both his hands driven deep in the pockets of his frock coat. His head was down, face obscured under his derbyshire hat, and he seemed to move cautiously, as if the blighting wind at his back threatened to pick him up and fling him forward over the ridge. Then he stood beside me.

"You're young Witherow, aren't you?" he said. "I've heard a great deal about your mother. She's a woman of much prayer, they say. A good woman—as your father's a good man." He glanced back to the grave, where father stood shoveling dirt over Edward Leam, then turned again to our view of the village. A ribbon of white breath spilled from his nose. "Did you know young Leam?"

I nodded silently.

"Does his death trouble you?"

I shook my head.

"I didn't think so. It didn't seem to." He withdrew his pasty hands from his coat and rubbed them briskly. "You're a strong lad, aren't you? What do you make of this ashes to ashes business?"

I kept silent, shrugged a little. He bore my reticence without any comment of his own, standing a long moment by my side, as though hesitant to leave me unattended on the ridge. We listened to the scrape and slap of the men's shovels, the soft thump of thrown dirt. He laid his light hand on my shoulder and said: "Do you know why we bury our dead? Because they disappear from us that way. It's in keeping with the Apostle's teaching: *We look not at the things which are seen, but at the things which are not seen: for the things which are seen are temporal, but the things which are not seen are eternal.*" His pallid eyes coursed my face. Then he started down the hill. "Peace to you, young Witherow."

I first learned the apprentice's name that evening at supper, when father questioned me.

"What did Josiah Lyte have to say to you this morning, Asher?"

Mother paused from her coleslaw. "The apprentice? He spoke to you?"

"Yes," said father, "they talked whilst I filled the grave."

"He asked me if I knew Edward Leam," I said.

Mother shot a glance at father, stared a minute at the fork in her hand as if remembering its use, then prodded the slaw about her plate. Father touched his beard.

"He said why we bury our dead," I told them. "He said something the Apostle said."

Mother's fork fell still again. She and father seemed to take up a
silent dispute. Father pushed his plate away. "There's little to fear
in a man of God, Abicca."

"A *boy* of God, more like. He's unordained yet, and talking with
a lad of five about death and the grave."

Father waved his hand. "I think he meant well. He just doesn't
know better. He's just unsure—still an apprentice and all."

"I don't want *unsure* scripture spoken to our boy. That Josiah
Lyte smiled this morning where he should not have done."

"Yes," said father. For a moment he worked his mouth glumly,
as though mulling the image of that smile between his teeth, tasting it. "Well, who knows how God's grace can fall on a man?"

"But to smile over the very grave? Who smiles over a grave,
David?"

Father lifted his palms, the skin still splotched in places where
the day's filth would not come off. "I don't know."

"Mr. Lyte told me you're a woman of prayer," I said to mother,
hoping to please her.

She gazed blankly at me, then cast another look at father as she
rose. She cleared our plates in silence.

{ 2 }

LATE EVERY AUTUMN THE RAINS CAME AND CAST A RICH BLUSH OF green over our dry hills. From then until early summer the whole earth softened and breathed as a body softens and breathes at a welcome touch. In these green days you could climb the steep Cumberland Rise to the plateau west of town and find the mountain restored to its truest appearance. Humped emerald against the sky, its hollows lay daubed in shadow, and at its foot the land flowed lush to the coast. The country spoke more vividly in these green months, like a voice cured of its long catarrh. The land seemed caught in fresh remembrance of how things had been in the beginning, in the age when mastodons plodded its swamps, long before the Spanish came with their yellow grass. The land bodied forth its remembrance.

In this season the earth felt more a home than ever the rest of the year. I plunged headlong into the autumn, sank to my ankles in mud, played in shoulder-high grasses. The country was already green when in December 1870, at barely seven years old, I went happily to work in the Black Diamond breaker.

That place was a hive of boys inside. We sat on slats astride chutes and hunched over a dark current of coal and slag, snatching at it with bleeding hands. Dust stirred thick up to the rafters and the rock in the machine's teeth screamed calamitously, like a dozen trains smashing into each other at full bore. The clamor blurred our vision and made us brace our limbs stiff. Our ears numbed, but still that jelly of sound went on tensing each wire and plank in our bodies. We bound our mouths with kerchiefs to screen the palpable air. We crammed our cheeks with tobacco to keep the dust out of our throats.

Somehow the monstrous roar was worsened by the lack of light. The few high windows stood filmed with dust, and up there upon the thick beams that stabled the roof only a choked glimmer fell. We would watch that minuscule light sometimes, in the seconds between tumbling loads of rock, when the clouds thinned and began to part in the air. Then the squeal and crash of rock again and the rubble pouring down between our legs and the big cloud dimming everything.

I took to my work in the breaker. The haze in which I bent my head for hours, the black pollen of the earth which coated me so profusely that I stood every hour to slough off its weight: there was something in all of it to which I felt akin.

Within weeks I'd forged a strong camaraderie with most of the boys, but with one particular fellow the sincerity of friendship ran deeper from the beginning.

Not long before I started, the watchman Boggs had become breaker-foreman. Regularly—if not hourly—I'd feel the sting of his quirt at my kidneys, his rod would whack my knuckles, or he'd slap one of my insensible ears with a brawny palm. In a steer-like voice he'd bellow: "No idle hands!" or: "Head down, hard at work!" or: "Back is straight, miss the slate!"

One day as the black rubble poured down between my knees, a stream of slate skittered in from the next chute. I glanced over to find the boy next to me sitting straight on his plank. He arched his back and stretched his arms above his head in flamboyant languor, his slight knees jutting outward. He was a little fellow, with lean pocketed cheeks and eyes ringed in shadow like a badger. His kerchief hung loose about his throat, crumpled under a white mouth that flashed a coy smile my way. He kicked up another spray of slag, and the chunks of slate went bounding into the troughs around him. Then that naked smile vanished as the boss's rod crashed down across his shoulders. He coiled over and took another thump at the small of his back. Even with the rumble of rock I heard him wheeze. Then Boggs's phlegmatic growl: "Back is straight, miss the slate!"

The boy's hands shot to work again and Boggs stepped back. I kept at my labor, resisting the impulse to turn my head. In my periphery I saw the foreman standing watch just behind us. For a long moment he was motionless, then finally he swiveled to pace to the end of the row, and I stole a glimpse at my broken neighbor.

The boy shot back an impish look. His grimy cheeks were veined pale with tears, but his smile flashed again. I thought I saw him wink, and then he was glancing down the row at Boggs. He stood fast with a big rock in his grip and flung it hard across the breaker. It struck the boss at the shoulder and burst in a spray of dust. Boggs spun around and came charging along the row of chutes. But Thomas Motion was already bent again to his labor, his bare fingers gliding over the rubble. Involuntarily my head snapped to the side. Boggs spotted the quip of my neck and thrust a blunt finger at me.

"Witherow!"

I bore his rage whenever he was unsure.

25

Without a word I stood and put out my hands, palms down. The force of the rod sent my arms whipping back like halter ropes yanked by a stud horse. I sat again and worked with dead hands. Left no choice but to sight what my fingers could not sense, I fought the welling tears. I did not turn again to Thomas, but I heard his voice.

"He's a bastard," he said.

⁓

I NEVER LOST MY APTITUDE FOR BREAKER WORK, HOWEVER RAW MY time in that place was. I met the darkness and the apocalypse of noise without resistance. Maybe I was built a little of blackness, a little of Nature's bewitched side. The dead breaker boy Edward Leam skulked in that place, but this did not disturb me. New carloads came clattering at the back of the grinders and tumbled through the raucous chomp of the teeth and I heard the snapping of child bones. The loads rumbled down and I saw vertebrae spilling from the jaws of the machine. I saw rib and heel and hipbone, femur and thumb clattering in the coal and slate beneath me. The wave of black dust floated upward and grew umber in the thin light, and I saw it as Leam's blood, dried and crushed to powder and mingling with coal dust, billowing out to bathe us. Leam was present every day like this. Every day he coated my person. Every day I snatched from the current his dismantled bones. And it wasn't strange to feel what I felt: that I was reconstructing him somehow.

In the evenings when the whistle blew and the grinders groaned to a stop, I joined father as he stepped out of the throng of surfacing miners. We walked toward home, the sky black and starry overhead, our breath steaming. In my first week at the breaker he came to me—dark against the darkness—and drew from a shadowy pocket a white handkerchief and rubbed my face roughly till the kerchief was indistinguishable against all the other blackness. He said: "Well, Ash, are you changed?"

I tongued a hunk of tobacco from my jaw and spat it to the ground. "No, sir."

A gray smoke rose from the chew. Father looked to it. "I know the necessity of that tar, but your mother needn't."

I nodded my understanding.

We walked down the grade of the company yard toward Main Street, where the light of the two whale-oil street lamps glinted copper.

"You're strong, Ash. If nearly a week's work hasn't changed you, it may be you're fitted for it, though I'd sworn no man was—and no boy at that."

"But you're fitted for it, father."

"No I am not." He stopped and cinched my arm in his deadlock grip. "And neither may you be. You have yet to crawl low after all. No man's fitted for it. We endure. Me and all these men."

He loosed my arm and stepped away. We went down into the flat hollow and to our house.

Father had felt this country's allure like the keen draw of a woman. Every young man holds to an illusion willingly so long as it bolsters his courage in the face of a big intractable leap—so my father must have envisioned America as an illimitable plateau of soft earth pocked endlessly with shafts. He was among the first in that long race of deceived fathers, hungry for vision, who have so regularly peopled this country since its birth not long ago. But this has never marred his character for me. Both he and mother were pilgrims of a kind. And for a while anyway they found a sort of happiness despite their troubles.

Mother had the washing barrel ready when we came in: warm

water and pungent lye. Father drew back in the rocker and undid his boots while she rushed to me and began plucking at my shirt buttons. Soon I stood naked and shivering in the knee-deep tub. I splashed handfuls of water on my front side while mother poured from a pitcher over my shoulders and back. I watched the black cake turn brown on my belly and arms, spreading into lines of grain before sliding off.

Mother circled to my front. In a brief, dread sigh she said: "Hands." I turned the palms up to her like stolen goods.

My first night home from the breaker she had started at the rawness of my fingers. Now she studied nightly the cracked bulbs of index and thumb and tall-man, worrying to cleanse the crusted blood free and stave off infection. She squinted into my flat palm, webbed with lines where the filth would not scrub out. She bent each finger to discourage the swelling and keep movement. When I winced, she drew up her breath as if she'd pricked her own hand while sewing.

"It's brutish," she said to father. "It's not only a gloveless boy that can pick slate." She cupped my skull in her strong fingers and pushed my head down to clean my ears. "You could do it in mittens, couldn't you?"

I rolled my eyes up to her and saw she was smiling.

"Yes mama, I could." That pleased her.

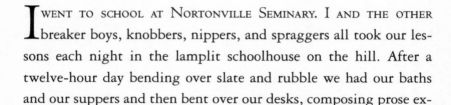

I WENT TO SCHOOL AT NORTONVILLE SEMINARY. I AND THE OTHER breaker boys, knobbers, nippers, and spraggers all took our lessons each night in the lamplit schoolhouse on the hill. After a twelve-hour day bending over slate and rubble we had our baths and our suppers and then bent over our desks, composing prose exercises, working out grammar, and figuring equations with our blackened hands while the night edged into deeper, cooler darkness.

During the daytime hours, as we labored at our mine work, the schoolhouse bristled with children from New York Landing. They came up in the passenger car at the rear of the coal train because there was no school down where they lived. They left their carvings in the desktops for us to run our hands over. We thought of them as strange and simple, their lives lackluster—down in the flats by the water. Ours was a cosmopolitan township, a community of stoic and well-rounded people. What kind of folks could they boast? In my desktop, chiseled in narrow slanting letters, was the name *J. G. Cobalt.* This person wasn't real to me.

Our school prefect was Gregory Evans: a dwarfish man with big yellow eyes that seemed to roll like marbles in their sockets. He talked in a soft way through his pinched nose, dolling out lessons like forgettable sermons and throwing a lamp-lengthened shadow over our desks.

Josiah Lyte taught the elder students of the seminary. I encountered him often, though I was not yet under his charge. As school let out and a flood of kids followed the path of light that spilt downhill from the schoolhouse door, the curious apprentice would stop me with one waifish hand at my shoulder. Always he fixed me with a protracted gaze, his nervy pupils scaling me from head to foot.

"Young Witherow," he said one night. "How are your studies getting on?"

"Fine, sir, thank you."

I watched my schoolfellows scatter down the hill without me.

"Does Mr. Evans please you?" he asked.

"Yes, sir."

"Of course you wouldn't tell me if he did not."

"Did not what, sir?"

"If he did not please you. Mr. Evans. As a teacher."

I was silent. We stood in the half-light of a schoolroom window.

Lyte leaned toward me and murmured: "He's a nincompoop and a terrible little grouch of a fellow. That's what you wish to tell me, isn't it?"

I faltered from answering. My feet stirred in their boots, but I did not move.

Lyte snickered. A stream of breath poured from his nostrils. He drew a finger along the brim of his hat as he looked up through the night air. "Well," he said, "though I'd favor that judgment of character myself, I can tell you that Mr. Evans knows his teaching. Learn from him. Learn well. Then you'll be prepared for my lessons."

"Yes, sir."

"He says you excel in his class. Not that I'd have doubted it."

For a long minute he stood gazing down the hill into darkness. I was unsure whether I might take my leave. He looked on the verge of speaking again at any moment, so I hung there in that dim light before him. Finally he turned to enter his classroom, gesturing for me to follow. From a row of shelves behind his desk he brought out a small book with a marbled cover, an ancient-looking thing, which he placed in my hands. "Here's reading for you," he said. "A special lesson."

I squinted at the book. Faded characters on the spine read: *Ovid's Metamorphoses. Arthur Golding.*

"I'd much rather you had it in Latin of course, but there's no helping that. Mr. Golding will serve you well enough."

The volume felt soft as kidskin in my hands, its edges turned in with use. The covers were fragrant with the yellow smell of ownership.

"Seeing as you're to be my pupil soon," said Lyte. He stood back from me grinning, as though measuring the effect of his gift.

I thanked him and bade him good night and started down the hill toward home. In the darkness below, the Main Street lamps burned reddish, and in the valley lay a glinting stitchwork of house lights.

{3}

DIM DAYS AND DARK NIGHTS—TIME ROLLED PAST IN THIS PLAIN equilibrium and only Sundays were punctured by light. I began to wear the darkness in my skin as father did— coal dust creeping through the slits and cracks of my hands, wandering under translucent flesh, spotting me. Around this time I also came to know the more furtive shadows—the shadows within, around which my body was closed like a canister; the shadows without, which lent me form like enveloping satin.

One night I moved alone through the darkness toward home, a schoolhouse window glowing high on the hill at my back. Only sound told me where I walked: the subdued thud of my feet in the dirt, then the rustle of grass—but was I in the grass?

From nowhere, a body slammed into mine. Stiff limbs forced me to the ground and my books tumbled into the blindness. The pages made a fluttering noise. I heard wild laughter and the scuffle of feet as the figure released me and stood.

"You're a cinch, Witherow!"

"Motion, is that you? Thomas?"

"It's like you just ask to be thrown down!"

I sat up and tried to distinguish his shape. I made out a slight contrast in the blackness.

"That's how Boggs can whale on you like he does," Thomas said. I felt him close beside me, sitting down in the dirt. "But you're smart for that I think. It's stupid to fight some things. Sometimes you shouldn't fight."

I saw a gray plume in the air and began to will his face into form. I could make out an outline. A brow and nose and mouth.

"Why'd you let me take your beating the other day, Thomas?"

"Cause you're better than me at that. I like to watch you and see how you do it."

"Do what?"

"How you take it. How you let Boggs whack away and you just take it."

"I don't understand."

"I mean you're smarter than me. You're calm."

My hands throbbed as I laid them against the ground to rise. I began circling in the blackness, feeling for my books.

"What're you at?" he asked.

"My books."

I heard him get up and enter the grass. I moved blindly a moment more, then felt something against my arm. He'd found them.

"You can see?" I said.

"Yes. I'm a born miner for it, huh?"

I took the books and staggered down the hill a little. I heard Thomas moving beside me. After a while his voice broke the black.

"Will you teach me how you can be that way?"

"What way?"

"How your blood can be so still."

I kept walking in silence. The few town lights swelled closer.

He said: "If you can, I'll teach you to see in darkness."

THESE DAYS WERE THE FIRST IN WHICH AUTUMN TOUCHED ME WITH A sense of dying, as it has done ever since. On Sundays, free of work to witness some daylight, I found the sky boiling and oceanic. I stood on the ridge-top and looked to the mountain, dark clouds like monsters of froth teeming about the twin peaks—blackish brewing-place, thunder belching terribly. And as the weeks shrank and dimmed, declining toward the winter solstice, the hills stood greener and shapelier against the dark sky, eerily colorful. It seemed a morbid charade—the land's last glimmer. At dusk the scintillating effect was peculiarly strong, yellow tree and emerald grass and russet earth: stupefying.

Thomas Motion and I went up to the flat ridge-top. We ambled east to see the tarnished mirror of the San Joaquin River below, its shine drowning slow under the dusk. To the west lay the humped valley of Clayton, Concord, Walnut Creek. South was Diablo—our Parnassus, looming and wigged in clouds.

We invited the blindness of night. Then night fell, hermetic and black. If a moon was up, a bank of cloud smothered it and at most I could see only imagined shapes.

I felt Thomas step away from me. "Watch!"

The rustle of movement. His body parting the black air beside me. A whisper of rock trodden upon. Then the sounds fading, the furrow of air closing again, and all was silent. Just a lowing wind and a dark sheet upon my eyes and the incalculable certainty of desertion.

Thomas walked with intuitive ease, without stopping or turning back. I was to follow.

"Eyes don't open against the black till they got no other choice," he had told me.

I stood alone on the ridge. I waited for form to come. But even in stillness: nothing. Only silence, thick and confounding as a riddle. I edged forward and strained to listen. Tried to trail the memory of Thomas's withdrawing noise.

Each step threatened a void. Stubs of rock beneath my soles. Rock: the familiar crunch. Rock yet. Then grass, cool against my shins. I paused, unsure which way I faced, tried to remember back the seconds along my path of sound.

I decided to turn a quarter left; that would take me back. I shifted and stepped, but my cheek grazed something coarse. The bark of a tree. A tree? I turned again and stepped: the hiss of grass. Where was the crunching rock now?

For a long moment I stood mapping out the darkness like a foreigner. Finally I started again, hands out in front, creeping. In that blackness, distances stretched like dough. Yards unraveled from endless skeins.

Nothing but the sound of grass.

I stopped again and stood, listened, crept forward, strained to hear. Stood. Listened.

It seemed I spent long seasons alone in that blackness. Space stood open before me, unfenced and yet as impenetrable as a wall. Then I would get to fumbling in some bush or low-grown tree. In scattered intervals I heard scampering in the grass, the slinking of a skunk or coon, the tiny screams of bats.

Suddenly the earth sloped down, dropped away from my feet. In my mind the huge firmament unscrolled and I fell through that emptiness, my body cut loose of earth and tumbling up through air. With a step I was anchored again, that blind hollow behind me now. I tried to penetrate the darkness once more, listening.

Something thrashed in the field, momentarily growing louder, and Thomas tackled me from the darkness, threw me to the wet leaves.

"Too much trying, Witherow! You can't try!" He dragged me up from the grass. "You have to move! You have to bolt like this!" His invisible fingers clamped cold over mine and he pulled me after him. I barreled across black earth—knees jarring as the ground leapt hard against my feet. Here and there the earth dropped into tiny craters and the wind burst from my lungs. Twigs lashed at my shoulders and neck as if the night itself had brandished claws.

"You have to travel! You can't pause!"

"Thomas, wait!"

"Make yourself see it!"

He dragged me across a wide lake of nothing. I passed through envisioned trees. I tore my arms against brambles where I'd pictured only space.

Then, like fierce eyes opening in night's face, the amber town lights winked below. Thomas released me. I could see him now, a flicker of darkness obscuring the light here and there. His voice was stark in the shadows, all its roughness embossed.

"So tomorrow you'll teach me."

"Yes."

At that, I heard him careering down the hill away from me.

I stood a while in the dark after his sounds died out. I willed vision to come. But again there was nothing: only the moist brush of my own breath on my chin and neck. So I crept in blindness toward the lights burning below.

T HOUGH OUR LIVES HINGED ON THE YIELD OF COAL, WE FOLKS OF Nortonville were really a people of shale and sandstone and lime. Geology is important. One can hardly know of what stuff he's composed if he doesn't know what's underfoot. Was it one of the Concord philosophers who stated that the greatest achievements of civilization correlate directly to the areas with the most abundant deposits of lime?

In Nortonville, the high ridge to the south was a thick spine of sandstone. And our declivitous valley walls were monsters of Cretaceous shale, risen long ago from the floor of the sea. They plunged down to our very doorsteps from all sides, buckling into furrows and ravines. Only beneath these hills, shelled up amidst tilting strata of sandstone and lime, were our black diamonds. Brown diamonds really, for it was stove coal we mined: sub-bituminous lignite. Young coal. In it only a quarter of the carbon of the black anthracite they mined in the east. And yet this young stuff was hard-made.

Some fifty million years ago, before our mountain was formed, our region was a broad primordial swamp, stalked by great Paleocene birds and mammals. Green plants collected in the muck and were leeched clean of air, made brown and stiff. Death, in the shape of plant stuff, germinated in the still waters.

Then the earth rocked, rubble fell into the swamp, and the vegetation sank deeper under the weight. The rigid plant-ghosts vomited water and air again and turned to hard peat. Time crawled on, and death was pressured toward perfection. But up came our mountain. It heaved its vast shoulders through the old swamp, crushing the peat beds in its fervor of birth, and death's black apotheosis was aborted. The mountain stood, flanked on the north by careening hills in which hard peat traveled at scattered intervals: brown coal, imperfect death, like blood crusted in a body. This lignite would turn to powder if blasted out, so our miners worked gingerly by hand with picks, chirp-chirping away in the dark.

Since the Clark Vein in which my father worked was hardly four and a half feet thick, he labored mostly lying on his back. He cleared those long, low rooms by picking discriminately at the jagged ceiling over him until it began to moan or creak, then he scuttled out of the way to let the coal fall.

Long, long formation. Then slow, slow extraction. And the end result of this huge process: lumps of turd-like coal that burned fast and dirty in less than an evening at the stove; a whole retinue of fleck-skinned laborers like my father; and long days of backache and bruising for the boys of the town. Nevertheless, our lignite comprised a full quarter of the coal burnt in San Francisco, and Nortonville prospered.

All the same, mother didn't take well to my blue-striped knuckles. She turned my soaped hands over in hers, brushing her thumbs across the swelling. She locked up her narrow jaw. I could see the silent rage stoking in her breast.

Father stood by. "This was Boggs?"

I nodded to him. My tongue was sticking in my throat.

The blue rims of mother's eyes burned fierce. "We don't take their pay for bowing to this."

"No we do not, that's sure," said father. "But this'll take care in confronting."

"—and never from an Irish hog for that matter!" mother spat.

Father drew up a breath and seemed to hold his tongue, looking long at me. He laid one black hand on the lip of the barrel and bent to mother's ear. "I'll have a word, Abicca. Don't worry, I'll have a word."

"Better ten or twenty! As many as it takes to pierce the boar's thick skull!"

"I will—"

"And if words aren't enough, God help our distemper!"

"He meant to punish me," I told them, shivering. "He thought he saw me pelt him with rocks."

"And did you?" asked mother.

"No ma'am, I did not."

Mother did not like it that both her men now came home covered head to foot in dust. After school each night she sat me down before bed and read earnestly from the gospels. *"Consider the lilies of the field, how they grow; they toil not, neither do they spin: And yet I say unto you that even Solomon in all his glory was not arrayed like one of these."* And as I undressed and wormed beneath my blankets, she recited the old Welsh legend of the seventh son of Madoc, a cautionary tale. I cannot think of my youth without thinking of that legend, hearing mother speak it. Odd, how those old stories thrive in the blood, like a kind of body-memory. The legend and my life have become inseparable. I can almost feel the scraping end-wood at our sawbuck table, that ragged grain where I sometimes dug my fork. I can smell the salted musk of our pork barrel. Clear as anything, there is the hot cast-iron belly of our stove, which scorched the triangular burn deep into my left hand before I was yet a toddler. I still have the scar. Through nearly nine decades it has stretched on my aging skin and now it calls to mind some distorted parody of an Odd Fellows emblem. I touch the unpigmented mark and mother is telling the legend all over again:

"The seventh son was seven times blessed by birth and yet he succumbed to the lure of the gold stowed deep below the earth's crust. Now, that gold was guarded by Arthur's sleeping armies— everyone knew it. One could expect nothing good from awakening them. But the seventh son, clutching the wind in his fist, would not be kept from such a famous treasure. He went under and took more than his share and broke the sleep of the soldiers. They chased him from the chamber and he was cursed with poverty and want all his long days after."

She had a white hair comb, a toothy thing made of bone. Often as she spoke she would withdraw it from her hair and lay it by on the bed stand. Or she'd let me hold it while I listened. On its spine ran loops of lacework and filigree, raised from the bone. My fingers traveled over that smoothness.

I believe those hours mother spent with me worked like elixirs for her, staving off her homesickness with Old World legend. She was a strong woman: ethically strong, strong in Christ, strong against circumstance. But even for all her strength, mother has etched herself in my memory as a figure of suffering.

I inherited from her the damnable headache, pain so fierce it set me to snapping thick twigs in my teeth. She bore frequent attacks all her adult life, but I didn't become aware of them until about this time, between my seventh and eighth years. It's strange and startling how life, in bits and pieces, enters the consciousness.

Every several weeks she became a stone. She slid back from the world, breathing hard and slow, blinking heavily, as though just her slumping eyelids were too much to endure. I was not to speak to her then, unless I chose to whisper to her from the Psalms—only the Psalms and only a whisper.

Even today when I'm wracked by this pain of mother's blood I breathe to myself the Psalms: *"Surely he shall deliver thee from the snare of the fowler, and from the noisome pestilence."* It brings comfort, though never relief.

Octogenarian that I am, I have cause to speak of anguish so various, so multifaceted, that younger souls would gape in wonder at the ingenuity of all those forces which descend upon one near the end of life. And yet it's different pain, the pain of those I've loved in my time, which draws my focus now. This is the stuff that finally matters and sticks in the mind. The closer we move to the big door at the end of the hall, the more we siphon off our tiny personal excruciations for a share in all that which has made our time significant. The hard-won histories of our friends and relations—our undiminishing currency.

Whenever the pain turned mother white, father and I would creep about the house, careful of the puncheon floor trembling at our boots. We brought her hot compresses for her head, stepping gingerly. Sometimes if she seemed to sleep, father would lead me out into the night toward the lights of the Exchange Hotel.

"This pain mother bears," he told me, "it's the curse of her womb. Since she can't know labor she knows another pain. Tis natural for her womanhead."

He told me this often, and I heard it several times before I saw my own birth for the exceptional thing it was.

In the lobby of the Exchange I would sit at a table with my books while father fell in among the men at the bar. Amidst a fog of tobacco and streams of spilt liquor I studied Golding's Ovid, deciphered the folly of Phaethon at his father's business, the reins of the sun-chariot in his boyish hands:

The singed cloudes began to smoke amaine. The Medes and Pastures
greene
Did seare away: and with the leaves, the trees were burned cleene.
The parched corne did yeelde wherewith to worke his owne decaie.
Tushe, these are trifles. Mightie townes did perish that same daie.
Whose countries with their folke were burnt: and forests ful of wood
Were turnde to ashes with the rocks and mountains where they stood.

Father crossed the lobby sometimes and sat with his chums on the settle nearby. Joel Aitken was a haulier in the Mount Hope Slope. He looked too huge a man to work in a mine—he had arms like oak branches. He flung his massive legs onto a table and spat frequently into a spittoon on the floor. He uttered few substantive words while the men rumbled at one another, but often his guttural earthquake of a laugh would tremor through the ranks and he would throw a ton of palm against a nearby back and affably wag his head. He leaned over to me once and fixed me with bloodshot eyes. His love for father made me peculiarly precious to him I think. The two men had worked on a team together in the early days of the town.

"What do you study, boy?"

"Ovid, sir."

"Ovid," he said. The name rolled untamed over his tongue. "Ovid . . . Ovid, by Jove!" He grinned with yellow mouth and winked, one sackcloth eyelid falling heavily. "Learning your Latin tales are you? That's well!"

His attention trailed back to the uproar of the men and he sat

42

upright in their midst again, guffawing at something and slapping the tabletop hard.

I returned to my book. In a moment Joel's voice was near me again and I raised my head to find him leaning once more.

"Have you met with Daphne yet?"

"Daphne and Apollo, yes!"

"No—*Daphne*," he said, "*hard-won woman* I mean. Have you? No? Well, you shall, boy! You shall! More than one woman has turned to a tree at *my* chase! You shall!"

He clenched my shoulder mercilessly, then turned to spit.

One night before the blue of my knuckles had faded, I was with father at the Exchange Hotel when Boggs and Buxton swaggered in.

Buxton was a watchman. He had a jouncing, bowlegged walk, as though his feet burned him when they bore his weight. He talked in Welsh but was proudly of Irish birth, and he took to Boggs in a way that seemed insidious. Really, his mixed culture served him even less than an undiluted Irish bearing would have done, and he and Boggs were equally despised. For Boggs's part, it needed a queer temerity for an Irishman to stand as a boss in a mainly Welsh town, let alone think to frequent the workingmen's leisure places.

I watched the two men enter and walk to the bar. Father set down his tumbler and grew quiet amidst his noisy fellows. The tendons in his neck flexed stiff. He turned to me and studied me in silence a while, then slid toward me.

"Not a word now, Ash. Come."

I rose and followed him across the wide wooden floor, then stood off a few feet as he shouldered up against the bar. He leaned close to the two Irishmen, talking and nudging Boggs with a wide-braced elbow. Some of his words drifted my way: "You'll not bruise the boy again."

Boggs glanced back at me. He shook his head and drank from his tumbler, father's mouth moving in his ear.

More murmurs and the subdued gestures of shoulders and heads. Father said something to Mr. Gwynn, the hotel owner and bartender, and Mr. Gwynn looked dismayed, stooping to bring out his ledger book from beneath the bar. He glanced askance from father to Boggs to Buxton as he leafed through the pages. Then he entered something down in pencil. Father turned and I stepped out with him into the frosted night.

We crossed the tracks toward our house in silence. A white fog lurked in the hollow around us.

"It's best to buy a man's drink in a grievance, Ash," said father at last. "Then if it comes to fists you know it's needful."

And as we came up to our house, he laid a hand on my back and turned to me. "Your mother would say different than what I've told you. That's well enough. You'll decide your own way. But you mustn't tell her what I've done. She'll not bear it well."

"Yes, sir."

"Good." He grinned. "You're growing up."

{5}

THE LONG DAYS IN THE BREAKER WORE ON. I DEVELOPED A wordless language with Thomas Motion as our lessons evolved. Everything could be made for discourse, everything a code. The fixing of a stare on a joint in the chutes. The altering rhythm of hand and slate. Left hand to ear: a warning. Thumb to knee: a signal for readiness. A tug at your cap: a request for more tobacco.

Our lessons were like this: As Boggs passed on Thomas's side, I leaned and spat a thick splodge of brown at the boss's back. He whirled round and yanked Thomas down off the slat and flailed his quirt across the boy's chest.

"Dirty little puke! I'll not take it, boy!"

I hunkered at my work while Thomas sprawled in the chute and grunted under the sharp whacks—one two three four five six—and then he would not bear more. At the seventh, he shot out his hand and snatched the quirt from Boggs, jabbed it hard into the boss's gut, then scrambled up and turned it fast on me.

"You stupid fucking Irish!" he screamed as the quirt ripped over my neck. "It was Witherow!"

With two great mitts at Motion's jacket, Boggs tore him clean out of the chute and jostled him to the wall. There Thomas took a number of hard blows across the ass, sobbing and holding his tongue with all his strength. Finally Boggs spun him around and prodded him back to his place beside me.

"I'll be damned if this will continue, boys!" barked the foreman, to be heard by all above the clamor. He stood near us for a time, angrily straightening his coat as we bent to our work. At last he took up his supervisory pacing again.

Thomas looked long at me, red-faced and grim. He snorted through wet nostrils and returned to his work without a word.

I allowed a few days to pass. Then I lit a fire again.

I gave Thomas the signal that all was clear, so he sat back from the chute and stretched out his stiff spine and neck.

"Boss!" I shouted, and Boggs turned to find him so.

The boss pounded off two blows of the rod and Thomas bit his tongue till it bled. He showed me that night at school.

"You see!" he said. Neat tooth marks ran like hyphens across the bluish tongue. "I did this but I didn't make a squeak. I'm doing good, huh? Not a squeak!"

"Better, Thomas, yes."

"Better, for damn sure, than beating you with the boss's quirt!" He heeled back and socked me so hard at the shoulder that I stumbled away from him.

"Yes, Thomas. Better."

As for me and my lessons—I was getting nowhere. I stood in the tall grass of our hills like a castaway, distracted by the dark rustlings about me.

I went forward in tiny jerks, all my weight tilted onto the balls of my feet, half-fearing I would come to the edge of the world with each step. I struck my head on low branches. And always Thomas would come ripping out of the dark to knock me down and pummel me. Blackness and nothing more fronted me at every try, inscrutable blackness through which Thomas would lead me sprinting in terror. I had blindness and terror, while Thomas simply bit his tongue and every day grew calmer under Boggs's rage.

THAT WINTER MRS. PRICE, THE BRAKEMAN'S WIFE, LOST HER SECOND son in ten months' time to the Black Diamond Company. The first boy, Charles, had been bucked from a runaway rail-car on a rainy morning as the coal train screeched down slick rails to New York Landing. Now Samuel—a spragger of ten—shattered his skull against an outcropping in the Clayton Tunnel gangway while hustling alongside the cars.

Samuel was buried beside his brother on Rose Hill. Practicing a superstitious piety like most good Congregationalists in our town, Mrs. Price arranged for the burial to be carried out at night, by the light of a few lamps. Any goblins of ill luck would find harder trafficking this way.

Mother and I were there among a crowd of workmen and their wives. Near to us stood Reverend Parry, head bowed and eyes squeezed shut, lips twitching in silent prayer. Josiah Lyte stood bleached by lamplight at the head of the grave, reading aloud from the little book in his white hands. He bent and scattered dirt over the coffin and his lean face broke into a notchy smile.

I stood there in that thick congregation of black coats and skirts and listened to the words of the death rite and suddenly—instantaneously—everything around me was illumined. Darkness

shuddered and went pale. Shadows slunk back and I saw the verdant green grass, the blue crystalline flakes in the quartz headstones
lining the graveyard. I wished at once that Thomas were there. I
could have bolted through the deep night without fear. All was
vivid, as in sunlight. The earth shifted and bulged warm under
my feet.

But promptly the lamp-rays quavered through filing shadows.
The mourners were parting, dark again, and my mind's sunlight
was snuffed. The earth at my feet sank and settled, as if with a silent
belch. Mother stepped away to greet some ladies. The unfilled
grave was left to the few men—Mr. Price among them—who stayed
to seal it.

I turned and started down the hill through the headstones. I was
seeking mother in the dark when someone behind me spoke my
name. Squinting back into the lamplight, I saw Josiah Lyte hasten-
ing toward me. His waxen face and hands gleamed against the
blackness. One of those weird hands flashed and gripped my shoulder and he began chattering with low voice.

"Asher Witherow, I saw you! I kept my eyes on you, you see. I
knew you for a remarkable young man all the time! The rare soul
will glow, without fail, of course it will! And strange that *I* should
see it, but I *have* and that is that—" He stopped and seemed to still
his tongue with considerable effort, then chewed his lips eagerly
and stared at me as though I might speak a language not his own,
which he knew a little of and was trying to recall. He clenched my
shoulder as if worried I might run from him. "Asher, I have *seen.*
I've seen the manner in which you stand on the earth. I've watched
your face at funerals, in the company of the dead."

I sputtered that I meant no offense, that I knew the solemn
thing death was. Mother said I was young still and intended no
harm in things I couldn't yet understand. I told him this.

Lyte shook his head. His mouth curved in a scalloped smile. "You've made no offense," he said. "I mean to tell you that—that I've seen. I noticed you first at Edward Leam's burial. I saw it then in you, only I couldn't speak of it surely enough. But *I marked you.*"

I saw now that his eyes were almost transparently green, the skin beneath them streaked with pallid rings. And his dark eyebrows were very thin, two tiny crescents like gills slitting his brow. He pulled me closer. "I saw the earth filling up beneath you," he whispered. "I saw the flowers at your feet!"

Mother appeared at my side.

"Asher—Oh! Good evening, Mr. Lyte."

"Mrs. Witherow, good evening." Lyte released me and stood straight again. "I was just speaking to your boy here—about the funeral. A sad event no doubt, but the Lord has his designs."

Mother cast her eyes at Lyte's feet, submerged in shadow though they were. "Yes he does, Mr. Lyte, that is sure."

"Your Asher's a remarkable lad, Mrs. Witherow."

Mother took my hand. She turned away. "Yes. Thank you, Mr. Lyte. Good evening."

"—And he does well in school I'm told. Mr. Evans says Asher has an aptitude for his lessons that's rare among boys his age."

Though I never knew her to shy from anyone, mother balked and stammered before Josiah Lyte. It makes me shudder to remember. She pulled me down the hill after her. "Yes. Well really, Mr. Lyte, we must go."

Lyte waved a waifish hand. "Good evening, then. Good evening, Asher."

"Good evening, sir."

And then I was walking through the darkness with mother. We picked our way down the graveyard path to the Somersville Road, then turned and moved up the saddled ridge. A soft fog hovered in the hills around us. Just beyond the crest of the road a cloud of it rose and churned like steam against the blackness.

Mother's fingers were frigid. With her free hand she clutched the weighty shawl at her breast. "Does Josiah Lyte speak often to you, Asher?"

"Sometimes at school he stops me with a word or two."

"What does he say to you?"

"He's eager about my learning. Asks me how school agrees with me."

Mother said nothing. Her skirts chafed softly in the dirt of the road. She had a way of drawing up into silence, exempting herself from what surrounded her, sometimes nurturing in this manner a terrible disapproval that would later be unpent. I always feared her quietness.

While we walked I began to read the texture of her palm against my hand. It was thick and fleshy, but the surface skin was callused and cold, ribbed like unstained maple. I pressed it and felt a slow heat seep up from its depths.

We crested the ridge and descended through the fog toward town, the Congregational church windows hazing yellow ahead of us. Mother sighed and dropped my hand to pull her shawl up. She spoke again and her voice was low and pointed.

"There are things that should not condescend to us, Asher— things that ask of us and are strong in how they stand. It's not our place to find them fitting or not fitting, because they're older than us, or worthier or holier. Do you see? Don't ask how school agrees with you and don't let anyone else ask you such things. Fit yourself to school and learn to agree with it. That's the best way."

"Yes, mama. I understand. I'll keep my head at my books."

"The grave," she said, "is no place for mirth!" The words jutted against the clouded night. It was clear she had not addressed them to me but to something inward with which her soul grappled.

At home we found father in the rocker by the stove, smoking his ivory pipe in a daze.

"Did someone walk you home?" he asked.

"Asher escorted me," said mother. She swept across the room to the stove, rubbing her hands.

"Yes, but you two fumbled through the dark no doubt."

"We made out. We're here after all. Our son's a fine chaperone."

"I just wish you'd take a lamp."

The kettle clattered from mother's hands to the burner. "But the oil, David. We needn't burn it if we can see well enough."

"Ah, my wife—who won't bear the escort of any good fellow with a lamp. And Maggie Hopkins having broken her neck in the dark just last year!"

"Let it be, David. We're safe and sound." Mother tapped at the tea leaves in a jar. She brought a parcel down from the cupboard, parted the paper, and squared out a yellow cake for cutting. "Mrs. Dolan asked after you tonight. I hardly knew what to tell her."

Father held his pipe at his lap. It turned to and fro like a tiny boat between his fingers. A thread of smoke zigged and staggered from the bowl. "Mmm. Yes. I reckon I just was not suited this evening." He spoke lowly down the length of his beard, which lay to his waist as he sat. "To bathe, scrub clean, then to stand at the lip of the grave, washed and smelling of soap. It didn't suit me tonight."

Mother sheared three slices of cake onto a plate and slid it into the warmer. "Josiah Lyte talked to Asher again this evening."

"Did he?"

"That young man takes a peculiar interest in our son. Asher says Lyte speaks to him often at school, asks him how school suits him."

"Hmm. Well, that's well enough I reckon." Father's eyes darted toward me, a speculative sideways glance.

"Lyte smiled at the grave again tonight," said mother.

"Did he?"

"Once was curious but twice is just queer."

"Yes," said father. His brow blenched in a quick wash of anger. "Tis queer. I wonder, has Reverend Parry noted it?"

"He's silent if he has. But I'm not the only parishioner to see it, that's sure. Mrs. Dolan, Mrs. Griggs, Mrs. Aitken have all seen it. We can only mistrust the man—the lot of us. And for him to speak like he did this last Sunday—Jonah swallowed by an angel and not a whale, Pilate as God's helpmate!—Better that Reverend Parry not compromise his pulpit."

Father got up. "Well," he said, hinging open the stove door to knock the ash from his pipe, "man and man'll clash sometimes. I guess it's more troubling when it's man and man of God—or *woman* and man of God for that! But it's all one, isn't it, not to see eye to eye sometimes?"

"Of course, but to have Josiah Lyte drawing out questions in our boy. Asking how school suits him. As though school ought to bend to his tastes. There's trouble waiting there."

Father slumped into the rocker again. He shot me a narrow grin, as though making me partner to the grain of salt with which he sometimes took mother. "But we can hardly forbid Ash to speak to him. Or him to Ash."

"Can't we! Why not?"

"Abicca, no! We'll not stir dust in this town. Lyte means no harm."

"But there's a long valley between meaning and *doing*—"

"If Reverend Parry isn't alarmed then should we be, Abicca? A man of God like him knows best."

Mother huffed. A bitter silence, sharp as a meat knife, halved the room while she poured the steaming tea into three cups and lifted the warm cake down. At last she made a little grunting noise, like a slight cough.

"I only wonder how long we'll bear it, David, before we see the cracks it makes in our lives. Such queerness on the part of a minister—"

"Abicca," said father. One soothing hand stroked the air as it would stroke a dog. "Enough now."

She brought us the tea and the cake and we sipped in silence. Father's smoke still lingered fragrant in the house. The stove settled with quiet metallic crackles.

After some time father spoke again, cake crumbling between his teeth. "After all Abicca, you said it yourself. We shouldn't ask how the clergy suits us. We ought to honor our ministers."

Mother's snapping voice was edged on all sides: "Then we shouldn't ask how funerals suit us either. We should honor our dead by attending, don't you think?"

Father blushed. He dipped the cake in his tea cautiously, as though it were a precarious labor. His eyes clouded up and he seemed to shrivel in the rocking chair, to shrink and double over as though some massive hand had deigned to fold him up and put him away in its huge pocket. For a long moment he sat there nibbling his wet cake. Finally he said: "The Lord forgive us."

"The Lord forgive us," said mother.

THOMAS LEARNED QUICKLY TO TEMPER HIS BLOOD. I WATCHED him get up and hold out his cracked hands and suffer the terrible rod without so much as unlocking his jaw. Before the new year had aged two months he was standing Boggs's wrath with a quiet firmness, silent under the strictest of blows, tranquil even when the boss bruised his hands blue.

It made me shudder. I had still not advanced a degree in my perseverance against the night—still stumbling, still lost, while Thomas had mastered himself. How could one so doggedly reform his own nature? I kept inciting the boss's rage, but Thomas's calmness seemed shatterproof, destined only to take increase. Soon he bore the whippings with a placid, distracted air, as though he stood with only one foot in the world.

When we were alone he was his roguish self again. He struck me in the dark. He threw me to the ground. He snorted with laughter. It was as if the lessons in the breaker had been mere experiments, challenging games to pass the time, having little effect on him in whole. But still, during those nights in the darkness with him I felt it for the first time: how I was rubbing up against some fell mystery which, though it might never unravel completely, would mean something great to me one day. I found myself holding to Thomas like a brother: bound to him, despite envy, in a sacred bond.

One night we stood in darkness among the graves at Rose Hill. The white headstones were swallowed completely in that black, yet I felt their nearness in my limbs, like cold water through the veins.

Thomas was giggling criminally. "Here we are with the dead," he whispered. "It's plain you need help, and nobody can see better— night or day—than dead folks."

His laughter trailed away.

Aloneness again. Nothingness. Wind stirred in the fringe of weeds at the graveyard's edge. The graveyard gate gave a moan of wood to wood, then the clatter of a latch and it was silent again. From the heights of the nearby cypress tree: the hiccupping of bats.

I edged forward. A step over a terrace edge. One foot extended from the high bluff of the world. Then—not falling—but the flattening of a stem underfoot and the surety of the solid earth.

All around me the charisma of death. Here: Maggie Hopkins, who broke her neck on the Somersville Road—her head now wrenched against the narrow coffin wall. Here: the crushed Edward Leam— flat puzzle of bone and cartilage. There: Samuel and Charles Price, embracing one another. I tried to enter their bloodless vision, to see with their eyes. I willed my sight hard through the black, as through the earthen ceiling of a grave.

First came memory, almost like vision. In memory I saw the rectangular plot of the cemetery. The rows of stones. The few trees among the graves: cottonwood there, cypress there, buckeye. The Somersville Road glowing wanly on the rim of the vision. And the cemetery path, near at hand.

I turned and walked toward the path, fighting dread at every step. The grassy earth seemed to urge into vision beneath me as I went, conforming to the picture.

Stepping. Stepping.

The way was clear, though dark yet. I found the path and quickened my pace. Gravestones trailed by in my mind.

I ran. I ran in that blackness on the hill, fast and wild between the rows of stones. Stones sailing past. Earth underfoot.

But this was only the ghost of sight, these were only airy spirits of stones, and I crashed straight into the fence, gasping as the wind was slammed out of me. I fell backward to the ground, breathless, my picture smashed.

Memory swallowed itself in the impenetrable darkness. I groped a few moments in the grass, lost. Then the terrible dread swooped down: dread of vanishing, losing memory of myself in that night, the way I'd just lost memory of my picture. Dread of illusion. The illusion of existence. Was I there at all? I could not see myself.

"Asher," I said, to hear myself. "Asher. Asher,"—as if the name were a path back to the place from which I'd begun to stray.

I murmured the name over and over until breath returned and I felt I could rise.

I stood and touched my face to feel my doubtful realness. Cold fingers, warm cheek. The solid anchoring of the tangible. The tactile. Good. I passed my hand before my mouth: moist wash of breath. I sensed my feet upon hard earth. Sedentary earth, out of which things grew, in which the dead were folded, over which moved persons and winds. Good. Thank God. I was there after all.

I looked about me: still there was blackness on all sides. Still I was afloat in that.

I felt behind for the fence—yes, there: coarse narrow picket under my fingers. So here was a boundary to the burying ground, its east edge most likely. Yes: from here I needed but turn up the slight rise and walk toward the older gravestones, near the buckeye tree. The image collected itself before me. Trees professed themselves. And stones. And the southern fence off left, with the Somersville Road beyond.

I let go of the wood and moved forward into the picture. Stepping. Stepping.

The shush of grass and the soft *pith! pith!* of weeds at my toes. Quiet dirt curling from the edges of my feet. Gradual tilt of earth, slanting toward me. Stepping. Stepping.

I tumbled, treading on air, foot falling through the disappeared earth — then earth slammed violent against my knees, chafing the heels of my hands. A ditch! A gully in which I lay, earth inclining on all sides.

I gulped the air. Tasted my red heart in my throat. Scrambled against the shallow walls. An uncovered grave!

But soon I had scurried out of it and, no—it was not a grave. A low dip in the ground. A buckle of earth. Not a grave. Not a grave . . .

But now I foresaw the terrain about me: a labyrinth of such dips, the ground endlessly pocketed, veined by a thousand scattered bridges of earth each no wider than my two feet side by side. I stood now on one such bridge. I could not advance without tripping again a thousand times.

I balanced there in that mottled blackness. My heart split open like a fruit, its acrid juice flooding the back of my mouth.

A sharp fist flew out of the black, ripping across my chin, and I heard Thomas Motion's high giggle as I fell. I landed ass to flat earth, head reeling in my sudden bearings. The relief of awful pain: that I'd been shaken from an abyss.

"No, no, Witherow! Too slow!" He stood somewhere above me.

"But I ran at first, did you see? Ran straight through the graves.

Laid out the picture and ran right through it—but then the fence was there."

"The fence is always there, Witherow. You just tricked yourself a minute."

His voice circled me now.

"You can't make sense of it, Witherow. You've got to quit that."

I set a hand against the cold earth, stood up and brushed myself off.

"You're goddamn slow, Witherow. When'll you learn? There's nothing to see! Nothing to look at!"

I heard the whisper of clothing, as though he were flinging his arms back and forth in the air.

"It's all just dark! There's nothing here! You worry too much you'll run into something! That's stupid. It's just darkness. It won't make any sense!"

I shook my head and made to move but was stopped by my blindness.

"I don't understand, Thomas. It's simple for you, but I'm made different and I can't do like you do. My eyes are weak!"

He shoved me then. His hands smashed the breath from my lungs. "Your will is weak!"

I lashed out at him. I threw a fist into the void, then another, pummeling air, my blows passing through him. But still his punches shot square and sure out of nowhere. He pounded my shoulders and gut. He seemed built entirely of shadow, immaterial, and yet apt in violence against the world of flesh. His fists came like gavels, relentless, with not a trace of their earlier humor. A brutal, evil force. I began to fear it.

"Thomas, please. Enough! Thomas, don't injure me!"

But he wouldn't hear. He had me beneath him on the ground. I struggled to breathe. My limbs were humming red.

My will shrank back and back, deeper under my skin. It seemed to want only sleep. I turned from the onslaught and pressed my face to the earth. I squinched up my eyes, my mouth, clenched my arms and legs until I was just an egg of a body.

A strange indifference slid over me like a husk. The rage outside muted to a blurry noise, a garble of thuds and grunts. Thomas's attack became a pantomime, all that splenetic energy turning abstract, inconsequential, finally evaporating and leaving nothing but a residuum of breath—my breath, level again and plenty. I sensed myself then: caught from long falling. Clutched. I lay, a seed against the palm of something vast.

At last I lifted my chin from my chest and saw Thomas standing over me, unobscured. Plain against the black sky. He glowered at me, his cheeks beating red. His nostrils flared and smoked.

I unlocked my arms, my legs, my fingers, unfurled them all over the ground like searching roots, watched them unflex and bend, bright in the shadowy air. And here was the burying-ground about me, clear as day. White headstones. Long tapered cypress tree.

I lunged at Thomas Motion, knocked him hard to the ground and heard his skull crash. A wrath, both taller and stronger than me, shot through my body like flame, seeking to cinder him.

Fist to mouth—dull, wet slap. Fist to eye—shattering jolt of knuckle to cheekbone.

He fought clumsily. His raging arms flailed useless against the poison pulsing through me.

I saw blood spurt vibrant from his nose to his neck. Another shot and blood sprayed the earth beside his ear. Scarlet. Bright in the darkness. My fists were certain and sharp and deaf to their own racket. Limbs flew brightly through the air. The senseless momentum of sledges.

Then his hands bolted up against mine, catching my wrists, and he looked toward the graveyard gate. "Shhh. Stop. Stop now! Quiet!"

I stood and saw, coming through the headstones, a yellow lamp and a form.

Thomas grunted to his knees. The figure moved closer and soon the margin of lamplight was splashing across the headstones just in front of us. Thomas rubbed the blood from his mouth with his sleeve. We heard a woman's voice.

"Who's there?"

We didn't answer. I made out the features beyond the light.

"It's Mrs. Price," I whispered.

Thomas seized my arm and tugged me with him into shadow.

"Who's there?" said Mrs. Price.

We edged back from her light. Thomas yanked me this way and that. But the lady could make out our forms and swung her lamp wherever we turned. She began stepping soft and slow to hear us better.

"Boys?" she said.

We made short dashes through the darkness toward the gate.

"Boys, is that you? Is it you, boys?"

Finally we darted right past her, through lamplight and all, and crashed out of the gate.

"My boys!" she wailed. "Ah my sweet boys, I knew you hadn't gone from me!" And her words trembled after us as we flew down the hill for Somersville.

The long slope sent us hurling faster than our legs could manage. We shredded through the tall grass, struggled to keep from pitching face-first down the grade. I spotted a hay wagon at the bottom and grunted: "There," and we both veered toward it as one. But as soon as we'd plunged into the straw, a godawful ruckus went up—murderous fussing and squealing and a tangle of kicking hooves. I took four or five sharp punts to the head before we waggled out and fell backward off the buckboard. We hit the hard dirt and lay there jolted while five white pigs tumbled after us squealing. They squirmed to their feet again, huffed out their displeasure, and went away fuming into the grass. Thomas and I watched them go. Then we blinked at one another and set to twisting and howling in the road. We rolled and choked and gasped for breath, every muscle flexed to aching.

"She's cracked!" Thomas wheezed. "Poor old bird thought we were ghosts up there!"

We drummed hands and feet on the earth. Finally, when the fit had left us and we could breathe again, we both lay on our backs in the tall grass where we'd rolled.

I wiped my dripping eyes with a hand I could no longer see. I turned to Thomas beside me but he'd vanished. Blackness and the hissing of grasses.

"I'm blind again."

"What?"

"I can't see in this dark," I said. "Just then, up there in the cemetery and coming down the hill, I could see clear as anything. I saw you. The stones. The road. Then the pigs. But now—"

"Shhh!" I heard Thomas scramble to his feet. There was a long silence in which he seemed to be listening to something. "It's Granny Norton."

I strained my ears. The noise grew nearer—the crush and squeak of a buggy, then the clop of hooves. It crescendoed before us and Thomas said: "Evening, Mrs. Norton."

The invisible horse went past and strained up the hill toward Nortonville. We listened till it faded off beyond the ridge.

"She's a witch," whispered Thomas.

"A witch?"

"That's what my mama says. Says she and Mr. Norton live separate now. In different houses." His voice quivered nervous through the dark. "I'd better get home."

He took my hand and pulled me through the blackness after him.

❧

THOUGH I SPENT MOST MY FREE HOURS RIPPING THROUGH DARKNESS with Thomas Motion, late that year another friendship somehow wedged itself amidst those boyish night-games.

Christmas time. Both daylight and evening the town lay green and cold under a gauze of winter cloud. Some days, light snow salted the two peaks of Mount Diablo. The men and boys started bringing small coulter pines down from the hills and into the houses, where they weighed the branches with candles and tassels. The Nortonville Women's Choir held a concert at the Congregational church. Mother sang that evening, clumped with the ladies on steep risers swathed in lamplight. Father and I listened from the darkened pews. Afterward everybody convened in the Good Templars' Hall for fellowship around three big vats of cider and little cups of bread pudding. Thomas Motion's parents were there, but he was nowhere in sight. I ducked through the bustling crowd and stepped outside into the night chill.

Everything felt idle out there. The cloudy air lent a tainted whiteness to the evening. Beyond that icy scrim, the town gave out only a tiny noise—faint echoes from the Exchange Hotel a half-mile off. I watched my breath flow in bluish steam. Some dim light spilt from the imperfect glass of the hall windows, dissipating in the dark a foot from the building. I dug my hands into my coat pockets and began crunching across the gravel beneath the angling light. As I rounded the side of the hall, I spotted a waifish figure,

the slight profile of a girl. She was standing on a wood crate, leaning into the glow at a window.

Black hair tied back from a pallid brow. Skirts waving softly
above lifted heels. She had her chin at the rough sill and just as I
spotted her she turned my way. Narrow face half-dark. Black eyes.
Chin delicate like a girlish elbow. The curling plume from her
mouth was gilded in the window light.

For a long moment she held my look and said nothing, stared
me up and down as if I'd caught her at some mischief and she was
judging whether she should trust me or run.

I'd never seen her before. Her hands tugged at a shapeless
woolen cape. I thought I heard her breath shudder with chill.

I said: "You're new here."

She moved her head slightly in what seemed a timid nod. The
line of shadow rolled softly on her face.

In a placid, husky voice she said: "Is that bread pudding they're
eating?"

I nodded. Then it occurred to me I was standing in shadows, so
I stepped forward into the residual light and said: "Yes."

She moved her mouth as if to speak, but instead turned back to
the window.

"Would you like some?" I said, but I could already see she
would. "You won't come in?"

She shook her head. "Don't know a soul in there."

I told her to wait and went inside the hall again. Moving
through the crowd toward the serving table, I glanced to the window and caught sight of the girl's face, pale beyond the reflections
in the glass. She was watching me, and I gave her a quick smile.

When I brought the warm cup outside, she was standing just
beyond the corner of the hall. I nearly ran into her as I came around.

She was already murmuring thanks, her two cupped hands coming from her cape. She spooned up a clod of pudding and a little steam ribboned upward. The silver glinted in her mouth and then she chewed quietly for a moment, swallowed, thanked me again, and said once more: "I don't know a soul in there. I just arrived yesterday. You're the first, you know."

"The first?"

"The first to know me. Not a soul before you."

Standing off the crate now, she looked younger than I'd deemed her a few moments before. My age probably. Perhaps a year older. She was savoring the pudding like some ambrosial nectar.

"I watched you standing about in there," she said. "You looked funny eating your pudding with all those grown-ups around you. I wanted you to come out here."

"You did?"

"Yes. I knew you'd be the first to know me."

"I'm Asher Witherow."

"Asher Witherow," she said, trying the name on her tongue, mingling it in the pulped pudding. "That's not what I imagined you'd be called. It sounds like the name of a dying thing. While I watched you through the window, I called you David."

"My father's called David."

"Is he? Don't you think it's a living name? I love David in the Bible. Such heroism. Such bravery and music." She turned and walked back to the window, climbed onto the wood crate again and stood there waving me near. I stepped up beside her, her figure so slight that we could both fit there.

"Which one is he?" she said.

"Who?"

"Your father."

"That one, there."

"With the long beard? Yes, he looks like a David. And do you have a mother?"

"Of course. She's there by that post."

My breath fogged the glass and the girl's fingers came up and rubbed it clear.

"In the green dress?" she said.

"The blue. She sang in the choir tonight."

The girl was silent a minute, her figure warm beside me. She made a little humming sound. "I think she's different."

"Different?"

"Don't you think so? What's she called?"

"Abicca."

The girl turned her shoulder to the wall and brought the pudding up between us. She scraped the last of it from the rim of the cup and sucked softly at the spoon. I watched the pupils of her dark eyes grow large again.

"I wouldn't have guessed her for your mother," she said.

"No?"

"No, but that happens sometimes. Is your father a miner?"

"Of course. And your father?"

"A miner, yes. We come from the Colorado black-towns. Las Animas County. Too much snow for poor mother—she had the whooping cough. I didn't like it either. Gray snow, always gray. There's color in this place at least."

She turned and set her chin at the sill again and gazed at the lamp-lit crowd inside. I watched her watching them. Her face looked keen with measured thought, a subtle intelligence simmering there. Something coming up slow like a heat from her depths into those sagacious eyes. Her warmth beside me seemed to express that stirring.

"Asher Witherow," she said softly. "We'll be friends now, won't we?"

I looked in the window again. "Yes," I said. The word fogged the glass. "Tell me your name."

She leaned away from the window and jumped down off the crate and stood holding out the empty cup and spoon. "Tomorrow."

I took the cup.

"I'll find you tomorrow," she said, and with a demure smile she turned and vanished in the darkness.

T HE FOLLOWING NIGHT I MET HER AS I WALKED UP THE HILL TO THE schoolhouse. She was sitting in the dirt at the edge of the light-path spilling down from the school door. She got up and said: "There's a creek down there a ways, isn't there?"

That big woolen cape still engulfed her.

"Yes."

"I want to walk down there. Will you come?"

"I'm headed to school," I said. I lifted my books like a meek kind of evidence.

She brought her lissome hands out of the cape and took the books from me and walked toward the dark spraggle of a coyote bush ten feet off the path. "They'll be safe right here," she said, stuffing them out of sight. She seemed to know I would not protest. She came back to me and gave me her hand and I went along beside her down the path to the Nortonville Road.

Just short of the footway to my house, we crossed into the north pasture and went out under the softly sheeting town lights toward the small creek bed. Cattle lay about in the shadowy haze across the field, big lumps in the fresh grass, their stumpy legs tucked under them for warmth. I could see the wisps of their silken breath.

"Do you go to the day school?" I said.

She shook her head. "No school for me. Mother's sick so I haven't the time."

"Is it the whooping cough?"

"It was. Now it's just sickness without a name. But enough to keep her in bed all day. I do the wife's work for her. I wash and cook, feed her and rub her legs, read her the Bible. Then father comes home and I lay out his supper."

We came to the thick pepper trees that rimmed the creek. We stood on an earthen ledge above the furrowing water and listened to the dark trill of it. The stream warped at a submerged laurel branch and caught the powdery town light and glinted blue. The girl stepped away to embrace a leaning tree trunk. With cheek to wood she gazed down on the tiny current.

"There's a great big river back in Trinidad," she said. "That's where we come from. The Purgatoire. It flowed right through the town. I've never seen a river so big. It was freezing up when we left it."

"Do you miss that place?"

"No. You could hardly go outside at night like this. Not without your toes turning blue. Here I get father's bath ready, I wash him and give him his supper, but then he goes out to the saloon and mother's asleep and I'm free."

She pushed away from the trunk and walked to a branch that stretched horizontally from the bank, like a great arm held over the water to bless it.

"Come here," she said, stooping and crawling out to its knobby center. The branch bobbed and shuddered. She tucked her cloak beneath her and sat swinging her legs. "Don't worry," she said. "We won't drown if it decides to break."

The tree trembled as I inched my way out. Then I was sitting beside her.

"There," she said. "It's not so frightening, is it? I didn't think you were cowardly, Asher Witherow."

"I'm not cowardly."

"Not at all?"

"I don't think so."

"Try to think of something you're afraid of."

"What?"

"Something you're afraid of. Maybe I can tell you if it's cowardly."

I thought long.

"I don't know," I said. "Broken glass?"

She watched her kicking feet a minute. Her dark hair ribboned down along her throat. I could see a tiny bulb of her spine at the pale back of her neck.

"If that's all you can think of," she said, "then you don't have to worry. You're not cowardly."

We stared down into the gliding creek. At moments I felt we could be flying somewhere. The water moved beneath us like a restless nightscape.

"So," she said at last, "with mother the way she is, I suppose we'll be evening friends, you and me."

"All right," I said. "What's your name?"

"Anna Flood."

Somehow it seemed right that she'd guarded the name till now. I watched her breath vanish in the dim air and the name was like some fine secret divulged for a tiny second and then closed safe again in our joint keeping.

"You're the first to learn it," she said, as if concurring with my sense of covenant.

We dangled silent above the water. Beside me Anna smelled faintly of laurel. The tree she'd been hugging had floured her with its scent.

{7}

AFTER A YEAR OF BREAKER WORK MY EAGERNESS FOR THE MINES had swollen as much as my fingers. I was eight years old, the age of most good knobbers in the pits, and it was killing each morning to watch father walk to the shaft without me. Time had come for the breaker to vomit me up.

No doubt mother was the one who wanted my mine work delayed, because father gave only a weak reason for not yet taking me below with him.

"It's not time, Ash," he said. "We must wait a while."

So I worked in the breaker as long as was possible without becoming an embarrassment to my family: a total of a year and a half.

At this time Josiah Lyte spoke to me almost every night at school. For a while I worked awkwardly at evasion. If I sensed him approaching I'd scramble off, calling back a "Good evening", as though I was on my way already and had just happened to notice him. If he'd not yet spotted me, I'd slip in amongst the other boys tromping down the hill, or would sidestep into shadow.

Thomas Motion, who'd smarted from my absence the night I went with Anna to the creek, questioned me crossly.

"Where were you Witherow, hiding? You'll never learn if you start ducking from me."

"I wasn't ducking from you, Thomas—"

"Where were you then?"

"Down at the creek."

"Doing what?"

"I don't know, Thomas. Walking I guess."

He stood before me in the dark outside the schoolhouse, stewing with something. Clearly I'd fractured some bond, had excluded him by telling him nothing of Anna. It was our first divergence and he saw it immediately and his esteem snapped like a dry oak twig.

One evening not long afterward, he saw me sneaking from Josiah Lyte and he squeezed an explanation out of me. Then he took up a countergame: if I were dodging into shadow he'd push me into lamplight; if I tried making off unnoticed among the boys, he'd shout my name and shove me in the teacher's direction.

One dark December evening, Motion claimed he would lead me clear of Lyte only to bring me around the corner of the schoolhouse and directly into the prefect's presence.

"Young Witherow," said Lyte, and clasped my shoulder so immediately I wondered if he'd enlisted Motion's subterfuge.

I heard Thomas tear off into darkness. Lyte glanced after him, then stared down his long arm at me, studying me in his sallow way. We stood at the rear of the schoolhouse. Dark hill and brush sloped up before us. A golden flask of window light glowed at our backs.

Lyte looked up into the night sky. "It's good to stand in the dark," he said, "and try to decipher the asterisms up there."

I said nothing.

70

"Though in this winter air you'll rarely have any luck."

His hand slipped from my shoulder.

"You don't fear me, Asher, do you?"

I was silent.

"Is it your mother perhaps? I think she dislikes me."

I bit my tongue and gazed at the ground.

"Answer freely, Asher. You're in confidence here."

My jaw unlocked and began to quiver. I tried but couldn't set it in place again.

Lyte leaned and cupped the back of my neck in his frigid hand. "Your mother's a good woman. Good like most of the folk in this village. I don't doubt that and neither should you. But—"

His glaucous eyes rustled downward, traveling the length of me to my feet, as though his glance were an ember that had cooled and fallen. Then he released me and stood tall again. His arm arced through the air like a scythe and he pointed at the dark wall of chaparral before us.

"Do you know what's beyond this ridge here?"

I gazed up into the black brush. I stuttered: "Yes, yes—" But the words choked against the quietness.

Lyte scowled. "No, no! I don't mean Clayton, Concord. Not the towns—"

"I know what you mean, sir. You mean the mountain, of course. Mount Diablo."

Lyte spun round. The eyes were wide in his gaunt face. "Yes!" He crouched beside me, gripped my shoulders and drew my gaze into line with his, up into the black.

Our joint gaze careered away. It scampered like a quick-footed animal through the root and thorn of the underbrush up to the ridge-top. There to the south sprawled the gorged Diablo.

"We began from those twin summits," said Lyte. "Further back

than we know, longer ago than we remember, you and I were nothing and there was only water and the two peaks. Then a voice from
the peaks called us out of the waters. We stood up in the shadow of
the mountain and the waters ebbed back."

A storm cracked over me. A thundering force. The rending of
something within. Something folding open in the body, beneath
the heart—the heart floating. Then darkness surrounded me again.
Lyte stood beside me grinning.

I panted and shook. I tried to gather myself, stepping back.

Lyte eyed me as I slunk from him. "You have the memory in *you,*
Asher."

I turned and scuttled away around the schoolhouse without bidding him good night.

I DIDN'T TELL MOTHER OR FATHER THAT LYTE AND I HAD SPOKEN AGAIN.
The confidence flared inside me with the irresistible thrill of sin.
It was so alarmingly simple not to speak, to clutch the secret deeply
and own it all myself. The clutching grew delicious.

I began to see Josiah Lyte differently. In my mind his image
morphed into something more alluring than fearful, something
magnetic. He seemed not to be bound up as most people were; he
stood back from all that—not that I could have put a finger on exactly what made him so unique. He was a manic sort of fellow to be
sure. Even now I remember him as unnervingly pale, bloodless in
the cheeks, ribbed with black nature. But I gave myself up to the
gravity that drew me to him, allowing that inward force to pull
with total strength, and in time something tore inside me. Then I
was changed. When he approached me again I spoke to him without guilt or qualm.

"Is it true," he asked me one night, "that you started talking in full sentences all at once when you were hardly fourteen months?" And he saw my surprise that he should know such a thing.

Lyte brought me after him into the schoolhouse. He pulled a book from the row of spines on his desktop and held it close to me. It was a red volume, gold letters along its edge, paper soft and beige. He fingered open the cover and drew back a vellum endpaper to show me the portrait of a gentleman in a high collar and dark cravat. The man had the look of a gallant, yet also of a country minister—two expansive, crystalline eyes and a large Roman nose. Oblong shadows sat in pockets beneath his cheekbones, lending him an air of rugged health.

Lyte fanned the pages under his thumbs. He read silently a moment, thumbed again, then spread the book wide and read aloud: *"Life is our dictionary."*

It was a bold, quick oratory, and Lyte's voice freighted it with a biblical magnitude. He looked up from the page and smiled triumphantly. "Ralph Waldo Emerson," he said. "That's true to your mode of learning, isn't it? Yes. And true to mine."

T HROUGH CHRISTMAS AND INTO THE NEW YEAR I SAW MORE
and more of Anna Flood, and Thomas Motion grew in-
creasingly remote every time I scrambled through darkness with him. We did not speak of the rift between us, though it
fashioned our former intimacy into a thing businesslike, a series of
frigid dealings—and we had no way of redressing that new hardness; it was in some manner beyond our jurisdiction. Still, I lost no
interest in my night-learning, and Thomas, despondent as he was,
did not abandon our lessons but took up a fiercer kind of instruction.

January days the mountain stood capped by long bars of cloud,
and January nights the cloud sank down and set to foaming along
the hills till the air grew tense with static. To me it was all darkness, a leaden froth. One such bewitched night, Thomas Motion
and I stole away from school and stalked through the shadows and
brush in the January foam.

"You're close, Witherow," he said. "You're almost there." It was
a sort of indignant admission.

He pulled me through brambles, leaf, thorn. I locked my legs at every step in terror of colliding with something hard in the blindness. Thomas clucked his teeth and shook my arm. "Goddammit, come on, Witherow."

We trudged up a sharp, long hill. Sound drew close around us, closet-like in the compacted air. We seemed to be moving up a narrow space—a ravine. I made out, by the wending of our course from the schoolhouse, that we were in the Black Diamond Canyon—a thin V slanting into the Cumberland Ridge behind the works of the Black Diamond shaft and the Mount Hope Slope. The early men, Hawxhurst and Henderson, had shoveled Nortonville's first coal in the old drifts on the northern pitch of this canyon, sacking it down along this rough trail to the meadow where the town now stood, then packing it out of the valley by mule. They hadn't lasted long that way. But even profitless labor wears ruts in the earth, so there was still this fair suggestion of a footpath leading straight up the cleavage of hill.

My feet kicked blindly at rock and downed limb as Thomas sped me along beneath the netted tree-cover. We mounted the last surge of earth and walked out onto the flat ridge and the air around us grew wide again. From here, in daylight, you could see Mount Diablo to the south, the San Joaquin waters to the north. But tonight I was afloat in darkness. I heard grasses hissing against our legs, smelled soil and pine and the vague tang of a faraway skunk.

Thomas dropped my hand. He seemed to vanish with the sudden lack of touch, though he stood somewhere in front of me in the grass.

Silence engulfed us. Space flowed vast before me and behind. It coursed left and right and diagonally across the globe, plunged over and upside down along every curvature of the earth, glided close along earth's antipodal bulge to speed back and flow over me again. My blood spread every which way through my limbs. My body diverged in all directions.

I have since suffered a stroke—*endured* a stroke, I should say, because I've come out of it with all my faculties, though I'm forced to do things slower these days. The seizure of my blood at the moment of the stroke was like a halting of the earth on its axis, like the depletion of this planet's magnetism. In that bizarre stasis I felt myself afloat, thrombosis detaching me from the earth's crust. That was the complete opposite of what I felt in my blood on this night with Thomas Motion. Extraordinary, to have lived both these moments.

Thomas rustled.

"It's dark here, huh? In big places like this, where there's just ground and sky and distance, it's darker than anywhere, though you don't expect it. You're close, Witherow."

Then he was near me. A voice in my ears. Breath upon me.

"This darkness is proof. Now you can know. There's no saying it, but this dark won't let you through. There's a different darkness—break that one open."

He punched me, his knuckles jabbing sharp against my sternum. Pain webbed my breast and I thought I heard glass splintering. The bony knuckles stayed digging at my chest cavity, wanting to tunnel toward my heart, which constricted now.

I stood still a moment, entranced by the pain, then shoved Thomas off. There was a trailing whisper of grass and I knew he'd left me.

I touched my breast. The blood had risen with angry heat there. I pressed my hand at the heat and listened with all my body, petrified. I felt I was stopping a terrible wound and I wondered if Thomas had indeed rifted a chasm in that spot. Then my heart leapt against my hand, slammed itself into the wall of my palm.

I gulped at the January cream, alone in the darkness, my body tremoring. Surely Thomas had abandoned me here. He'd had enough of my ineptitude.

Space compressed itself around me, drew inward with a compacting force.

I heard the yowl of something wild in the openness below.

My hand could not keep against the pressure. My heart gushed out in a spray of blood. Blood roared thick for several moments, then slowed and thinned and spread like a stratus cloud in all the depressurizing space, pooling outward on all sides. The air soaked up the color like a cloth.

Next there was emptiness—vacuous and sucking, as though the night had puckered its dark cheeks.

Finally all that space poured inward, flowing in countless intersections through my body. It was an ineffable convergence—I stood crossed and recrossed, as if held fast under some immense, supernormal knot. I looked inward and saw that I was like a cave. I turned and entered that cavern as though entering the earth.

And here was a landscape: a field of tall grass. A coyote bush prickling against the darkness. A pine. A cottonwood. And here to the north: the white river flowing, definite as though in daylight, lands hazy beyond.

Turning: here was the mountain in the south, huge in the night.

Not long before, Josiah Lyte had told me this mountain was once the world's center, that it had borne the sacral names of the native peoples. The Ohlone called it *Tuyshtak,* the Nisenan *Sukku Jaman,* the Julpun *Oj-ompil-e,* the southern Miwok *Supemenenu,* and *Kawukum* was the word by which it was known to a nameless tribe. Now the names struck in my heart like colossal bells. And all of that was in me: the grassy field, the dark horizon, the mountain and its many names.

The big shape stood lucent against the sky, as though rimmed in light. Then the pleated slopes quavered into motion, pockets of hillside shadow lurking sideways, and a furtive plume of breath brought out a form against the mountain-face.

Without a sound, a cougar stood before me in the grass, contour of muscle camouflaged in contour of mountain, flank against flank. I stood fixed before the two burnished eyes glowing low in the air. I held my breath.

The animal grew clearer as if by a change of light. In its tawny fur was a luster as of moving waters. One great forepaw hovered above the grass. Then it lowered its head, dipped its muzzle into the warm liquid of my scent, and its eyes rolled upward. We stood there a while, I and it, the dark gaze slinking over me. I saw that it had emanated from someplace deep and old within the mountain's core, taking form for the nocturnal hunt. Its two shoulder-peaks rose from the riverbed of the spine. I saw the sleek descant of the haunch.

The mountain rippled and the animal slipped away through the field.

I breathed again and walked toward where it had stood, the suggestion of its body in the grass. The mountain enlarged before me and it seemed I could enter into it as into a house. I wanted to be like the cougar had been: noiseless shadow and strength, leonine body of hill and hollow, part of the mountain's palimpsest.

Thomas found me slinking in the grass, hunched over like a creature. He was smiling as I'd not seen him smile in weeks.

"You've learned it, Witherow. We're done. Now we can sport in the darkness!"

We bolted through the grasses together, dodging trees, clods of earth exploding from our feet. The night air was ginger as satin against our faces. We were at one with shadow.

From the ridge, Thomas led me down an eastern slope and over a swale of green into a bowl between hills where the tall oaks cast a wide canopy. I was right on his heels when he turned and halted me with his rabble hands. The wool of my trousers rested wet and heavy against my legs. The night dew hung cool between my collar and neck. It was late now, but I did not think of this. I thought of the slender lion watching us from the brush.

Thomas jerked his head to the side and scrambled up a fold of earth, toward the steep hill-wall to the east. He pried back some spiny juniper fingers and ducked into the brush. I followed.

We came to a low arch yawning black in the hill-wall. He turned to me. Against that black he appeared radiant, a light in himself. A cool draft purled out of the passageway behind him.

"In?" he said, tossing his head again. And he vanished into the tunnel.

I heard his feet shuffling in leaves and I did not hesitate.

The blackness engulfed everything as I entered. It took a long time for my sight to adjust, and still I could make out only texture: the rough walls close on both sides, the layered leafage underfoot— as though my eyes could not see, but could touch. The crude vault of the tunnel grazed my head as I walked.

"Thomas, I can't see."

We kept walking. The tiny nickel of light at the tunnel mouth shrank to nothing.

Blackness deepened, ink-thick. The chill draft gained force as we drew near the long esophagus of an airshaft.

Thomas turned and I walked against his raised hands. A current of air whistled upward just behind him.

"Now down," he said.

I heard him scuff and barely made out the dropping of his form against the dark wall. He lowered himself feet-first over the ledge into the shaft.

I edged forward, my feet scooting among leaves, until I heard the leaves twittering up on the channel of air. I crouched and found the ledge with my hands, then turned and swung my feet over in that wind and slid down. The magnetic blackness tugged. I dangled my legs along the wall, panting against that pull.

Motion heard me from below. My limbs were dislodging tiny pebbles from the rock.

"There're spikes," he said.

I swung broad and high and low until I touched one with my ankle, a small post, secure in the wall. I found another near my waist, solid like the lower one, so I let go of the ledge and spidered myself between them.

I worked my way down between these spikes, resisting the suck of gravity. Thomas was somewhere just below me. We might have been floating there in that disembodied place, but I felt the rock against my forearms and knees and told myself we weren't. We weren't.

"Thomas, I can't see."

"I know. I can't either."

Where are we going? I ask this question every time my memory moves down again into that January night, down again into that pitch-black air shaft. The question is a koan beneath which my life has moved for the last eighty years. There's never been an answer and I suspect there never shall be; the koan itself is the answer, however inscrutable. And meanwhile, out in a country well past the boundaries of thought, I am inching along the rim of a cliff, the sheer bluff of my own heart, one leg braced on solid earth, one dangling over a chasm. All of this is a mystery.

I scaled down and down. My muscles locked hard as I clung to the spikes. The lungs of the closed earth fumed upward. Thomas hardly made a sound. I thought to call to him but could not spare energy for words. After some time though, the spikes came warm in the dark, oiled from his hands, and I was assured he was there below me.

We sprawled and retracted our invisible legs. We rubbed our full bodies down the length of the earth. Our minds closed against everything above us. There was nothing upward, nothing overhead, only this long descent. We were in the blackness like ants in a tube. We crawled deeper down the throat of gravity, playing against gravity like insects.

Finally I heard a shuffle below. Motion had reached the floor.

I clambered on till my legs dropped free of the wall. Then I released the spikes and fell. Earth did not catch me at first, and for a moment I swore I would keep dropping through blindness to the deep center of things—but then earth shoved at my feet with an impact that bent my knees and sent me squatting. I pitched forward and braced my hands against the floor: coarse slat of wood. The tracks of the mine.

I stood and sensed Thomas beside me. But he was still silent.

The air was dank. I knew that smell. The same one clung to father at the end of each day. The underworld wind rolled from far off, churning toward the shaft. We heard scampering along the floor near our feet, the whine of rats, their little bodies brushing by.

Thomas moved along the slats and I followed the trail of his sounds. Black clay squashed under our boots.

"There's no light," Thomas said. "Everywhere there's a little light but not here."

We walked a few moments, tentative and slow against the carbon black. Then Thomas turned around and we walked a while the other way. But our exploration seemed clamped up at both ends by something invisible and mean, unwilling to lay a path for us. Our walking bodies wanted a horizon and stopped when they were given none. We were inside the horizon.

"Dammit," Thomas hissed.

We walked very slowly for a long while, till it seemed we'd

passed beyond most of what we knew of the earth. We moved in some dark wet compound of dream and frozen time. Sound grew shallow, like words in a closed mouth. Muted chafing of foot against slat. Muted gush of clay under boot.

There was a plash and slop in front of me, a confused grunt and the dull smacking of limbs stirring in mud. I stopped and heard Thomas come up cursing.

"Goddammit, Witherow, I fell into something. Dammit, the shit's all over me!" He spluttered repeatedly, trying to expel something from his mouth.

Moments later, when the flame lit the gangway, I would learn that he had slipped into a shallow bowl beneath the slats. A steady muck had sluiced down from the room overhead and collected there in a tiny swamp.

I heard him freeing himself of the sludge, then the angry flap of his clothes as he tried to swat his hands clean. I heard the grating of fingers to scalp and made out that he was wiping his hands in his hair. I stood wordless through his fit of disgust. Then there was silence as he studied something in the blackness.

"Good. It's dry," he said. "Didn't think we'd use it but I'm glad it's dry."

He brushed past me and moved a few paces back along the tunnel. There came a low scraping sound, then his voice again: "Dammit. Witherow, come here."

I drew up to him. I knelt near his voice.

"Here. Take it," he said. His freezing hands seized mine. He pinched a matchstick between my finger and thumb. "Take it. My hands are all greased. I can't get a strike."

With one hand I touched the ground near my feet, then walked my fingers across the damp dirt until the iron rail of the tracks rose against my touch. I scratched the matchstick across the metal and a small flame burst the darkness with incredible light.

We glanced about. It was as though the light itself had discovered us at our trespass. The gangway track rolled straight off into shadow in both directions, the tunnel roof and walls timbered with great beams. Overhead, the wall gaped with the dark mouths of chutes. The floor was all puddle and clay, black, and on the one side was the terrible pudding Thomas had fallen in.

I looked at him now. He was black to his belly, his arms sogged to the elbow. The muck had splattered his face and his hair stood up in dark clumps. I rarely saw him in light at all while I knew him, and here he was in the naked glow of a matchstick: covered in black as in shadow. I saw our breath billowing white and shivered.

Thomas was holding a short, blunt taper. He tilted it toward me.

"Light it," he said.

—My mind wants to jump forward now. Suddenly I am thinking of the spring that followed fast upon this late January night. It was like the first spring for me; from it I have known every spring since, and each has been terrible with new life, each a ruthless combustion. A monstrous wind stirs and shreds the long cloud bars at the mountaintop. In their ripping the clouds insinuate—have insinuated ever since that night—the soft, tearing scream of new flame. I hear terror when the sun splits them.

—"Light it," he said.

And a tongue of flame leapt from candlewick to cuff. Fire growled from the swinging arm. Thomas whipped himself about, torso spinning. I saw the fire stretch like glue across him and both his arms were suddenly lashing orange. He fell back against the tunnel wall.

In my memory I want him to scream, but he is quiet as he was, whimpering only. He struggles against the wall somewhat, a blur of black fume and light. Scuffling to his feet again, he comes up with skull aflame, face and hair engulfed. He flings his head side to side like an animal with prey in its teeth, clods of fire falling from his ears.

I want to see his face enraged against the burn, but there is only the impotent bucking of limbs. The tunnel is all alight. Heat rages. Thomas turns, confused in the brightness, and walks straight into the wall. Then again. And again. He wants to tunnel into that spot of earth, cool himself in the darkness he knows.

He stumbles and slumps down against the wall, then catches himself and begins to run on into the tunnel, deeper, the blaze going with him. The slats trip him up and his legs catch in that bowl of muck. His body's fire slurps up the muck and Thomas bursts bright in a new snarl of flame.

I want him to fall, to crumple forward, to succumb, but he stands there stuck upright and burning.

I race to the shaft and climb without effort, as though lifted on his rising heat.

BONE

{ 1 }

In my long life I have come to hate winds. But *HATE* is the wrong word, because I've never had a visceral nature; my blood has always flowed with a leaden surety, moderate even in whirlwinds. No—*hate* is imprecise, too shallow a term.

But the impudent spring winds of our Carbondale region, so rude with frost, have long jarred my memory. Even if I am walking in the static heat of a summer afternoon or gazing through the immobile air over a field, they still wear upon me. I clench my fists and grimace—an involuntary reaction, a physical reflex much like the spasms of a stroke. And then I see it for what it is: a kind of life-will at work, rising against the wintering. Something inside me is as stubborn and impregnable as granite and resists the wind's erosion. Yet all the same I am worn smooth. I cannot deny it.

That year, 1872, spring arrived in the first days after Thomas Motion's death, and nature was pagan in all its festivity: azure sky, white light, early blossoms. But still those winds began to blow—those vituperative gusts with all their withering freeze. They came raging between the two round-topped hills at our valley's northern mouth, as though in vengeance against the sudden spring. Our little houses shuddered and the winds railed under doors. The smokestack's gray exhaust sprayed the town, tiny particles mounding into lumps of ash against the buildings. We wrapped our heads like Bedouins, squinting against the sting. An incessant crashing filled our ears, like an avalanche of salt; it edged us toward a docile madness, the blunt unease of a paranoiac dream. Our bodies warped beneath our clothes. Our bones softened and paled like driftwood.

Only now do I see that this was the first spring—this season after Thomas Motion's death—that the winds ravaged inward and left me, as they have done ever since, bewildered by my own resistance.

Merely eight years old as I was, I learned in but a few hours' time to wrestle against that bright blaze that had eaten Thomas before my eyes—that meteor-fire whose beauty would burn too hot in me if I opened myself to its wonders, if I spent a breath in testimony to it.

So there was wind and flame, both. I saw us folks of Nortonville teethed upon from all sides. Recoiling from that, I kept silent about my place in Motion's death. Silence was my grotto out of that squall, out of those sparks that rivered down the leathering air.

But silence, as I now know it, is both a demon and a builder of things. To one in metamorphosis (and we are, all of us, always in metamorphosis) it is like a pitted fruit in an infant's mouth: impossibly succulent, and all the time poised to slip backward down the tongue, to lodge like a quiet boulder in the throat. It is the very bloodstream of this world, yet silence can carry awful poisons in its roiling current.

The night I ran home from the fire, I slept in my parents' bed at father's side. I had nearly crashed into him on the dark footpath outside our house. He was coming home late from the Exchange Hotel. My body was still steaming from all the running and he stopped me with the grip of one great hand at my arm, then stood before me in shadow while I caught my breath. The smell of Thomas's smoke covered me faintly.

I gulped at the air and said: "Where's mother?"

"Inside. She's laid with the headache all evening. You just now home from school?"

"Yes, sir. Been up over the Cumberland Rise."

He looked so motionless and tall in that dark: my father—real in a way he hadn't looked before. He filled the night air with a presence that seemed knitted from some fabulous element. I thought to tell him then of Thomas's burning, thought I heard the words spilling out fast—but too fast! Too fast—that I could relate a death in the space of a moment. So I said nothing.

I glanced at his knees and felt him fixing his eyes upon me. He squatted before me and I smelled his closeness: the pale odor of lye over a day's sweat and grime, the pungency of beer from his beard.

He squeezed my arm.

"Where've you been tonight, Ash?" His voice was as tight and plaited as a binding of rope.

"Up the Cumberland Rise. Like I told you, father."

"Running around alone up there?"

"Yes, sir. Getting my night eyes. So I'll be ready when I go below."

He tested my claim with a dogged stare. Then his hand wandered in his beard. "Your mother'd think you awful late. Good thing for you she's to bed already. Best she doesn't know you were up there on your own head."

"Yes, sir."

Still he squatted there before me. "Did you take a spill coming down?"

"No, sir."

"You look it though. What's happened?"

I answered him quickly and felt no danger of letting slip a word about Thomas. Thomas was weighted firm under the silence now.

"I met a cougar up on the ridge."

"Tracking you?"

"No. But we both got a start, I think."

He took my chin in his hand and moved my face as he wanted it. "Mm, yes. That'll rattle a boy I reckon. You sleep with me tonight." Then he guided me into the house.

Only now does it occur to me what father suspected that night: that I'd gotten caught up alone with Josiah Lyte. So maybe mother's apprehensions, though he parried them off with reason and talk, touched him quick in moments of unease, and the first thing that should cross his mind at the sight of trouble in my eyes was abuse at the hands of the curious Lyte.

In bed beside father, I lay long awake. His great body inert and hot beneath the wool, thin nightshirt over rough-hewn skin. He breathed loud in his sleep, sending out thunderous vibrations like a lion. Beyond him mother moaned. The headache was troubling her dreams.

In the early morning hours I heard the wind rattling under the floor.

⌁

I KNOW NOW THAT BENEATH THE WORLD'S WINDS, DEEP IN THE IMPASSIVE heart of rock and vegetable, there resides a dark and elemental silence, an indomitable thing that turns this world hour by hour. In those days my own silence was drawing me close to this powerful substratum of Nature, this noiseless pulse. And that was no domain for a boy. None for a grown man at that.

Even today, though all the awful tumult of those boyhood years is passed, I sit here troubled by this fearsome silence. Who masters it? What god might I blame for all it has wreaked in my life? If I put my ear to a growing oak, the most I hear is the sigh of tree-joints under the press of the wind. Or if there is no wind and it is quiet and I am very lucky, I might detect the low scrubbing of a beetle. Or maybe the *tacka-tacka* of a jay's beak. But where is the noise of the living tree itself?—the creak of its dilating rings? What dark hand is gripping it to fashion its annular growth and decay? And how am I gripped? The mystery has haunted me for years and years, for I was first gripped in these days after Thomas was killed, and I felt it like terror.

The truth is there's no listening to this noiseless thing as it squeezes the world. Such listening is the work of remembrance—it always happens too late. I've come to accept this. Man shall never invent an instrument fine enough to tune the waves of the great silence in its working hours. And it's never so simple that he might turn to read his own heart like a meter. We are powerless to capture its effects, and then we're given memory.

So here I sit, ancient in this overused body, and I am a vain instrument of sorts. Because I'm still alive, the silence still flows in me. It's in there, mastering my every moment, compelling this old body into all kinds of contortions: wrenching me, bending me, tying me into knots. No doubt it's the very thing at the bottom of all these memories; through them it is stretching me back in order to send me flinging toward the grave someday soon.

While I hang here stretched taut with so much stored motion, these arthritic limbs of mine remain pitched in muscle and marrow to the dread clang of a great tuning fork. And this is what the long hum seems to say—this is the best guess I can make: Inside me and inside all things the world is pure silence, yes. But then too there's an outside silence, and they rub, these twin silences, like air fibers before a storm. Their friction drives the engine of event. Silences grind, and things happen. Everything—incidental, monumental, wondrous, terrific, harrowing—begins like this.

But how is it a child could host such a colossal thing? And how does the child reckon with that once he's grown?

The next morning in the breaker the boys were already murmuring of Motion's disappearance. The slat next to mine lay empty, and Boggs paced along the row of chutes.

"Who's got word of Thomas Motion?"

"He's run off, sir," said one kid.

"No he ain't," said another, "he's dead somewheres."

Boggs stopped before the talker, a red-haired twig of a boy who twisted round on his plank. "You know about it, Burns?"

"I know what his pa told my pa this morning."

"What?"

"That he's certain of something awful. Certain Thomas got ate up or fell someplace and broke his neck."

Boggs turned and looked my way. As if unwittingly compelled to assign me penance, he barked out: "Witherow! Today you keep one foot in either chute, you hear?"

So I set my plank end to end with Motion's and straddled the chute rail and all day long my two hands did the work of four.

By evening, most of the town was privy to the news of the missing breaker boy. Though Mr. Motion had but murmured his presentiments to a brakeman during his short walk to the works that morning, he might as well have posted a notice at the mercantile. A child gone missing stirs a dread that is tenfold to that around a child found mangled or misused in the brush someplace. Then too, unease was to Nortonville a thing like plasma in the limbs of a body. Such was the nature of a town peopled as much with superstitions as with working folk.

At supper that night, I swore my every movement dripped with criminality. Mother served us brown beans and hunks of beef and as I sawed at the meat my arms and hands looked murderous and vile. Father gulped buttermilk from an old jar he treated as a glass. The cream stood in his mustache like divots of glue.

"Some men'll go out looking tonight," he said. "Most likely the boy went headlong down a bluff."

"A search party already?" said mother. "My, that's quick."

"Aye. Town can't stand the mystery for long. We both know that."

"I didn't know Mr. Motion had called for it is all."

A trail of grease went splashing from the full fork in father's hand. His cheek bulged with beef, the jaw champing words and meat alike. "He hasn't done," he said. "No need to wait on that. It's a matter for the whole village."

"I suppose it is."

"The party's all company men. We'll start at the Exchange and go up over Somersville one way and up the Cumberland the other."

Mother shook her head at her plate. "God help you find the boy whole."

We ate in silence, the meat smacking between our teeth. The minds of both my parents seemed elsewhere entirely. They appeared not to notice me at all. They never knew the intensity of my friendship with Thomas—I don't think anyone did. He and I had raced about in that outside darkness which no one else thought to frequent. But I'd believed surely mother and father would read everything from the distressed signs of my body. I had thought I'd glow maroon with the whole history, such that they could stand me up and review it all—my arrangement with Thomas, our night-races and breaker tests, his bright expiration—clear as the visions in a stereoscope.

So maybe I didn't look as awful as I felt. Maybe my silence had smoothed everything out, even the blame that coursed inside me, that heated my hands and made them look to me so deadly and red. Perhaps that didn't show.

I thought I should say something. I might invite their suspicion otherwise.

"Do you think he's dead, father?"

Both of them turned to me then, their chewing mouths strangely slack. So now they *were* considering the possibility of their boy after all, the things his reddish hands might hide. I tucked one hand beneath the table. The other lay in plain view, grasping the fork, and I could not remove it—it would not go at my command.

"Oh, dear," said mother. And she gave father a long look, then slid her eyes back at me. "You knew him, didn't you, Asher?"

I said nothing.

Father stared at me, though his fingers rubbed the wood of the table beside his jar as if working salve into a wound. "We don't know yet, Ash. Nothing's certain yet."

Mother leaned. "Did you know him well?"

"No, ma'am."

This is the very first bold-faced lie I ever gave my mother. It came slipping out of me without effort, in a manner like something fashioned, preformed. It seems to be one of Nature's strict dictates that as the body of a boy grows, and whether he would choose it or not, he is by some fell strength unknown to him stretched and pulled away from his mother. The pattern is begun from the moment of conception: the child goes outward and outward on the breaking of some irreducible wave. He is fashioned from seed, sustained by some endogenous juice, delivered, and after a time commanded to lie and deceive, to squirm and wrangle toward some independence, some separateness he might never have chosen of his own volition. It's yet more muscular work of that great *something* that's got us always in its grip.

"No, ma'am," I said. "Not well. But I knew him."

Mother's face looked rigid and angular.

"Mr. Motion believes he died," I said. "Doesn't that mean it? His pa knows best, doesn't he?"

"Maybe so," said father. "But what's most needful is we find the boy."

As soon as he'd swabbed his plate dry and gobbled his soaked bread, father rose and got his hat. He took his Davy lamp from its place near the door, gave mother and me a grave nod, and went out.

They found nothing that night, a band of fifteen men dispersing into the hills and tracing the long, curved rim above our valley. I went up to the schoolhouse and could hear their voices over the chatter of the kids streaming in the darkness around me. When I came out of the schoolroom they were still up there calling. Motion's name fell through the night above Nortonville, lobbed down the hillsides in every direction, like the wayward shuttlecocks from some futile contest in the dark up there. I went back down the hill to our house and the name multiplied in the air around me, all those voices propagating the name till the night was overrun with it.

When I came to our door I saw that I couldn't go in. Mother's lamplight burned softly at the windows. That inside quietness in her presence would unhinge me. So I sat down on the stoop, my boots planted on the frozen footpath, and hugged myself against the embroiled winter air. Now and then I could see the broken membranes of light from the search lamps floating high in the darkness. The Black Diamond Canyon, penciled with trees, flickered clear and then the blackness was whole again.

A tiny stream of white smoke appeared and I heard a voice, words dissolving in that white.

"Has your father gone up there?"

Anna was standing at the side of the stoop, lit softly by the window gleam. She had made no sound as she approached. I thought she must have been lingering nearby the whole time, watching me from the shadows. She hugged the awning post with one slender arm and glanced up into the flickering trees.

"Is your father in the search?"

"Yes."

"Do you suppose they'll find that boy?"

I shrugged. "Maybe. Maybe not."

"What if they don't?"

I stared off. I did not answer.

Anna hung back. I could feel her eyes on me.

"Can I sit with you?" she said.

I said nothing, but scooted over on the boards. She came and sat, her damp winter smell stirring after her.

"Don't you wonder," she said, "what'll happen if they never find him?"

I shrugged.

"Once in Trinidad," she said, "four men got buried in the mines. Way down under a huge pile of rock. They could never get them out so they had a funeral without the dead people. I suppose that's what they'd do—just give the boy a funeral all the same."

"If they keep looking," I said, "they'll find him."

"You must've known him," she said.

"Yes. I did."

"From the breaker?"

"Yes."

It was somehow automatic that we should talk of him as dead. Everything seemed simpler with Anna—she and I could skip over speculation. We fell silent a minute and gazed away toward the Cumberland Rise. The lights up there were now submerged in the black again, the dark line of the ridge barely distinguishable against the night sky.

"How late will they look tonight?" she said.

"Till they're tuckered I guess."

I felt the seam of her cloak brush my shoulder. She was leaning closer.

"Do you wish you were up there with your father?"

"No."

"He's a good father, isn't he?"

"Of course. Isn't yours?"

Her shoe made a grating sound in the dirt. She bent forward and looked at it as though its motion surprised her. A long finger of black hair hung vertical from her brow. It looked very fine and soft.

"He disgusts me," she said with quiet voice. "He's a savage. So stupid with work. Have you ever seen him?"

"No."

"He's ugly and cross-eyed. I hate it when he comes home. I feed him and bring him his fresh clothes and just chew my nails till he walks out for his night whiskey. Then I can run away. I can come find you."

"Is he bad to you?"

Her eyes narrowed on the dangling strand of hair. She twisted it between finger and thumb. "I'd run away entirely if it wasn't for mother." She curled the hair behind her small ear. That ear looked like a tiny blossom in the half-light. "Would you come with me?" she said. "If I ran away one day?"

"Where?"

"You could decide." Her gentle weight was against me now. "Not Colorado, that's sure. Maybe San Francisco. Have you ever been there?"

"No. My father has been."

She turned her face on my shoulder and I scented her breath.

"Could you leave him?" she said. "You love him, don't you?"

"Yes."

"Me too," she said. "I hate it that I must love father as I do. Does your father beat you?"

"No. He would never. And if he did, mother would wallop him."

We laughed.

"And do you love her?" she asked.

"Mother? Of course."

She shot to her feet and crept fast to the side of the house.

"Anna?"

"Come here."

I got up and found her standing at the far side of the front room window, one shoulder edging the frame.

"Anna—"

"Shh. Don't spoil it. Just look."

She crooked her neck and held her face next to the glass. A bar of light slanted across one dark eye.

I stood opposite her and peered in.

"You're too close," she whispered. "She'll see you. Step back."

I tucked my body into shadow like hers, twisted my head beside the window.

Inside, mother was in her chemise. She stood at the stove making lye, spooning wood ash into a pot and stirring. The pale fabric near her torso was streaked dark with the trailings from the spoon. Her eyes looked heavy-lidded, her gaze sunk deep in the simmering broth.

"She's different," said Anna.

"Different?"

"Yes. Can't you see it about her?"

"See her difference?"

"Yes."

I stared hard through the curvy glass.

"She stands apart," said Anna. "See it?"

When I didn't answer her, she said: "She's different from your father, for one thing."

How could Anna see that? I studied my mother's hand twirling the wooden spoon.

Anna said: "The first time I looked at her in the Templars' Hall I knew it."

Mother swiveled a bit and pinched up some dried flowers from a plate on the sideboard. Anna jerked back into shadow. "Watch out."

I backed off. I could see the girl's smile, dim and wide in the grayness across from me.

"You need practice," she said. "But isn't it fun to spy? Don't people look curious this way?"

I cocked my head again, tried to see in from the shadows.

Anna said: "It's safe now." She had her face in the light once more. "Look at her, will you. She doesn't even suspect us. Have you ever seen her like this?"

I hadn't. She looked as I'd never seen her—I think she looked less mother than woman. It seemed she suddenly had a name, seemed she'd only answered to a name till now, but now the name was hers. Somehow I knew that would change again once I went inside, once her solitude was broken. We were outside now, Anna and me.

My cheek lay against the coarse house-wood. I could feel on my face the radiant coolness of the windowpane, though I didn't touch it. Anna looked spellbound in that half-light. Her white breath rolled gently against the glass without fogging it.

After she'd gone, I sat on the stoop again. I don't know how long I roosted there, but finally the lamps came wavering down and sheeted the valley floor with a patina of gold. Father came through the houses and found me shivering before our door. By the light of his Davy lamp his body looked red and liquescent.

99

"Waiting on me, Ash?"

"No, sir."

I knew I needn't ask what they'd found, and he didn't offer a word. He put out the lamp and I followed him inside.

Mother was in the rocker with her Bible. She rose and helped father from his coat. "Nothing?" she said.

Father didn't answer, but kinked his brow and blew a snuffling breath out his nose.

We dressed for bed and put out the lamps and father slumped down beside mother with a grunt. Their bed creaked as he twisted beneath the blankets, then the house was silent but for the tiny hiss of the embers in the stove. After a time I heard mother mumble.

"Going out again tomorrow?"

"Aye. And if nothing turns up by lamplight, there's talk we might halt the mines a day."

"Oh, dear."

She lay wordless a while, then: "It does play at the nerves though, doesn't it?"

"Aye."

"To think what mischief the boy might've suffered."

"Aye. It won't sit well, Abicca. You can count that as certain."

Then they were silent and I heard father's sleeping-breath. But I lay awake, and it seemed that Motion's name still dithered in droves through the January air.

THE FOLLOWING NIGHT THE NAME WAS AGAIN AFLUTTER UPON THE sundry voices as I went up to the schoolhouse. The men were still calling after school, when Josiah Lyte took me into his room and bade me sit with him. The desk rows imprinted the darkness around us like a tartan. Crickets screeched beyond the closed doors, over the crackle of the schoolroom stove.

"This Thomas Motion is your friend, isn't he?"

"Yes. He is."

"Are you afraid for him?"

I said nothing.

"Afraid of what they might find?"

"No." Somehow, despite all the complicity tackled up in me, this wasn't a lie.

Lyte sat back. He webbed together his spindly fingers. "You don't fear me any longer, do you Asher?"

"No."

"But you did before, didn't you?"

"Yes."

"*Why* did you fear me, Witherow?"

In all of this I found myself answering involuntarily, as though Lyte were drawing me out by some imperceptible magnetic spell.

"I can't say, sir. Cause you're a teacher, I guess."

"But there are *adults* who fear me too. How is that?"

One of Lyte's pale hands fluttered and alighted on the small inkwell of a desktop nearby. The fingers rode the curved shape, then withdrew again.

He left his question dangling in the dim air.

"You and Thomas," he said, "I've often seen you two going off after school. Always romping in the dark together."

I felt the dint of his insinuations, clearly as if he'd clutched me with his bloodless hands. But he didn't touch me and there was only a quiet ease between us—no condescension, no threat. I read his intuition and I wasn't frightened by what he knew: that I carried the secret of Motion's disappearance. He slouched in the small desk chair before me, eyeing me with all this inhumed in his narrow face, and there seemed some soft confederacy between us.

"My mother and father were missionaries," he said then, as if sealing our new bond with the stamp of sudden disclosure. He got up and vanished in the darkness and I heard him feeling among objects. He came back holding something big in his hands. I watched a globe turn beneath the rays of his fingers.

"Here," he said, and pointed to a triangular shape, a country like the ear of a dog. "I lived here. In India." His fingers crawled over the tiny country, antennae-like. "I spent my youth here: Deccan, Bihar, Patna, Agra. Do you know anything of the people who live in this place, Asher?"

"No."

"There's a saying among them: *The wise man does not grieve.* Can you understand that?"

The words seemed in some way fiery and bright, as though I must squint against their dazzlement.

Lyte said: "These people burn their dead rather than bury them. They set them afire on the riverbank. Or they send them floating down the current to the sea. They don't hide death away. Can you imagine such a place? Such people."

Lyte's mouth moved against the glow of the lamp. The trim, dry lips popped softly.

"I broke faith with my parents," he said. "They took me to India to spread the grain of Christianity at their side. My mother and father walked into the villages to disseminate our brave Christ and the Christian fear of death. But I fell away from that. I found a new seed in that country. It grew up in my heart, Witherow—the seed of Brahma, of Vishnu, of Shiva. How could I have helped it? As the seed grew I heard, of all things, Christ's voice. The Christ who says: leave home, hearth, family, to follow me, and don't look back."

He put the globe aside and leaned near me in the darkness. His words had become soft and raw, disemboweled shapes in the still air between us.

"My parents came to fear me, Asher. My father and mother, both. Even them. I think I'll always be feared. But you—" he held a long finger aloft in the air and for a moment his words escaped him. He brought the finger to his mouth and with his teeth briefly tugged the skin off the knuckle. He said: "You ought to know something of those three names, Witherow. Brahma. Vishnu. Shiva. They form a circle."

He told me of the three deities and of their domains.

"They are the Bringer, the Keeper, the Taker," he said.

He drew an invisible ring in the space before me, his finger circling several times—generation after generation.

"Their names are three but they are one," he said.

As if smoke trailed from his finger-end, I saw a silvery line arcing cleanly in the air. I saw the three names patterned along the circle's course, like the points of an inset triangle. Origin and Essence and Emptiness, then Origin again. Though Lyte's talk arced as roundly as the form he drew in the air, I simply lost myself to all he was saying—and somehow it was clear to me.

"So the wise man doesn't grieve," he said at last, and for a moment he sat there studying me, such that his knowledge of Thomas and my silent burden grew patent in that space again, like a thing that had been plainly spoken between us. "I think you knew it already, Asher. You see how we know things sometimes, though they've never been taught us?"

I did see.

FATHER CAME IN LATE FROM THE SEARCH THAT SECOND EVENING AND sat silent by the glow of a candle, nursing a saucer of tea. Mother and I had gone to bed already and the house was dark. I lay on my back, listening to the gurgle of his throat as he drank, the ticking of the rocker as its gliders sawed back and forth on the flooring. I heard the big bed squeal somewhat, then mother's feet padded softly across the floor.

"The works'll sit quiet tomorrow?" she said.

Father didn't answer.

"There's word already of something blackish in the town. That boy gone vanished for three days now and not a trace. Had Mrs. Dolan for tea today. She says you can see the stamp of something evil in poor Mrs. Motion's face. She called on the lady early this morning, came straight here after. Says the poor mother's eyes are like the mercury for the dark stuff astir in the village. Says you can just read the temperature of the badness hanging on to her. Says it's high."

She stopped and still father said nothing. The house was silent. I think mother stood in one place on the puncheon floor all the while. As I stared up into the shadows over my bed, I pictured her in her chemise and stockings, fixed in the dimness before father's rocker, like a slender wraith materialized before a medium. Finally I heard her voice again.

"And there's already a name being talked—"

"I know it, Abicca." Father's voice quavered thin, as if in grief.

"He's the first to draw a question—it's only natural. I told you the women mistrusted him."

"What matters is we find the boy."

"The women have the sense for such things. Could be he's brought something darkish to this town."

"The boy's what matters. Those whispers'll spark a brushfire, Abicca. We'd best find him soon or God knows."

"I don't know as I believe it yet myself, but I think of him and how he settles on Asher. What does he want with a boy small as that?"

"We'll find the Motion kid and it'll be plain he met his own end and all this'll pass. You'll see, Abicca."

"So you think him dead?"

The rocker groaned and father's footsteps went trembling over the boards. His saucer clinked at the basin. "Come to sleep, Abicca."

"A body'll raise the roar, David, not quieten it."

"There's no roar, Abicca. Only rumor. Come to sleep."

⁓

IN THE MORNING, AS SOON AS THE SUN WAS UP, FATHER WENT OUT WITH a search party now tripled in number. Not a single workman went underground. Because the Black Diamond operators would never stand for a mere faction of truants from their pits, all the teams stayed away from the works that day, a mass acknowledgment of the dread necessity that the missing breaker boy be found. The bosses were left to throw up their hands.

So forty-five men scattered across the hills above the idle works, hollering the name that had in three days become a malediction to Nortonville, while the rest of the labor force, left to bide the whole of the nervous winter day, convened at the Exchange Hotel and at Sharp's Saloon to wet their consternation in the palliative of drink.

By noon Motion's name had fallen a thousand times to the valley floor, and the steely air, which had grown electric in a multiplex of voices, grew quiet again as the party came down for their midday meal.

It was an unsettling quietness, to be sure. A dead quietness. Mother sent me out to the Good Templars' Hall with a packed dinner for father and as I walked past the noiseless breaker I felt I went by some great carcass, some dark bulk hollowed of substance. Beyond the breaker the brick smokestack jutted skyward like a cenotaph. And suddenly I saw that all this quietness, all this mimicked death, had its brief lineage in me. Everything I knew of Thomas Motion, all the terrible knowledge my body gulped inward and inward as if by some unstoppable reverse secretion—all of that had somehow fashioned all of this: the lifeless breaker, the insensate tower of bricks, the inactive trestle overhead. In that horrible moment I realized the preternatural force that had gripped me and the whole village—and it was not something outside or above, but something indwelling. So inner things transformed outside things—even such inner things as could be encased in the tiny limbs of a boy.

In the Templars' Hall the men slouched about on benches or huddled at the little stove rubbing their hands. All were bundled in coats and hats and looked as I'd seen them only on Sundays. Clearly they'd brought the outside quietness into the hall with them, for their talk was numb-lipped, murmurous. It seemed unmanly and perverse, so unlike their usual stridency when gathered in the Exchange of an evening.

I saw father leaning in a corner. Joel Aitken sat talking to him from a bench nearby, gnawing his words while he crushed a green apple to cream in his teeth.

"Hello, Mr. Aitken."

"Ah, here's the boy with some grub for his pa."

I gave the bundle to father. He said nothing, but shouldered away from the wall and dipped his nose to the fragrance of the covered food before parting the cloth. Then he chunked off some yellow cornpone and stuffed it in his mouth, backhanding the crumbs from his beard.

He didn't look at me. His face was set in a dim stare and his eyes were pinpoints. He looked only at the food in his hands while Joel spoke. Joel had the staring face too. The gravity of two men set hard upon their task. I stood there unseen.

"We'd best spread far south as Horse Haven," said Joel, "if we hope to settle this by dusk."

Father shook his head. "Better we look close before we spread out."

"We've ranged the country three days already."

"Haven't yet gone underground."

Joel was turning the bitten apple in his two hands like a ball. He tilted his head sideways. "Well, there's a few air shafts up there on the Cumberland, that's true."

They ate in silence. Now and then their eyes traveled a little, gray glances crossing at some indeterminate point. I stood a few feet off, loath to trespass on that area where the joint thought seemed to ferment with silent force. From the hall behind me I heard the muttered talk of several men: voices sober and pensive flicking Motion's name about between the names of places. Then, amidst the patter, startling as a swallow dropping into grass, the name *Lyte*. And almost exactly at the same moment, Joel Aitken's eyes coming up with the words: "That Lyte's stirring talk, isn't he?"

"Aye, but that'll finish today."

"It's no trifle though." Joel twisted his apple stem till it came off in his fingers. "You hear about Martha Griggs? Coming home from Somersville the night the boy was lost and thought she saw a corpse candle up on Rose Hill. Stopped by the west gate all terror-struck and peered through the darkness and what does she see? That young minister walking back and forth in the graves all alone with a taper in his hand. My wife has it from her just yesterday. Back and forth like some ritualist. Now what was he doing up there?"

Father said nothing. He was plucking olives from the cloth and chewing as if in solemn Eucharist.

"And what'll the town do," said Joel, "when they all learn of that? I told Louisa to keep mum, but Martha Griggs'll tell it everywhere."

"There's nothing to that," said father. "If Lyte was on Rose Hill, he couldn't have been with the Motion boy."

"Aye, but what wickedness was he about? That's what folks'll wonder. It's known he keeps with Sarah Norton sometimes. She was near too much before he ever showed up. Folks'll take fright."

Father spat the dark pits from his cheek into the cloth. Anger creased his face like a sudden pain. "These folks'll stir their hogwash till they think it medicine."

Joel smiled bitterly.

LATER THAT DAY, JUST AS THE AFTERNOON SUN WAS STARTING TO DROP, a man's lone whistle pierced the voices above Nortonville. The long echoes of Motion's name sizzled out and a tone of low alarm sounded from man to man across the hills. I stood in the wet grass before our house and imagined I saw the trees trembling up there, the scattered party racing to the whistler from all directions, men converging on a noise like termites upon a column of heartwood.

Mother was hacking with a spade at the dirt in our growing patch. She stood up and listened. "Lord be praised," she said.

Within half an hour Main Street was astir with noise. I went running through the grasses and climbed the rail bank to get a vantage of the ruckus. A crowd of workmen was flooding from the Exchange Hotel toward the works. I went down among them, jostling up the grade till we all roiled at the foot of the smokestack.

There was a definite logic to the uproar, a oneness of mind in the bustle of all those limbs and faces. Working my way up front I saw a vanguard of party men, thirty thick, coming down to the shaft mouth fresh from the Black Diamond Canyon behind. Their rank met the Main Street rank and stopped short of merging, as though they were two warring forces sighting each other before the clash. The whole multitude began to seethe with broken phrases, news running a crude circuitry atop those many heads and shoulders. The word *airshaft* flitted on all sides, the word *dead,* and the men became a single ungainly organism breathing deep with the answer to their three-day mystery. We all remained there soaking up fragments.

Bringing him up here—way back at the Upper Black Diamond, but—
Even I soaked up those bits of news, though they could give me no relief.

Only way to get him out whole—burnt up like paper—Witherow and Aitken are back there—
Up front there was a commotion around the hoisting derrick. The cables groaned. An empty lift clattered to a stop. A corps of the party men filled the lift, and the groaning cables let them down. The long frictional noise seemed to me some slow, penitent keen given out on my behalf. Because I could not myself speak.

The derrick halted and we all stood there a great while as the dead breaker boy traveled in the arms of the men that long mile from deep beneath the Cumberland Rise to the foot of the shaft. In the course of an hour the multitude grew, trailing out behind to the steps of Noakes's Butchery half way up Main Street. The sun dangled a palm's width over the canyon ridge, the winter light flattening out and stranding in a filmy bar above the tips of grass.

Finally the cables squalled again and the lift came up into view, now clumped thick with men. They broke apart slowly like something eroding, and in their center I saw father's back, the shoulders humped. He stepped rearways from the lift and the men gave him the berth of another few paces. He was handling one end of a long board, a makeshift litter on which Thomas's body rode charred and quivering like a brittle leaf. Joel Aitken had hold of the other end (the head or the foot—there was no saying) and the two of them crept gingerly into the crowd, their eyes locked fast on that boy-like cinder between them, as if they feared the slight wind might scatter him to bits.

The crowd made very little sound as it beheld the sight. I watched father working backward amidst all the people and it seemed he carried some bleak offering for their appraisal, passing along the row their parted bodies made, head hung down in deference. Thomas went by them, a lump of carbon, like some rendering of that most basic element from which they were all concreted, some inverse reminder of their own sedimentary nature. And the onlookers' eyes as he went past gave back a terrible reflection of this realization among them.

The crowd stood in place as father and Joel Aitken walked slowly toward the houses in the valley. Only a clutch of pious folk followed after at a distance, men with their hats in hand, their wives wringing faces and fingers like empaths already carrying the sorrow Mr. and Mrs. Motion would soon find delivered to their door. I trailed along myself, well behind, and watched from a section of grass as Joel and father set the litter down on the stoop of the Motion house. For a minute they stood together before the threshold. When Mr. Motion came out they gestured meekly, stepping back as he knelt to the detritus of his boy. Then they went away slow with eyes on the ground before them.

The Black Diamond operators bore a swift community outrage over the poorness of their night watch. In an effort to deflect criticism, one watchman was ceremonially dismissed within a day. The company promised publicly to bolster its guard. This was the first aftershock of Motion's inexplicable end. Everyone knew there would be others. Having seen that disfigured thing the earth discharged, there was no letting it be.

{ 2 }

I N A THRONG OF WHIPPING COATS AND SKIRTS, I STOOD ON ROSE HILL
and chased Josiah Lyte's words out into the wind. His mouth
moved ineffectually against the oceanic roar. The pages of his
black book fluttered under his thumbs. The small grave lay open
before him. A veil of dirt unraveled from the graveside mound and
hovered over the hole. Down there: the gleam of the lacquered oblong box. In that surface a crude reflection of sky: black shine,
white windswept stars.

Lyte read from the Psalms, and the Psalms flitted from the hilltop into the night above Somersville: *"Hear my prayer, Oh Lord, and
let my cry come unto thee. Hide not thy face from me in the day when I am
in trouble, incline thine ear unto me: in the day when I call answer me
speedily."*

Father and mother stood behind me at the grave, their bodies
pressed to my shoulder blades, their hands upon me.

The previous evening, moments after that stark delivery to the
Motion house, I went up to father as he stood with Joel Aitken before our door.

"You won't come for a drink?" Joel was saying.

Father's mouth lay in a straight line through his beard. His eyes were set on something low, as if he fixated upon the muck spattering Joel's trousers.

"No," he said. "Too tired."

"All right then, Witherow, I'll raise one in your honor." Joel palmed father's shoulder a minute and his mouth shaped a smile that his eyes didn't seem a part of. He went off down the footpath toward the rail bank and I went inside after father.

The house smelled of cooking meat.

"I've fixed a steak," said mother softly. She stepped to father and kissed him and stood holding his two hands.

He kept that low-set glance, eyes grayed off at some intermediary plane between him and her. He pulled his hands away and held them from his body.

"I need to wash, Abicca."

"Of course. Asher, fetch your father a towel."

I went out and took one from the line and when I came in again mother was at the stove, talking into the pan.

"I'll scrub those for you if you get them off. You'll have to take supper in your nightshirt of course, but that's no matter. A man works at such nasty stuff as you needs his clean clothes. Needs a big supper. Needs his bath. It's a lot of good you've done though, David. You've done a lot of good."

Father was already bare-chested and bending to the basin. I brought him the towel and he set it by on the washstand without looking at me. He stared into the soapy water and his hands began working up little rapids. He scrubbed for several minutes, then cupped water in both hands and splashed his chest and arms, rubbing the soap over every part till he stood there oiled and streaked. He lifted the pitcher and tipped it near his collarbone and water ran down his trunk. He tipped the pitcher at each shoulder and let the rinse flow to his wrists. Then he plunged his hands back into the basin and scrubbed them again.

Mother got the steak from the pan and slabbed it onto the platter over some potatoes. She set the platter in the center of the table. I sat before my plate and waited. Mother stood by the table a moment, giving indirect looks toward the washstand, then went back to soak the pan. It seemed father would not bear any premature comment from us, so we hung listening to the foamy splash of his hands.

At last he made a murmurous sound, though he did not pause his scrubbing. Mother stopped the pan from its clatter, and we listened for something more.

"I can't see it," father said. "I can't see—I don't see the good of it."

He had the look of talking to the infinitesimal dirt lodged in his own fingers.

"There he was. Stuck in the slats in that dark. Just like somebody standing up in front of us. But when we got close I saw it was bad. I saw there'd be nothing to do. And I wondered, what good to bring him out? Even as we carried him I wondered. He was falling apart between us. I don't see what good—"

He stopped and lifted his hands from the water and took up the towel. We waited as he rubbed himself dry, then waited as he went and got out of his trousers and into his nightshirt. Finally he came back and sat down and mother sat opposite and nudged the platter toward him.

Now on Rose Hill, Josiah Lyte's voice entwined the Old Testament song of David: "*For my days are consumed like smoke and my bones are burned as an hearth. My heart is smitten and withered like grass, so that I forget to eat my bread. By reason of the voice of my groaning my bones cleave to my skin. Mine enemies reproach me all the day, and they that are mad against me are sworn against me. For I have eaten ashes like bread.*"

Someone howled—a thin little woman, weeping in coughs and shrieks. It was Thomas's mother, who never knew me. I'd seen her before, but we'd never spoken and she'd never learned of my camaraderie with her son. Our town was just large enough, our valley just wide enough, for such strangeness. She hunched and pressed two knobby fists to her eyes. Her husband stood behind her and clapped his hand gently over her mouth and murmured in her ear. In the lamplight her cry flapped upward and tumbled like a great moth.

Josiah Lyte smiled. He doused the coffin with a fistful of wet earth, his white hand floating upward, describing an arc against the shadows, dirt trailing from it. His eyes met mine as he spoke: "Blessed are the dead which die in the Lord: Yea, saith the spirit, that they may rest from their labors."

My feet began to burn. I looked at the ground where I stood. Something stirred beneath my boots, an undulating shape like a body arching upward. The fed earth grew tumescent, quivered like a squirming blanket. The grass prickled up at the sides of my feet.

Another wail tremored along the lamp beams and Thomas's mother lost all decorum as Lyte closed his book. She fell against her husband and muffled her terrible keen in his coat. The black mourners dispersed and a shovel began raking dirt into the grave.

$\backsim$

I NEVER WEPT FOR THOMAS MOTION, AS I'VE NEVER WEPT FOR ANYONE in all my life. Even now, though I've reached my final years, I'm not inclined to weep for anything. If I sound cold of heart, I fear I'm not to answer for that. My life has been a difficult one, I suppose, fraught with early death—and I don't believe I've just grown colder through it all. Instead (and as feeble an explanation as this seems) I think the earth has slowly become a counterpart to me—not a nemesis, but an intimate and querulous thing to which I'm engaged in struggle and sustentation alike. Anyway, whatever happened to me started back in these boyhood days. Though I sought to fight it then, I don't fight it anymore. I no longer shrink from the earth's bringings; neither do I mourn the fates she exacts. I see that I'm like the hunted deer—helpless to redirect her whims or her patterns by decision or self-will. And like the deer, I am part and parcel of her blossoms, her pods, her shoots, and her jolts, her fires, her decay, all.

In fact, by getting all this down at last, I'm standing up on the sheer bluff of the world with my toes stuck out into the void and my nose to that wind so rife with brimstone, and I'm crying at the top of my lungs: *Come end, come end!* Yet it's silly, because I know the great black hole won't receive me till I've tied my guts into sailors' knots over regrets and dreams and other torments I'm helpless to alter.

I never wept for Thomas, and today while reading the old Sanskrit words of the Hindu faith, I think I found a kind of eulogy for him: *The self is not to be sought through the senses. The self-caused pierced the openings of the senses outward; therefore one looks outward and not within oneself. Some wise man, however, seeking life eternal with his eyes turned inward, saw the self. The small-minded go after outward pleasures. They walk into the snare of widespread death. The wise, however, recognizing life eternal, do not seek the stable among things which are unstable here.*

Obsidian darkness; gloom without gradation; ether-blackness; the blood of earth: despite my early resistance, I've come to pass among and through these things without dread. But for a long time—and how very long—it was not so. And still, my friendship with Thomas Motion has remained a specter by my side—a sweep of heat in empty rooms. I've dreamt his image for many years.

"Witherow!"

I hear his raspy voice.

"Witherow, this way!"

I wake into dream. We are moving through stagnant air, in the murk of some unlit place. Our blind feet brush against grasses, snap twigs.

We claw up into a narrow mouth of rock in the ceiling above us. Light floods our senses. We emerge into a church: wood floors and rows of pews and tall slanted ceiling—like our Congregational church but utterly unlike.

There's a rustle of paper and a clatter of wood. Thomas is stomping through the pew rows, knocking the hymnals from the benches. The books tumble to the floor and he walks over them. Under his tread they turn to ash. His stride sprays up cinders.

"You didn't go in for that hogwash they were telling us, did you?"

"Who? What do you mean Thomas?"

"The father the son the holy ghost—they talk about them like they're big merry bedfellows. Bollocks!"

Suddenly he's in front of me, his nose nearly touching mine. In his eyes are embers.

"The Father creates us the Son preserves us and the Holy Ghost brings us our death. The rest is just the hogwash talk of men."

A light spills upward. There's a flame flapping in Thomas's cupped hands. He kneels and lays the flame, like a baby bird, on the floor. It throbs there obediently. Then he steps once and kicks it hard. A long scar of flame goes sputtering right up the aisle and shatters against the humble pulpit. The pulpit-cloth shivers into a mane of fire. Soon the whole altar is alive with the blaze.

"Thomas!" I shout above the chatter of flames.

All at once there is silence. Stillness. He turns to me, unsuspecting, and around us the church is intact again. Everything untouched.

"Thomas," I cry, "you mustn't!"

But he smiles coyly. He ticks his head and I look down at my hands. A ball of flame glows in the bowl of my fingers, tame and pulsing. And though I've just protested, I do not resist as he lays his hands on mine and guides the flame toward a window-dressing.

The red-orange tail lashes hotly up the wall, glares in the stained glass. Black smoke ripples up the pyramidal ceiling, a monstrous caterpillar teething at the beams. Clouds unfurl along the lower walls. Through an interstice of smoke the yellow-painted walls of my family house appear. I spin around. Our sawbuck table is engulfed in fire, my parents' bed ablaze, the sheets leaping.

"For Lord's sake, Thomas!"

He is neck-deep in flame, smiling large.

"Thomas! This is my house! We cannot—"

"It'll burn, Witherow. Keep your temper. It'll burn. But is it the Son or the Holy Ghost?"

The ruinous tongues lick hot. I am glowing redder by the minute. I stand in the pyre till the world is bright, every shadow expunged. I wake with a heavy peace.

AFTER MOTION'S FUNERAL, MOTHER WAS LIVID.

"What a despicable scene that was," she said as she placed three red bricks in the warm belly of our stove. "Josiah Lyte and that smile of his! There's something ungodly in him, David. He means to undo us in some way. And those Psalms! I'm disgraced to think of poor Mrs. Motion standing there, hearing her son burnt up all over again!"

"I know, Abicca."

"And how crass of Reverend Parry—letting that boy manage the funeral after all the talk in the village."

"But there's a chance he's heard nothing yet."

"Well, he ought to hear! There's already much being said among the women, you know. If he's still deaf to that, then I've a mind to bend his ear myself. We're not Irish Catholics that we'll bear these horrid ministers."

"I know, Abicca."

Mother was a captious woman, it's true—and mostly she dispelled her misgivings in fiery talk. But now she resolved herself to action and made her first direct scrimmage against Josiah Lyte that Sunday at church. It was our family custom to arrive early each week, sitting prayerfully while the altar boys lit the candles and the organ wheezed into song. This week mother led us to our seats.

Father stopped in the center aisle. "This isn't our pew," he said.

Mother turned. "Whom does it belong to?"

"Mr. Clayton, I think. The Lassells. The Woodruffs."

"Well, surely there's room for us," she said, and took a seat.

"Abicca, they'll come here—"

"Really, David, are these people Christians or Colonialists?" She folded her hands atop her skirts. "I don't think they'll tax us."

And so we all sat, though father glanced about a lot as the congregation began filling in around us. Mr. Clayton arrived and took his seat beside me, but I did not look up at his face. Then came Mr. Lassell with his white-haired wife. After a moment, a few indignant whispers shuddered across the sanctuary and father stopped looking around. A small host of bodies stood about us in confusion. Spouses hushed each other. Someone's wife sniffed bitterly at someone else's husband who was slow to move. Soon it was plain to everyone that some fragile equilibrium had been thrown off, but no one could tell where the aberration lay and no one would admit to being so easily perplexed and each family silently resented every other family for the disorder.

Mother sat straight and prim through all the subtle clamor, a flowery cap clipped to her up-pinned hair. Father clamped his hands together in his lap. His freckled cheeks throbbed burgundy above his beard.

Finally the congregants sorted themselves into their accustomed pews and at once a subdued murmur began trickling through the church. Mother stared ahead at the pulpit, burying an impish smile. To her left sat Delilah Woodruff, the stocky black-haired wife of

D. S. Woodruff—superintendent of the Nortonville Seminary. Mr. Woodruff himself sat at his wife's left, and beyond him the four young Woodruff children: Daniel, Dessa, Drake, and Debbie— aligned like a row of milk bottles.

The superintendent was a lean, tall man—so lean that he seemed monstrously tall. Even seated in his Congregational pew, he cut a height equal to most Nortonville men. I looked at the profile of his rectangular face, dark eyes couched in long slabs of skin. His body slanted in his shirt, for he had only a single arm. He wore the derelict sleeve rolled neatly to the shoulder and pinned. Naturally, this bindled sleeve seemed his chief trait to the kids at his school, and was the reason he prompted every one of us to terror. Though that was the fashion of a few armless miners in the town, it looked especially terrible on him for all his length. Rumors flew among the kids that he sometimes made examples of students at random. All of us quailed at the thought of his one long arm wielding the whif-fled paddle, an image so frightful it nearly civilized some wilder boys when they pondered it—though God knows we took worse things in the breaker. At any rate, this man was the husband of the lady mother sought out, and was the employer of Josiah Lyte.

When the service ended that day, mother stood and turned to the black-haired wife: "Mrs. Woodruff, would you care to come to tea at my house this Tuesday morning?"

So Delilah Woodruff became the object of mother's increasing warmth.

⌒

THE NIGHT AFTER MOTION'S FUNERAL, MOTHER HAD LAID A WARM brick from the stove between my blankets, snuffed the lamp and gone to bed herself, but I lay long awake, listening to the wind.

Listening to father's breathing, his lion-lungs shuddering my head-board.

I thought of the grasses outside, the brush along our valley walls, the naked crest of Rose Hill, patterned with stones. I thought of Thomas, silent and brittle in a nailed-up box under piles of earth, closer now to the warm brick of the earth's core. I saw Josiah Lyte standing above the grave. His yellowish grin. His white hand fist-ing dirt from the shoveled mound. I felt myself moving toward him. Somehow, he seemed my sole ally. I could not then think of everything I was bringing down upon him, though someplace deep within me I knew I held something that was terrible to him, pre-cious to him. I simply moved toward him and it was then that mother and I diverged—branching sharply into opposite direc-tions, though we would course in the same orbit around one man.

⌁

ON A SCHOOL NIGHT SHORTLY AFTER MOTHER'S GESTURE IN CHURCH, Lyte brought me into his empty room and bade me sit near him in the lamplight among the desks.

"I watched you at Thomas Motion's funeral," he said. "You didn't weep."

"No."

"Did you weep before that night?"

"No."

"No," he said, as though confirming my quiet answer for the benefit of some audience who listened from the dark beyond the lamp. He nibbled at his lips a moment. "So you didn't weep and you weren't afraid. Are you afraid now?"

"Now? Here?"

"Yes. Afraid of what will happen now they know he's dead."

I sat very still and tried to stare down the feeling in my breast. I sensed something hardening in there. Some backward process seemed at work, like the swelling of a mutant organ amidst my vital ones. There was fright there, yes. But it was different than the fright Lyte was asking after; it was closer to him than he could know. And it was encased in my stony silence. How could I say this fright to him of all people? He was my only ally. I thought of him walking back and forth on Rose Hill, candle-lit as Martha Griggs saw him. I thought of mother—but then the thinking stopped and I could barely fathom my own apprehension.

"You had it again," he said. "Standing at that grave, you had that same thing I saw before—that efflorescence, that queer élan of yours. I saw the thawing at your feet."

He leaned close, nearly whispering.

"And then that smile—your smile at Mrs. Motion's cry, just the same as your smile at Leam's burial, at the Price boy's funeral as well. How could *I* keep from smiling at the sight?"

I taloned the rough seat beneath me, gripping the wood and clambering backward in my mind to Motion's open grave, to the graveside of the Prices, of Edward Leam. Memory disentangled me from myself. I moved amongst the black crowds at Rose Hill, separate from my body.

There I stood, lamp-lit amidst the dark mourners at those earthen holes. I looked small. Lyte funneled the dirt from his fist again, over Edward, over Samuel, over Thomas. Mrs. Motion shrieked and a wide grin split the funereal mask of my face. Then Lyte's smile flashed: crescent of teeth like a naked sickle.

The schoolroom furnace creaked and tapped, the last solids in its belly turning to cinder. Lyte was still leaning close.

"I remember the Ganges, Asher, India's sacred river. How it snaked after me! It seemed to be everywhere at once. Even if I couldn't see it I could feel it, like it followed me through the streets. I remember those corpses floating down it to the sea, vultures swooping to tear them apart. Sometimes my mother would try to cover my eyes when we walked by the banks. I wouldn't let her. I threw off my mother's hands to watch the bodies drifting. The vultures rode them like rafts."

In the quivering lamp-glow, the white ridges beneath Lyte's eyes were strangely lustrous.

"You, Asher—you smile at your chum's grave. How is that?"

His gaze was like something heavy and dark upon me. It suddenly seemed too much. I shut my eyes. In the black of my lids I saw the earth bulging warm beneath me. My two feet side by side on the soil that spread its lips to swallow Thomas Motion.

"How is that?"

I opened my eyes. Lyte's anemic face hovered, disproportionate and large.

"You were with Thomas at the moment of his death. What was it to see that?"

My hand shot out and grasped his sleeve. His voice, his words, wrenched me into sudden movement. I perched on my seat, wringing his coat's wool in my fist. He seemed to wait for me to speak, but though that mutant organ within me flamed huge and raw, nearly to bursting, I made no sound.

Lyte saw my breathlessness. He said: "This world is fire, Witherow. And we have the fire in us."

He grasped my hands and brought them to my ears. Then he covered his own ears and fell silent. I heard something rumbling beneath my palms, the roar of a furnace somewhere down in my limbs. Fire gnawing. Lyte and I sat long in this way, listening to that blaze. I breathed deep again.

Finally we dropped our hands. He told me of the cremations in

India: the black, rank smoke of the burning dead. He uttered from memory a Hindu verse. *"His fire itself becomes the fire, fuel the fuel, smoke the smoke, flame the flame, coals the coals, sparks the sparks. In this fire the gods offer a person. Out of this offering the person, having the color of light, arises."*

Conflagration. Blistering of limb under flame. The ravenous appetite of a little spark. I saw all of it now as the inception of light. I'd seen Motion licked blue with fire, succumbing to that.

I held my left hand to the yellow lamp, ran the finger of my right hand over my old burn. The scar spread from the notch of my thumb over the sinuous bones toward my wrist—a crude diamond of unpigmented skin: that spot where our stove had touched my infant hand.

Outside, the crickets shrieked. I heard the wind lowing along the walls. A heathen susurration, the approach of the forbidden. I shuddered. I wanted the forbidden to come. I stood and moved past Lyte, out of the yellow circle of the lamp. I couldn't be still. A pressure was growing in my blood. Something bore down against all my young loyalties, like a flood against a dam. I paced between the desks, the pool of lamplight behind me. Then something gave way and words took shape.

"Thomas showed me how to see in darkness," I said. "I couldn't see before that. And in the daytime I showed Thomas some things. It was like that, like a trade. We went up the canyon that night and I felt it happening—I felt—"

My youth cut back the words, lopped the heads from the flowers of my thought. Still Lyte sat there with a terrible eagerness in his face.

"I saw the mountain. I saw a cougar—the cougar came from the mountain. Then we went up to the Cumberland and Thomas took me into the airshaft after him. It was dark—pitch dark. I could see now, you know—but not in there. In there we couldn't see anymore at all. Not even Thomas. There're places like that, I guess. We climbed down there and walked around."

My voice fell flat over the floor, like a bolt of canvas dropped down. I wanted to rise again from my seat, though I already stood. I wanted to dart through the shadows, to shout, to fling my arms out wide. My heart ached like a swollen fruit in my chest.

"Thomas tripped. He fell into something—something wet. I could hear it splashing. He gave me a match and then I saw him. I saw where we were. He was soaked in the stuff—he was black from head to foot. My father calls it *goaf* I think, but it just looked like mud. He had a candle in his hands—"

Then I was deep in the telling of it, something inward bursting slow like an abscess. Lyte sat craned in that lamplight and my words traveled out of the darkness toward him. The darkness seemed conductive, made the words possible. I told him slowly of Thomas's death. I found myself struck deep with an awful thrall like praise. I spoke soft, but it seemed I nearly sang of the effulgence I'd seen. And then it was out of me. It was out of me—and yet I hadn't told him all I knew.

I stayed there in the dark and for a long while Lyte sat staring at his lean hands, his neck curled over the upturned palms in his lap, as though he held my secret there. As though the secret itself gave off that pool of light around him and he was wondering at the glow of it.

"I see it, Asher," he said without lifting his eyes. "It's clear."

But standing back from him in those shadows I saw that it wasn't clear. I saw all that he didn't yet know, all that I'd thought to tell him when I began. So my body tremored toward speech again.

"Mother had tea with Mrs. Woodruff," I stammered. "She means to do something to you, I think."

Lyte didn't move.

"Mother disliked your reading at Thomas's grave—the Psalm."

Now he looked up. About him was a deep silence like a loosening of long hair over his face. He sank back behind that curtain, motionless again. For a moment it appeared plain that he understood.

"Your mother dislikes me, Asher," he said. "But it's not your fault. I trouble her, I think. Why is that?"

I stood silent. I might have answered him, but that I felt so far on the wrong side of things now. I hadn't made him understand. I seemed to have muddled something that had started very clear. And before I could muster words again, he stood and said: "Come," and carried the lamp to the front of the room.

I followed him to his desk and he raised a book in his hands, lifting the lamp to the open pages and reading aloud: "*When we have broken our god of tradition and ceased from our god of rhetoric, then may God fire the heart with his presence.* Do you see, Asher, how the Christian death that my parents taught became so alien to me? How I walked along the Ganges and that teeming river made it all different?"

I looked in his eyes. I said nothing.

"Is that why I trouble them?" he said. "Because I don't squint at death, they think I don't fear God? It's *my* death after all. It's inside of me the same as my birth. Christ knew that."

He edged nearer. Something sickly smeared his countenance now, something pitiful, like a hunger.

"Why are they troubled?"

He appeared to need something of me, and I saw, helplessly, that it wasn't the thing I had tried to give—so I found myself staring down at my two hands, which were opening and closing like mechanisms.

When I looked up again, Lyte was smiling. But immediately a

splinter of pain cracked that smile. "I wonder what your mother would have had me read that night. At the grave. If not that Psalm, then what?"

He closed the book and put it into my hands. It was that red-bound volume of Emerson that he had showed me some time before.

"Shall I take it?" I asked.

"Yes."

As I went away from the schoolroom that night I felt I carried Lyte's loneliness down into the valley with me. I walked through the dark, and behind me, up in that schoolhouse on the hill, he seemed so innocent of everything I knew. That innocence drew a big circle round his feet, cordoned him off from all that surrounded him, everything and everybody. I had thought to cure him of that, but somewhere I'd gone wrong. Maybe I was too young to make it plain, maybe I was a coward. Anyway, I saw the truth of what would happen—and it was a terrible truth: he would learn without me. He would learn too how I possessed none of the innocence he did. How I had carried the knowledge into his presence and held it away from him, just beyond the margin of his loneliness, even as he laid open his heart to me.

I went looking for Anna Flood. It was the first thing that occurred to me, as if some sure comfort was to be found in her, though I knew I couldn't tell her anything.

Her house was tucked back behind Main Street, a little shed of a place off the curving footpath that trailed between Sharp's Saloon and the mercantile. I hoped she'd be there, hoped her father had not yet come home. I approached the back way, walking along behind the row of Main Street businesses. It was dark and the ground was strewn with refuse: the jagged slats of cracked barrels, broken shelving, balls of tangled wire, bits of tin and bottle glass. Someone's goat stood tied to a gnarled post. Its rectangular pupils followed me as I went past.

I was relieved to find Anna outside, taking bedding from the line at the side of the house. Her face, deep-set in the trance of work, looked more stern and woman-like than I'd seen it yet. But then she glimpsed me approaching and her regular look returned.

I asked her if her father was still out.

"Yes."

"And your mother? Is she asleep?"

"Nearly, I think."

"Can you come with me then?"

She told me to wait and I stood back as she stretched the bedding out in her open arms, doubled it closed and folded it. She dropped it into a basket and her hair fell free as she bent and lifted the basket. Then she disappeared inside.

She seemed to be a long time. I stood in the shadows before the house. The noise of Sharp's Saloon came in spurts through the night. The tethered goat paced with little crunching sounds. At last Anna came out again, her eyes glowing darkly as she hurried toward me with one pallid hand held out from her cloak. The hand was warm when I gripped it.

We went out behind the businesses, crossed Main Street well clear of the saloon windows so her father wouldn't see us, and found ourselves seated side by side on a slant of packed earth in a dark recess beneath the rail trestle. We sat there an hour or more, the night frost numbing us both through our clothes.

"Is it all right?" she asked.

"What?"

"I don't know. You're not sad are you?"

I shrugged—but then I thought how she could barely see me, so I spoke up. "I don't know."

"It's a sad time, isn't it? The breaker boy and all."

"Yes."

We didn't need sight in that darkness anyway. As I'd somehow known she would be, Anna was exquisitely tuned with me into some fine silent parlance. We could sense each other out clear as anything. A whole vivid feeling between us, as though we were touching one another. We hardly spoke much more than this that night, and the terrible course of everything around us did not change, but it was a wonderful comfort.

⌒

THE FOLLOWING NIGHT AFTER SCHOOL, LYTE STOPPED ME BEFORE HIS classroom door.

"Why didn't you tell me, Witherow?"

I felt something fall inside me, a great sinking weight, like blood unpent from beneath my scalp, plummeting down through my belly to my heels. I felt I might drop my books.

"I thought—I think I tried to tell you," I said.

Lyte's eyes looked burnished and hard. He stood in his greatcoat, shadowed to his nose by a derbyshire hat. Steam jetted white from his nostrils, blurred and clung to his dark figure like a faint aureole. He turned and pulled the door shut and rattled his keys in the lock.

"You tried?"

"Yes. I did. I thought I could say it, but it went wrong and then it wasn't possible anymore."

He twisted the doorknob once, then turned back again and stood looking at my throat. His mouth was a narrow seam. It stitched his clamped jaw to the rest of his face. In that half-lit face I saw how grave things were now. How he held my secret uncertainly between us.

130

"Reverend Parry says I ought to be careful. Says he wouldn't have given me Motion's funeral if he'd known of all the whispers in town. Your mother called on him, Witherow."

"She did?"

"Yes. Things are bad already. She made that much clear."

I twisted on my heels, moved to the low step before the classroom door and sat there, my legs slackening under the weight.

"You didn't say a word about it, Witherow."

"But I did. I meant to. I told you about mother. Didn't I say that?"

Lyte faced me, tall and lean in that dimness. Behind him the hazy rim of the hill gave way to darkness and cloud.

"You told me much last night," he murmured, "but nothing about all they're saying."

"I would have done."

"You would?"

"Yes."

"But you were afraid."

I couldn't answer. The words were icy and hard in my throat. I couldn't swallow. My chest heaved.

"Now it's with me," said Lyte. "Now it's all with me, isn't it?"

I felt the need to squint as I looked up at him.

"So you'll tell?" I said.

I heard the keys clicking softly in his pocket.

"Shall I?"

"Yes," I said. "I wish you would."

"Then where are you in all that, Witherow?"

"What?"

"What part have you done? If I'm the one to tell."

I stared at his black shoes. They were rocking softly in the dirt, tiny rails of dust rising at their edges, momentary imprints.

"It's for you to tell, Witherow. Isn't it." His voice was sheer and firm, but quiet. "You're to face that yourself. It's yours."

"But I can't. I can't, and things'll get worse. Someone else has to do it."

Lyte knelt, his mouth sinking into view before me.

"I'm sorry, Witherow. But don't you see? Even if I thought they'd believe me, it's not my part."

"But things are getting so bad already."

"Then you mustn't hold out. I don't believe you will."

"No?"

Lyte seemed preposterous to me in that moment. He stared blankly at my eyes. Not into them but at them, for mine and his both were varnished beads and they met without joining. I saw him take my last word as an abject kind of threat. Its meaning settled in his face and the cowardice of it spawned an amused smile.

"No," he said once more. "I don't believe you will. And I'll wait on the strength of that belief."

But he couldn't know the tremendous mass which held me from speech. I sat curled on the crude board of the schoolroom step. I hugged my books and in that doorway my body became a fist. Lyte held my own duty before me like a rebuke and a challenge, and his foolishness made me wretched. Why in God's name would he commit himself to the little hands of a boy, as if it were all some inebriate's trivial game?

"You should tell them yourself," I said again, but he was rising now and turning and he didn't seem to hear. "It'll get worse."

I stood and moved after him.

"You don't understand, Mr. Lyte. Martha Griggs says she saw you at Rose Hill that night."

"Well, I was up there, yes."

"But why? What will you tell them when they ask you that? She saw you stalking through the graves with a candle. They'll think it wickedness. How will you explain that?"

He slowed then, his chin angling sideways. He spoke to me over his shoulder. "I won't. I can't. But if you care to walk up there with me now, maybe you'll know what to tell them."

He moved briskly ahead of me, down the curving path which lay purpled under the night clouds. I followed, felt myself dragged along after him, as if after a punisher.

We said nothing as we passed the derrick, the trestle, and walked along the rail bank toward the Somersville Road. Our muteness was like enmity between us. Lyte never looked back to see that I followed.

There were still a few people in the streets, mostly workmen come out in the bracing air to send their pipe smoke into the evening cloud. Several men were clustered near the door to the Exchange Hotel, their shadows pitched out into the yellow light. I did not look at their faces. Then Lyte was huffing up the road, his breath hazing around him. His shape cut through the breath and behind him trailed smoky outlines one after another, each collapsing centerward. He remained twenty paces ahead, and as I crested the Rise I saw him unlatching the gate at Rose Hill's southern fence.

When I entered the graveyard he was standing far off among the headstones at the center. Beside him the cypress tree shot high into darkness, itself dark, like an artist's horsehair brush standing endward from the fist of the earth.

I found him talking before I was within ten feet. From the depths of his greatcoat he had produced a taper and a match. The light shook across the tablet lying flat at his feet.

"Here's an Aitken," he said. "Daughter of your father's chum, isn't it?"

I looked at the inscription.

Clara, Daughter of J & L Aitken, Died Jan 1 1862, Aged 7 years 5 mos 12 days.

"I didn't know they had a daughter," I said.

"Weep not Father and Mother for me," Lyte said, reading, "For I am waiting in glory for thee."

A wind skimmed down from the crest above us. It swirled through the fence posts and headstones and tickled the candle flame till it gave out. A blue-black strand of smoke unraveled from the naked wick. Lyte dug in his pockets and brought out another match.

"If any townsfolk saw that just now," he said, "they'll swear it was a corpse candle."

He knelt and scratched the match on the daughter's stone and lit the wick again and cupped his hand against the wind.

"Have you ever seen one of those, Witherow?"

"A corpse candle? No."

"Do you know what it means?"

"Yes. It means death's due somebody."

"Do you believe that?"

I looked at the Aitken stone again. I rolled my shoulders.

"I come up here every so often," he said. "Sometimes I walk among the stones. Pay them a visit, you know. Read their messages. Sometimes I find a dark place to sit."

He paced left to where the grass stood taller at the edge of a waist-high wrought-iron fence. I went and stood beside him and looked down at the tablets coupled there in that enclosure.

"Another daughter to someone," he said, and bowed the candle downward with both hands.

A small, round-headed stone lay heavily fringed with grass. At

its top a soft relief embedded with grime, the forms there enunci-
ated by the dirt: a bending willow tree with a little lamb shaded up
beneath its fronds.

"Read it, Witherow."

"Martha Etta. Daughter of Joseph M. and Martha Piercy. Died
Dec 24 1859. Aged 2 years 11 mos & 16 days. Too sweet a flower
to bloom on Earth, she is gone to bloom in Heaven."

As if perfectly satisfied at that, Lyte stood again and started
walking toward the southern edge of the burying ground.

"I'm not the only one to come here at night," he said. "I've sat
over there under that big oak and watched folks pass through the
gate, bend over a stone, tear up the weeds at its edges. Most of them
come at night, Witherow. Why'll they expect an answer from me?
Why not interrogate everyone who comes? I was here some time
ago and saw you and Thomas Motion dallying around."

My heart stood thick in my chest. I saw Thomas and me thrash-
ing each other on the ground amidst the graves, racing out past old
Mrs. Price.

"You saw us?"

"Yes. You see, everybody comes. But I think it has little to do
with the dead. It's not about them. Here's one."

He squatted before a standing stone and the candlelight sent the
stone's shadow fluttering back and forth like the head of a green-
broke horse.

"Tis God lifts our comforts high. He sinks them in the grave.
He gives and when he takes away, he takes but what he gave. In
India, Witherow, there are women called *suttees*. Ever heard that
word?"

"No."

"They're widows who throw themselves into their husband's

cremation. They do it so the husband isn't shamed by a disloyal wife, some say. Some say they do it for pure grief. Some say because death has no dominion over those ladies. Can you see that? Can you see flinging yourself away like that?"

I said nothing. I felt he had me at a full arm's length, and yet he was somehow gripping me fast at the same time. It made no sense that he talked to me this way. Talked to the craven boy for whom he'd proxied himself. There seemed a pregnant absence of malice. It bewildered me and I softened—felt my anger, my compunction, slowly enervated. Suddenly we were two up there in the graveyard. We were intimates in some fiercely quiet grapple.

"Anyway," Lyte said, "whatever their reasons, the suttees comport themselves according to some knowledge of the world that you and I can barely fathom. They give up their illusions completely."

Again he was pacing ahead of me as he spoke. I watched the candlelight shudder outward from his shoulders and arms, as if he tore paper into strips and sent it flitting off while he walked.

"So for them also it's not about the dead, you see. It has to do with they themselves."

He stopped then and turned round and spoke to me with the flame jouncing brokenly from his cupped hands, spattering his long cheeks.

"I'm just now twenty years old, Witherow, and already the world's weight is on my shoulders. All its machinery. All those restless gears. Under that I fold up, you see, fold up like a sheaf of letter paper and forever after I pass all my days front to front—inwardly, you know. I think and hope and fret and remember. And soon I lose hold of the other part of things: the earth's skin everywhere around me, the great table I walk upon with edges on all four sides."

He stopped and his mouth became a seam again. He stood there cupping the flame and said nothing more and I saw that our grim contest would keep fixed between us, my silence and his, under-thread to our peculiar bond.

"Read this one," he murmured now.

I crouched to the tablet between us, a flat pediment cracked through from its left edge to its right. I twisted my neck and read the epitaph sideways: "Write the errors of your Brother in sand, but engrave his Virtues on the tablets of enduring memory."

⁓

THE NEXT TIME I SAW ANNA FLOOD, SHE AGAIN PROVIDED COMFORT she couldn't have measured. We were down at the creek after school, the cool night abuzz with insect noise. We sat on our laurel limb above the water, and everything that I carried unconfessed, all that which weighed me to the hard earth day and night, needed no unburdening for the breadth of our entire hour together. I could never have spoken of it anyway, but Anna was such a presence, so profoundly absorbing, that the great need itself fell away while I was with her. She was my one refuge from all that bore down upon me. I could not have known how that evening would end, how suddenly all this would be changed.

When we left the creek, I found I could not allow her to walk home alone. I was still too deeply enveloped in her comfort. Together we crossed the meadow and went by my house, toward Main Street, then picked our way through the shadows behind Engler's cobblery, behind the mercantile. As soon as her house came into view, Anna gasped softly and clutched my arm.

"What is it?" I said.

"That light in the window."

"Has your father come home?"

"No, it's too early still. Mother must be up."

She hurried ahead of me through the dark. I saw her shape flitting black against the mild house light.

In sotto voice, I called good night, but without stopping she murmured back: "Stay a moment." Her front door clattered and she vanished inside.

I stood there in the dewy night, uncomprehending, tense that her father would come charging drunk from the porch any moment. Beyond the curtained window, faint forms moved here and there. A voice, thin and plaintive, rose up toward a kind of screech, then halted. It was not Anna's voice. It was followed by a sudden banging noise, as though something had been knocked from a shelf. Anna appeared in the doorway, the door held tight in one hand behind her. She was waving me near with frantic gestures.

"Asher, please come. Please come help. She's in a frenzy."

In one apprehensive jolt, I found myself on the porch, but another banging noise stopped me short. Anna vanished inside again and the door swung ajar. I saw her in there. Her back was to me, both her elbows lifted high as she struggled to grasp her mother's flailing hands. The two were strangely quiet in their scuffle. Beyond their muffled grunts, there was only the noise of their feet scrabbling on the floorboards. The blunt slapping of their limbs.

"Shut the door, Asher!"

I went in and closed the door and stood with my back pressed stiff against it. Anna and her mother were circling now, clasping one another in a desperate sort of dance. A chair lay overturned on the floor behind them, one of its rails cracked. I saw Anna's heels scrape backward as her mother wrenched her sideways, then caught my first glimpse of the sick woman herself. She was hardly bigger than her daughter, trussed in a sagging nightshift which betrayed sharp and fleshless shoulders. Her two bloodless hands clawed at Anna's sleeves. She pressed one sallow cheek to her daughter's breast, her face jammed there like an infant hugged too tightly, her thin lips trembling agape, red-rimmed eyes fixed wide. I saw her catch sight of me then, those eyes shining in sick horror, and the yellow arch of her teeth glistened plainly as she sent up a wail. She started flapping like a butchered chicken. Anna fought to restrain her with a rough embrace, shoving her backward toward a disheveled bed at one end of the room.

"Hot water, Asher!"

"What?"

"The kettle! Heat the water! She needs it hot!"

I glanced to the stove in the corner. A charred kettle sat atop it. I lifted the lid and found it full already. I moved it to the burner, then squatted and opened the stove door, set about stoking the fire inside.

At the other side of the room, Mrs. Flood was muttering in terrible fright as her daughter forced her into the bed. Anna clapped her palm hard across the woman's mouth, but when she got to flailing too much, the words jittered clear again.

"Who is he? Who is that wretched boy? He's come to do it hasn't he? He's come to drag me to his pit!"

"Hush, mother, hush. He's our friend. He's come to help us."

Soon Anna had her down on the bed and managed to swaddle her tight in the blankets. Mrs. Flood began to calm somewhat, her mutterings subdued to a panicked chatter, but still Anna deemed it best to remain there, pinning the lady on her back.

Braced across that bony form, Anna stared into her mother's restless eyes and stroked her ashen forehead.

"Don't fret, mama dear. You'll have your compress in just a moment. Then you'll sleep again. You'll sleep long and deep. Don't fret."

At last the lady's twitching lips relaxed, her mouth fell slack, and her eyes went graying off into some waking dream. She didn't even flinch when the kettle began to hum.

Anna eased herself off and stood up beside the bed. "She's better now," she said, and stepped toward the stove.

"You don't need a doctor?" I asked.

"No. See how calm she is?"

"What was it?"

"A terror."

"A nightmare?"

"A waking nightmare, yes. She used to have them every night. She's been better these last few months. This one was bad because I was gone when she woke."

"Dear God," I said. I was trembling from the scene. "What did she say when she saw me?"

"Don't think of that. That was nothing." Anna poured from the kettle into a bowl. Several blue strips of cotton floated up in the steaming water. "The compresses keep her calm. It's all we can do."

She took the bowl to the bedside and set it on the floor beside her as she knelt. She dipped her hand into the water, wincing at the burn, fished out the strips of cotton, wrung them gently and plastered them together before draping them across her mother's brow. Mrs. Flood blinked wildly, as if some bright light were shining through her ill trance.

Anna murmured something, but her back was to me, so I drew closer to hear her.

"She must have lit the lamp when she got up. It's a miracle she didn't burn down the house. She's so clear sometimes. Then sometimes she's like a baby."

I didn't know what to answer. I stood there looking down upon the sick woman, that emaciated skull plopped on its pillow, black

hair tangling out like a mess of carrot weed. Anna pressed the scalding compress against the brow and the blood-tinged circles under
Mrs. Flood's eyes burned dark.

I saw it then: the horrid nature of this woman's malaise. The
glossy bulbs of her eyes jutted from her head like calcined stones.
Her hollow cheeks lay sucked into her jaw. She was withering in
every respect, as if some slow fire peeled at her from all sides. I saw
her splayed out on a web of flame, her descaled limbs pinned to a
blazing mesh—not to the stained pallet of her bed. Her fire was
plucking her apart with terrific slothfulness.

I started back. I think Anna saw my sudden cringe, for she
turned her head a little.

"I'd better go," I said.

Then I was at the door and Anna had said nothing. I ducked out
into the night, thought I heard the cool air give off a pacified hiss as
my warm body entered it. I ran home, plunging hard through the
darkness, and within minutes I was climbing my porch steps. I
think I knew that some poison thought would now sever me from
Anna Flood, for I spent that entire night squirming in my bed,
wild-hearted in a fit of dejection, sick with all that I could not speak.

Anna's mother was frying day and night, and something within
her—something inexpressible—was staving off the fire's triumph.
Anna helped her in this. But that night, while peering out from the
deep clutch of her conflagration, Mrs. Flood had known me for an
enemy. Now I would not look at her daughter's face without seeing
all this there. My error, my secret, would reflect from those dark
eyes. I was not strong enough for that, not hard enough. Not yet.

In the following weeks I'd find Anna awaiting me after school
and would speak with her a while, but I could not bear much of
that, so we never spent another whole evening together—not for a
long time. Soon she had grown cautious of me, as if she sensed the

troubles she induced. We fell away from one another like demagnetized things. Maybe we both knew deeply that this estrangement would not persist forever, but we couldn't have foreseen the manner of its reversal, the kind of quiet sclerosis that would take effect before things changed again. Anna and I would never again be children together.

{ 4 }

THIS WORLD, VERILY, GAUTAMA, IS FIRE. THE EARTH ITSELF IS ITS fuel, fire the smoke, night the flame, the moon the coals, the stars the sparks. In this fire the gods offer rain. I remember the rains of that year's prodigal spring. They pounded down in torrents even until May, as if wild with fear against the coming blaze of June.

I was to start in the mines that summer. Those rains seemed to draw curtains between me and my initiation, pushing summer back. Gray slush everywhere underfoot, mud mingling with the coal-dust dragged from the air. Puddles swirling black. Dust guttering from wet oak canopies, smearing ghost trees across the ground. Still, mid-May came, though cloudy. My time of induction.

On the eve of my first day of work, father took my shoulders in his hands.

"A boy can't go down that mouth of earth with the wind in his fist, Ash."

We had long been conscious of my coming passage, but had spoken nothing of it yet, nothing save a month before when father had tossed off to me the starting date, like a heavy thing shaken temporarily from his shoulder.

Now he said: "I've made plans with the foreman to start you off low. You'll be a nipper on the Clark Vein."

Mother shuttled to and fro behind him, bearing our used plates to the basin. I caught a sidelong glance from her.

"I thought I'd work with you, sir. Thought we'd be side by side."

His eyes flickered shut a second. "This is best, Ash."

"But Jim Griggs went straight to work with his pa—and most the other kids too. We could pick twice the bushels they do."

"Ash, it's decided."

I saw he was firm and I let off my plea.

"Anyway, I'll not be far off. Joel and me are just down the seam from your door. You'll see, son. It's best."

He turned from me to take down his pipe. He and mother exchanged silent glances as he plucked a wad from his pouch and stuffed the bowl and lit it.

Our gabled roof rattled like a snare under the rain. Father walked to the porch window and sleeved the steam from the glass. He watched the silver curtain coming down off the awning. His voice was plain, as in sadness.

"That's not all, Ash," he said. "You'll come with me tonight."

"Where?"

He turned. He held the pipe-stem level in his hand and looked at the fizzing bowl, seeming to speak to it. "To the Exchange Hotel."

Mother clattered a spoon.

"Abicca, I've decided it," said father quickly, not raising his eyes. "It needs to be. A boy cannot, all of a sudden one day, become less of a boy, but he needs some turn in his character."

"David, I'd thought something of temperance—"

"I'll not hear it, Abicca."

144

"But a boy so young, David!"

"Aye, and not so young that a man's life is his before he's tasted it, I hope!"

They looked long at one another.

"It needs to be, Abicca. He'll have a hard forehead in weeks. We wouldn't just throw him down there, would we? It'll be this once only, then we'll forbid it. But it needs to be."

Their icy impasse seemed to thaw a little. They both looked at me. Mother drew close and knelt and stared into my eyes, as though she studied something strange to her.

When it came time that night, she gripped my arms and stuffed them into my coat sleeves, yanked the wool tight about me and fastened the buttons. She slid her callused hand over my brow, displacing my hair—warm touch at my head, as if testing for fever. Then she settled the brim of my hat into place and guided me out after father, wordless at our going.

THE MUD WAS DEEP AMONG THE HOUSES. I MOVED AFTER FATHER'S hunched figure, toward the rail tracks. Our boots sank and smacked. Rainwater poured from our brims.

The rail bank rose before us, its incline all slicked, the little upward footpath washed out. Father leapt up to the flat of it in a few quick, long strides, then turned and pulled me up. From the tracks, Main Street ran wide and straight before us to the wall of the southern ridge. The tall whale-oil lamps glowed red along its edges, smudged like chalk in the streaked air.

We managed our descent from the tracks and turned toward the Exchange Hotel. In the empty street ahead of us a figure stooped near the rail bank, yanking at something low. As we approached I made out a woman's form: dark skirts and cloak. She held a frail, bone-handled parasol askew in the air as she bent.

Father said: "Evening, Mrs. Norton." His voice was strong against the thudding rain.

The woman jacked straight as if spring-loaded at the knees. Her round face shone from a hood.

"Oh, good evening, Mr. Witherow. Oh my!"

"Didn't mean to startle you—"

"Oh, no. It's just the rain. The storm—" She looked up at the sky and seemed to float from us a moment. "Isn't it gloriously loud?"

In one mud-spattered fist she held a clump of dark leaves.

Father gestured to the bush at her feet. "May I help you?"

"Oh, not by any means. You're very kind, but you won't muddy yourself for my sake. You might hold my parasol for me, though."

Father lifted the small thing over her, lacy and useless as it was, while she crouched and tore at the bush, stuffing her cloak with wads of wet leaf. Her skirt hems soaked in the shoe-thick mud.

"I was just coming home from a call at Mr. Scammon's lodging house—a baby, still-born to Mrs. Peets, sadly enough—when I smelled it. Do you smell it in the air?"

She stood again and cupped her two hands over nose and mouth and sucked a long breath.

"Ahh. Black sage. Rain-washed. The fragrance is on my hands now." She held out her dirty palms, and by the way her eyes had brightened, she looked like a child who'd clutched a dragonfly in her fist. She had smeared her cheeks and chin with mud.

"Yes," said father. He bent a little and nosed the wet air. "I do smell it."

Sarah hunched over and set to plucking again. "Our village is the farthest north that one can find this black sage," she said. "Don't you find that auspicious? There're a great many auspicious

things about this place, Mr. Witherow. I hope you're praying, by
the way, for our good Josiah Lyte. He's been put in an awful mess. I
beg your pardon, but I know you're not of the same mind as Mrs.
Witherow on the matter. One can see that about you."

Finally she had all but stripped the little bush to twigs and filled
her pockets to bulging. She rose and turned to father and me.

"Ah, dear. I believe there are just a handful of us, Mr. Witherow.
Those who see the damage it does to the town, you know. Such a
bright young minister."

Her gaze sank downward as though after some falling thought.
She appeared to take note of her filthy hands, turning them over,
amused, disinterested.

"One can make good use of rain-washed sage, Mr. Witherow. Matter of fact, Mrs. Peets could use a strong tea of it now. I'd best be off."

Father handed her the parasol and bade her good night.

"Good night, Mr. Witherow. Good night, Asher."

"Good night, ma'am."

She plashed off along the rail bank as we entered the Exchange
Hotel.

The lobby was thick with men, the wooden floor shuddering
and mud-caked. A fire blazed in the stone hearth. Father received a
dozen hefty slaps on the back as he steered me through the crush to
the fire. We peeled off our coats and laid them with our hats to dry.
On the settle before the hearth, I sat down in a row of men. Father
withdrew to the bar.

A massive arm fell against my ribs.

"So we've a new nipper here, huh?"

Cale Carver grinned at my side—hoist man from the Black Diamond shaft, bachelor with wide mouth and sparse hair. He had a
great thick-set brow which looked somehow like a jaw. It was
flecked with liver-spots that would better suit someone older.

"Yes, sir. Tomorrow I start in the Clark Vein." I stamped the mud from my boots, needing to make some deep, indisputable sound.

Cale slapped my thigh. "Well! That's what I have from your father. Very good, very good. I say—he's a good man, your father! The doors're a good spot for a lad to start below. You'll grow real accustomed to the works that way."

Father returned, his face warped in the smoky light, long beard limp and rain-pleated. In one hand he held a tumbler of beer, in the other a short glass of yellowish liquor which he passed to me. He had a serious air, as at a delicate task.

"You drink this, Ash. And no hurry about it, but I want you to drink it all."

I held the glass to my lips, felt the blaze. Within me, the fierce stuff welded itself to the fireplace heat.

Father drew up a chair and watched me over his jug.

"I say, Witherow, you've a fine son!" Cale lifted his own tumbler in tribute. "He's a company man yet, and the young roof of this town too!"

Father gave a wan smile.

"To the young roof of Nortonville!" said Cale, hoisting his cup again and drinking. Then he palmed my back and leaned close, breath of beer and smoke in my face. "More than six thousand long tons of coal each month—that's what these men pull out of this earth! And I watch every car of it flying up the shaft, more and more cars every day!"

Father was peering through me into the fire. "Mrs. Peets's baby came out limp tonight," he said. "Sarah Norton told Asher and me a minute ago."

Cale held his tumbler between his knees and studied the floor. His shoulders folded in and he seemed to narrow in stature. "What a pity," he said.

I drank another spot. I rolled the venomous fluid over my tongue, tasted the rude vapors, then let the scald plunge in. It illuminated my stomach under my clothes.

I lost myself in the welter of men. The world before me became a series of lantern slides. An elbow poked over the back of a chair. A pair of legs flopped upon a table, big boots among ashes and empty cups, clods of mud peppering off the treads. A grizzled face leaned and spat. In a corner somewhere, somebody squeezed an accordion. A gray weft of smoke trailed over my cheek. Cale had kindled a long cigar. He looked distant through the screen of it.

A big hand braced my knee. "Ash. Ash, you're through."

Father ferreted the empty glass from my hands and slipped away toward the bar.

Cale's grin flung wide behind the smoke, but his head looked awful and small. The stogie at his lips misshaped his words. "He takes it for a portent, you see."

"A portent?"

"That Sally Peets birthed a corpse tonight—it's a portent to your father. Takes it for a gesture from the Fates, with you going down tomorrow and all."

I glimpsed father at the horizon of men, slim and dark amidst the uproar, handing his empty tumbler across the bar.

"He's a superstitious one, your father. We all are, you know—have to be, I suppose. But your pa—it's different with him. Troubles him so. I can see it, you know, for I watch the men come in the morning and go at night."

Father was returning now, moving along the tilting floor with a fresh mug of beer. The room heaved, delaying him: the long journey of a single moment. This is perhaps the purest image I retain of him. It's strange for me now, to be older than he ever was, to look back upon him as upon a youth.

Cale set to talking again as father sat.

"That Josiah Lyte's come into pig's feet, hasn't he?"

"Think I just caught wind of it at the bar," father said. "Something happened this morning, they're saying."

"Hell, I just heard it myself stepping in here tonight. All the blokes are thick with it."

"What?"

"Eddie Payne's kid, works as altar boy sometimes you know—he was going round in his little robe after service putting out the tapers with one of those bell-snuffers and his sleeve goes ablaze."

Cale lifted his tumbler high and waved his cigar at the general area of his own arm aflame with imaginary fire.

"Poof. Like that. Just like he'd bathed in whale oil that morning. Well, most the churchgoers were gone outside already, but there were still half a dozen or so yammering rear of the pews. They turned round and there was the Payne boy flapping wild at the altar. For a minute they didn't know what's what, then George Minett came to his wood and dove on the poor kid. They tumbled round over head and ears and that got it out and when they sorted themselves little Payne's sleeve was all charred to hell but he wasn't even singed. Then all the souls in that church, every hairy peak, turned around and who did they see'd been standing there all the time?"

"The young minister," said father.

"Our young Lyte. Standing with not a finger raised. Lord knows I've no bone to scratch with that boy, but it's terrible queer."

Father sat silent. The many shadows from the crush around him merged black and by the fire's light he looked raised and spectral amidst that.

There was a gorge of hours that night, or maybe of moments, as I plummeted to sleep by the fire, sitting upright in all the noise.

Then father roused me with a shake, bade Cale Carver good night, and led me out into the street.

The downpour had softened to a spray and water billowed weightless in the air. Our boots plashed in the thick road. I thought a lamp glowed somewhere off, for everything looked gilt-edged: my father's form ahead of me, the brow of the rail bank, the puckers in the wide field of mud beneath our feet. We were wordless in that glinting.

The air wheeled and pitched, as if thick with a drove of insects. I thought I recalled some leaden words of the evening, but my mind was all cack-handed. Then I was calling ahead to father, my mouth fashioning the words of its own accord.

"They're all after him now, aren't they father? Isaac Payne near got burned cause of him."

Father kept walking.

"They think he's done something awful. Well, they don't know, do they? They don't know what really happened to Thomas Motion."

"They'll talk and talk," father said. He stopped and stood in the road without turning while I caught up.

"Father?"

He said nothing.

"Father, don't you suppose it was accident? Lyte couldn't have half a part in it, could he?"

I came upon him and he set to walking again.

"Don't mince air, Asher. They'll talk and talk."

I looked up at a silver sky. The steep walls of the world reared sideways and I stumbled to my knees. My shins were glad at the coolness of the saturated earth.

Father did not turn round. "Come on now, Ash."

I rose and followed him home, into the vertiginous warmth of our little house.

That night I dreamt of emptiness.

5

RISING WITH FATHER BEFORE DAWN, I FELT THE EMPTINESS FROM my dream upon me. It seemed to have turned me inside out like a blouse. I stepped into my coveralls and followed him out into a muggy purple.

Mother had packed me a lunch pail like father's. The water in it sloshed as I walked, fruit pieces floating in there. In my free hand father placed a narrow Davy lamp. We went up the valley grade toward the tall derrick and the lamp spread a low amber before us, lighting my emptiness in a prescient way. Around us, figures verged through the mute streets. By the time we came to the shaft mouth we were among thick ranks of men.

Father waved a finger at my lamp. "Put that out now, Ash. You'll need it later."

I snuffed the flame and the apparition of the dead light swam in my darkened eyes.

The cables whined in the derrick. An iron cage clattered and something whooshed downward.

"Ours is the third lift, Ash." Father led me up to the mouth. "When we're inside it, you give me the left and stand in front."

"Yes, sir."

We watched a company of men step onto the shuddering platform. There sounded a hiss and a screech and they dropped from sight. After a few moments an empty cage appeared.

"Now us, Ash."

We filed in. Men large all about me. The floor of the thing dropped from under us. My feet nearly lost their touch, then met the swift falling.

Darkness sucked hard at my eyes. Then small lamplights began to flicker on around me.

"Now, at day's end you find me at the foot. Third car up'll be ours. You'll stand in front and left, just as you are, understand?"

"Yes, sir."

Our long fall tautened and slowed. Something jolted us from below. We moved forward into a wall of blackness. I distinguished the scattering of the other men, blue lamps floating away. A dense pillow filled my mouth. Sulfur in my throat. I heard the cage roar up behind me.

Father's voice wedged itself close in my ear. I watched his head-candle bobbing above, felt his hand at my shoulder.

"When you're shown to your door today you mark your way, Ash, understand? If you walk right of the tracks in the morning, then keep to that side at day's end too."

"Yes, sir."

"Now come."

He led me somewhere in the dark. Flames moved round like constellations, some tiny, some large—it was impossible to tell their distance. The blackness held no depth. Dimension folded in on itself.

Now father was speaking to another man. The bassey thrumming of a pump obscured their voices, but I watched their two faces
hovering above me in candlelight. Father bent to me and roared
over the noise of the pump. "Here's your boss, Ash. You follow this
man." He nodded assuringly and drew away in the blackness.

The man's yellow-lit face sank closer. "I'm your foreman, John
Plight," he boomed. "Follow me, son."

We walked through the flat blindness. Direction defied itself in
the restless drifting of lamps all around, flames passing through one
another, withdrawing lights beguiling me as they floated past the
opposite way. Soon the rumble of the pump had faded and we
moved through a narrow tunnel, slats underfoot. I heard the dull
trilling of hidden waters. Sound came dense, blunted against the
black walls. I heard faint bellows and calls sounding stale from
some corner of that tunneled place. In the foreman's wavering light,
the darkness around us seemed to breathe.

"Now, your job's to listen, son. You'll listen hard for the roll of
cars, for mules, and for men. When you hear 'em, you jump up and
open your door—quick like so they get plenty of clearance. When
they've gone by, you shut the door fast."

Deep in the body of the walls something yawned and creaked.
On our left and on our right thick lumber legs pulsed momentarily, faded into blackness again.

"That's all you do," said John Plight, staring down at the slats
ahead of his feet. "It's a crucial task, as the air'll turn wrong if the
doors don't shut. You've got to stay quick—no dozing off and no
leaving your station."

"Yes, sir."

We moved in silence a long while. At last we came to the door,
a body of thick vertical planks, hinged on one side and closing off

the passage entirely. Plight shoved it open and held it while I went through. Then he let it fall with a boom against its posts.

Beside the tracks there he showed me a plank laid over two low blocks. This was my station.

"Sit down here, son."

He stood back from me, fists at his hips. "Now open her!" he shouted.

I scrambled up and grasped the handle and threw my weight back. The massive wood came heavily off its posts, then caught the swing and groaned open.

"Now close her!"

I ran hard against the door till it thundered shut. John Plight nodded and gestured to me to sit again. "That's fine," he said. "Good and spry!" Then he yanked at the door and vanished and there was nothing but black.

I fumbled blind till finally I got my lamp aglow. Then I sat in the mellow light, listening for the noise of Plight's feet withdrawing. Nothing. I heard water trickling down the dark throat of tunnel behind me, the intermittent crackle of wood and earth. It seemed I sat in the lightless hull of a great ship.

Time dropped into some dead pocket here. It lay devoid of motion or variance, lifeless as a crust of hard bread. I pressed my ears into the wood of the door, tense that something should explode the silence.

Occasionally in that long season of darkness a distant crumb of noise would travel down from the breasts the men worked and jitter under my door. A blast? The clamor of loaded cars? Rock falling in the chutes?

I perched there and pictured the toil in the distant tunnels. A flash of powder blasted shadows from the wall. Then shadows were gouged from the seam and piled high in the fat cars. Eventually these shadows would burn to emptiness in the bellies of stoves.

Off in the darkness behind me, the flat passage rolled deep into nothing. I lost sense of a horizon and felt gravity sucking me down that way, the tunnel tilting and becoming a shaft. But I glanced at my lamp and found it upright and did not fear.

Soon the great emptiness of last night's dream had engulfed me. Soon there was only emptiness, simple and salient, like a cold wet cloth over my being.

I think now of those old caves in Lauscaux, where boys went deep into the unlit rock loins to confront the hard intersection of youth and manhood. There in the dark, 40,000 years back, they created the first human art, flung animal spirits over the walls, surrounded themselves with great bison. Some people think they put the pigment in their mouths, swirled it in saliva, then spat it in colored sprays, great forms above them.

There are painted caves high in our own Black Hills too, on the eastern side of Mount Diablo. Long ago the native people, the Volvon, ground pigments and spread colors over those rock walls. As for me, nine years old, I sat that day at my dim post in that artery of earth and painted the black walls with a new knowledge of emptiness.

But I soon got into the rhythm of things down there.

Traffic along the tunnel came with an unnerving thunder emanating from the rock. I envisioned a great rending of the sediments, a cataract of rock crashing along the gangway, the earth folding in upon me. But I would gather a sense of things and spring up to drag the door off its posts.

The ragged ears of a mule would flush from the darkness, then the animal's rumbling burden—a train of loaded cars. Jim Hopkins, the driver, sat perched on the foremost car, hollering mule-commands. If it wasn't Jim, it was Isaac Payne or Jack McCarthy. Every mule driver was a boy a few years older than I, each one schooled in the same pugnacious manner. Often he would fling his whip as he passed, the leather tongue snapping at my arm or thigh. Then the cars would fade down the tunnel and I'd slam the door.

I got used to taking my midday dinners alone in the darkness. Tearing mother's bread in my blackened hands. Tasting the tin in the water I tipped from my lunch pail. Listening to the rats, the gathering scamper at the crunch of an apple or the fragrance of salt pork.

Sometimes I scattered a tiny dinner for the rats, to amuse both me and them. They came with their miniature hands, collected the scraps, filled their narrow mouths, sniffed about my boots, then darted back into shadow. Watching them, I had the feeling that I fed the earth, or some beast of the earth far off in the darkness, to whom they brought the repast. The emptiness, deep in those tunnels, had a hunger I could hear.

Each morning, descending with father, I could not help thinking of Madoc's seventh son, who had gone into the earth along some dark diving path. I was akin to the mysteries of his legend. And at night, coming up to the place of earth and air, brush and star, I left father's side to climb the Black Diamond Canyon to the Cumberland Rise. I thirsted for the separation of elements: hill and sky, grass and cloud. The variety of twilight.

Standing atop the ridge, I looked upon the mountain's great shoulder blades sprawling the valley. They glowed brilliant green even at dusk. The mountain seemed to have been waiting there all day long, impassive and weathering. I understood it had always waited—autumns and summers blushing up and down its slopes like the changing coats of an ermine. I had no secrets before it. It felt me fumbling in its belly by day, no different than the teams spooning the marrow from its bones. So each night the mountain gave audience to my silent contrition. The angular bowl of its canyon stood full of gloaming sky. I wanted to lie down in that V.

∼

AFTER THE ALTAR-BOY INCIDENT, AND IN THE CHOPPY WAKE OF THE gossip it stirred, a great many people stayed away from church. Reverend Parry was finally compelled to keep Lyte from the pulpit for an indefinite term. In the meantime, though, our town's yield was swelling, fuller cars than ever coasting down the rails to the water. Twenty-eight thousand more long tons of coal than the year before. Nine hundred people in Nortonville. Over three hundred men and boys employed at the pits. Four large mercantile stores, six saloons, the county's best public school, two Welsh literary societies, a fine baseball club, a brass band. Yet I remember this first year of mine work as a palled and ashy time. The daytime heat pressed down. Our verdant hills turned yellow, and black dust hung corpulent in the village.

One July morning, as I walked with father through the already oppressive air to the shaft, he drew away into the knee-high grasses to cough. In the dim light I saw the spill from his mouth: burgundy spattering the yellow weeds.

I'm sure his lungs had got clouded long before, but he had kept discreet. Now he bent there, hands braced on his knees, half-turned from me. When he came to me again, blood glistened in his beard.

"Don't fear that, son," he said. "It's out of me now. The body gets it up that way. Gets clean again."

That summer too, for no reason at all, I started to suffer the damnable headache of my mother's blood. A drilling pain at the rear of the skull, like an auger steely and cold. Then the pressured vise-grip at the crown and brow, spreading, clawing at the brain. I spent insufferable days supine on the puncheon floor beneath my bed: needing that hard flatness beneath me, unable to bear the seething light.

Father took it for a womanish thing. He never spoke a word to me in my maladies, never asked mother why I was under the bed. In the pits, it shamed him to tell the foreman the reason for my truancy.

At home in that midday heat, I lay across the puncheon with my cleaving head riddled by feverish dreams. I saw myself enrobed beside Josiah Lyte, staring upward from the flickering radius of a church candle. There in the dark reach above us, the altar boy Isaac Payne went circling in a trail of fire and smoke, the one flaming sleeve of his vestment like a ruined wing lent flight, rather than robbed of it, by the ravishment. He turned slow loops up there, growing blacker for all the amassing smoke, till the haze he emitted appeared to harden in some terrible plumage that clung to his limbs, and he became a demagogic bird, a courier-beast come to dispatch all the mistruths my silence engendered. I called out in that smoke: *Come down! Come down you devil bird!* But my words themselves took form as columns of vicious wings, black bat-like things that screeched upward in a melee of noise and mistake.

❧

THAT AUGUST I MOVED UP A LEVEL IN SCHOOL, JOINING THE OLDER boys in Josiah Lyte's classroom. By now my meetings with Lyte were a regular affair. We'd long since made a habit of night-walks together, long saunters into the hills above Nortonville. The other boys noted it and for a while I was an object of mild suspicion, but then they began to deal me their salient neglect. Hoping for a clue to my own bewitchment in the afterblaze of Thomas Mo-

tion's body-fire, I had read what I could from the Emerson volume
Lyte had given me. We talked of it while we walked. He recited
long sections from memory, the meanings coming out in the flow
of his voice. Now and then he spoke to me of India, lost in his rev-
erence for that place.

We ambled along the high ridges through the Indian summer
air and looked down into the dark Diablo Valley. He had taught me
the names of the people whose country this was: the Volvon, the
Chupcan, the Julpun, the Ompin, the Saclan. Now he showed me
the flat rocks where they had ground craters while mashing buckeye into bread and salves. They had ridden the waters of Marsh
Creek and the San Joaquin, he said, on boats of bundled tules. They
had gathered mussel shells and hunted grasshoppers. They had carried obsidian-head arrows in quivers fashioned of fox hides, the animals' limp snouts nosing their shoulders. And the great mountain
that fed them, clothed them, sheltered them, had been their pro-
genitor in the very first days—back when the whole valley was an
ocean and the two summits were islands.

And he told me how that huge shape had come beneath the
devil's moniker. There were a number of stories and by midautumn
I'd learned most of them. I had known the mountain in the years
before, but with Lyte I came to *feel* the mountain. I came to sense
that wide Diablo Valley like a body stretched out below. The
mountain bulged in the valley's chest, like a heart. My days pulsed
in time with it. Somehow this was liberating. Somehow all the
grim pressure inside of me took on the slow and fateful weight
of the earth's palpitations, just as terrifying as ever, yet more inevitable. It was almost as though Lyte, by some sardonic design,
meant to initiate me into knowledge of that grinding process, that
slow and intractable momentum which would govern my secrets as

it governed all things, that force against which there is no resistance that is not futile.

⌒◞

M OTHER CLEARLY KNEW I WAS CONSORTING WITH LYTE, THOUGH
she kept from raising a word about it. It seemed now that I
worked underground, now that I walked uphill in the morning
with father and the other men, a passage had been marked; now it
would be retrograde for her to speak to me as she had always done,
no matter the extent of her shame or disapproval. Still, I couldn't
expect her to sit by, and despite the unspoken laws of my growth
she had methods.

Arriving home from school one night, I found her and another
lady at our table. They stirred as I came in.

"Oh, Asher. Mrs. Woodruff has just come by for tea." Mother
rose to warm the kettle again.

"Good evening, ma'am."

"Good evening, Asher."

Delilah Woodruff was a disproportionate creature: two dwarfish
arms, an absence of neck, and hardly any torso. She appeared swallowed by her pale blue dress. She waved a midget finger at my books.

"Just home from school, young man?"

"Yes, ma'am."

"And how are your studies going?"

"Fine, thank you, ma'am." I piled the books near the door.
"Where's father?"

"At the lodge, I think," said mother.

Mrs. Woodruff squirmed round in her chair. "I understand you
and your father saw Mrs. Norton some time ago."

"Yes."

"During that terrible rain, was it?"

"Yes."

She tut-tutted her teacup. "Abicca, that woman will wander the streets at the strangest chance. Hides away in that house all the time, then comes out in a pounding storm. She was muddied head to foot, is that right, young man?"

"She was pulling up sage by the rail bank," I said. "She'd just been to see Sally Peets."

"Mrs. Peets is pregnant again," said mother as she bent to the stove.

"That's fine news," I said.

There was an indecipherable silence. I remained near the door, on the margin of some unnavigable feminine circuitry.

Mrs. Woodruff spoke to mother.

"It's said in town that she's lately taken more to witchery and potions."

"Well, David thinks well of her—"

"And they do associate rather a lot—she and Josiah Lyte, I mean. What a frightful pair, isn't it? That Lyte boy means to study under Sarah, it seems. Strange thinking for someone appointed to God's work."

Mrs. Woodruff nibbled daintily at her cup, slurping soft and swallowing quick so as to speak again.

"Sarah was midwife to me for all four of my children, you know, but that was some time ago. And seeing her in such a state yesterday, sniffing at leaves down in the hollow, I simply cannot abide!"

I left them and slipped out into the darkness, walked through the dry grasses toward Main Street.

The evening was black and clear. I went along the railroad levee, toward the big skeleton of the hoisting derrick, then passed beneath the trestle where it lifted toward the breaker house. Those wooden limbs and iron runners slanted up through the air, asleep and unrattled by the wheels of cars. I felt myself a shape at large in the machinery's dreams.

Down along the rail bank yellow light puddled outside the Exchange Hotel. Figures moved there, going in and out. A piano rang from that distance, jangling and fading with the rumble of men.

I climbed the slope toward the works and scaled a jagged culm bank. Up there the air felt cooler, softer. Main Street lay before me—the whale-oil lamps glowing, a number of windows still lit. But the town was calm, lethargic almost, everything embraced by shadow. I watched the few people wandering the streets, the forms within windows, the sheet of stars rolling overhead like the punctured scroll of a Pianola. The sense of stillness was palpable and somehow quenching. Then, as if the quiet night itself had respired deep, the whole of that chiaroscuro seemed to gain in depth and dimension and the scene drew wide on all sides till I found myself enveloped in a soft and vivid diorama. I felt suddenly untethered, disburdened of mass, as though the evening passed no judgments.

It became a habit of mine, then, to clamber atop a slag heap and imbibe the town's slumber. I often thought of Pwyll, the legendary Welsh prince who sat on the visionary mound near his palace, where he first saw his beloved Rhiannon ride past in golden robes. Was it this same mystifying bulge in the world's girth that kept him there till she came?

❧

THE YEAR MOVED WITH A GLACIAL PACE. LONG CORRIDORS OF DAYS, sunless and lamplit. Long walls of rough-hewn hours declining off into shadow. I think my interminable weeks of solitude down there at my post, always poised for the thunder of cars amid the constant rumble of the works, weathered me and instilled an ineffable kind of hunger or thirst. I aged in that first year the way rock ages—settling deeper into motionlessness. I took on the earth's empty hunger.

At some point in my succession of lone dinners down there, I learned to trap the rats as I fed them. I had only to cup my empty pail over them, then with a sheet of scrap wood I could lift the pail and turn it to look inside. The slinky curve of the bodies against the tin. The oily fur bristling at the spine. Scratch of incisors, gnawing for escape.

Sometimes I trapped two in the same pail and watched them fight. They screeched and flung their snouty fingers against each other, chomping savagely at the back of the neck. Sometimes they bled in my pail—watery blood on the tin. I freed them before one killed the other.

Once I had trapped a pair and they had just got to sparring when a long train of cars came through. I left the pail to fetch the door and when I came back both rats lay dead under each other's teeth, coiled over the tin in a kind of S, the weight of them thick in my hands. I pawed out a small grave in the dirt and emptied them into it. They stayed linked as they tumbled out, so I covered them up joined as they were. It struck me how quick their deaths had come while I wasn't watching, and I began to wonder how many deaths I had just barely forestalled. Then it became a sort of study for me— to trap a pair and watch them fight and learn to recognize the instant just before the life cut loose. It was a game of seconds really—moments thin and decisive. The fight boiled furious, never flagging, then dropped off all at once, and somewhere in the midst of that was the moment of difference wherein the vital thing fled and that which had been there was suddenly gone.

Over the course of a few months I watched a dozen or so rats die in my lunch pail. I buried them all in that wet darkness and gave up the game. The mystery was too much. I stopped trapping them and started feeding them again, letting them scurry across my boots.

Those rats really ranked among our minions down there. A scramble of their little bodies all in one direction was a sure warning of something amiss. They often flooded a gangway just moments before a wall crumpled, and sometimes a lucky miner had the sense to follow them free of doom. For me their scamper helped signal the arrival of cars. In time I even came to feel them comrades to me. I trundled off into the darkness like them, to squat and shit in the dirt.

Often, to occupy myself in that dimness, I sat and chewed over the things Josiah Lyte had told me. I imagined India's reddish sands: baked by the sun. I saw the dark waters of the Ganges. The billowed hood of the cobra. Or, since my lamp was too poor to read by, I tried to call up Emerson's words—saying them over in my mind till they had furrowed themselves there. *We are afraid of truth, afraid of fortune, afraid of death, and afraid of each other.—The world is his who can see through its pretension.—Thought is devout and devotion is thought. Deep calls unto deep.* The language had a rhythm innate to my own thought patterns, even if I didn't comprehend it all.

I studied the brownish portrait at the front of the book—the young gentleman's countenance—and that face flashed up in my mind as the dithyrambic phrases flowed. One night Lyte told me Emerson was now an old man, silvery and close to seventy. I balked fiercely at the idea. I could not fathom the stubborn contradiction of image and fact, so I denied it and Emerson remained that youthful gallant to me. *The young man reveres men of genius, because, to speak truly, they are more himself than he is.*

Tunneled up down there, I often thought back along the crusts of earth, sent my mind running down the memory of those long, arterial caverns, envisioning the sea that had spawned everything overhead. The great rock musculature around me became a terrain deep within the waters.

One Sunday about this time, in a foolhardy effort to gauge the temperament of his congregants, Reverend Parry invited Josiah Lyte to the pulpit again. As if the occasion inspired him toward beginnings, Lyte preached from Genesis 1 of the face of the deep. He recounted the Miwok tale of our valley's primeval abyss, telling of Wek-wek and Coyote-man who brought the land from the waters, even as God had said: *"Let the waters under the heaven be gathered together unto one place, and let the dry land appear."* The sermon's paganism embroiled the churchgoers anew and helped again to galvanize my mother's crusade. But the next day I rose from my bench and brought my lamp close to the tunnel wall and found the countless strange insignias in the rock. Embedded forms. Whorled shapes, tails and tentacles swirling. The bodily imprints of marine animals, and tiny fanlike shells, clear as anything. They ran the whole length of the wall, slanted up and sloped down again, following the undulations of the strata. Sure etchings in the old bone of the earth. Memory in rock. Echoes of the sea.

"The people hated my sermon Sunday," Lyte said to me that week while we walked beneath the dark umbrage of the hill pines. He high-stepped through the dry grasses, where the monstrous cones of the coulter pine lay scattered. "I'm not surprised," he said. "I half-expected it, you know. Then Reverend Parry upbraided me—in as genteel a manner as ever, of course—but still, there it is. He didn't approve."

"Will he keep you from preaching?"

"If he were wise he would. But he said he didn't want to put me down again. He confessed it's probably foolish of him, but he believes if he reads my sermons over each week he'll be able to hamper down anything objectionable. Reverend Parry's a pantheist at heart. I don't know how he manages it amidst all these moralists."

Soon Lyte fell silent and we walked a long time without a word between us, following indignity all along the hills, like so many snaking paths. He said nothing of my responsibilities to him, and I felt myself red-handed and weak. This muted me, shamed me, even as it impelled me closer to him.

He flung his head back in the shadows. "It's folly, isn't it, Witherow?"

"Isn't what?"

"The way they disfavor what's true," he said. "They hypnotize themselves and each other till they've forgotten their flesh and blood, till they believe in all the fakery they've stirred up around them. Scrambling after dead gods and reenacting all the old catastrophes. But where is Nature in all that, Witherow? Where's the living stuff we haven't stamped out with our heavy Roman feet?"

We came out of the trees to a wide shelf of open grass. The night was luminous with moon and star. Lyte spread his arms to the sky, standing there in the meadow, a blank form against the many constellations.

"Do we really stand in places like this and think ourselves deathless, Witherow? We'll smother ourselves in that, don't you think? Convention will become our god. Its heavy hands will shut the book on everything important, everything sacred."

He turned to me, his green eyes glossy and phosphoric.

"I've seen it, Witherow. My own mother tried to clap her hands over my eyes—over the Ganges and the ancient traffic of the dead."

Abruptly, his breath seemed to leave him and he dropped his glance to his feet. From the hand at his side his lean fingers twitched among the stems of tall grass. He clenched a yellow bunch and tore it up from its root. It parted from the earth with soft breaks: the snapping of tendons. He passed the long stalks through his pensive hands, then stepped toward me, the hair of grass falling along his legs. He gripped me suddenly in a grave, secretive way.

"You, Witherow, must not suffer it."

I muttered: "Yes," though his meaning was still unclear to me.

He glared hard at me, plumbing the depth of my sincerity, I think. I bore the push and pull of his hands.

"All this . . ." he said. "You're larger than all this, can you see?"

I felt the blasphemy of his words. They cracked away at the thick husk of my upbringing.

"Can you see," he said, "how by all their sophistry they would have you shut the pages of so much which needs to be?"

My eyes dropped from his and he shook me. "Can you see?"

He seemed thirsty for language. His eyes slipped to my mouth and he stared there with a new vengeance.

"Can you see," he stamped his foot madly, like an animal, "how all this would smother God in you? How you cannot stay a Christian?"

"I think—" I said. "I think—"

"Day by day, Witherow, we're made to forget the words of Christ himself. No man shall serve God *and money.*"

With an impotent little shove he unmoored me from his grip and moved off along the hilltop, back into the trees. I sensed a sort of expulsion in the push of his hands. I stood there bewildered. Lyte's sharp enmity trembled in me, a new and combustive force, like a hot seed he'd implanted.

And Lyte spoke no differently at the pulpit the following Sunday, eschewing his written sermon for an extemporized one. He preached of Christ storming through the temple, throwing over the moneychangers' tables, and called for all people to "route out the currencies that profane the temples of your heart!" He spoke of new crucifixions: Christ, hung not from a cross, but strung to the irons and timberings of the locomotive—his flesh pierced by railroad nails. To the townsfolk, it was a slew of unintelligible omens and they would not be goaded by this dubious Cassandra whose hands no doubt bore the whiff of a boy's demise.

It was Josiah Lyte's own zeal, understood to be plain evidence of his infernal nature, that shoved him irrevocably to the outer verge of Nortonville. Having too long lacked some concrete clue to implicate him in Motion's death, the people now seized upon his impious proclamations like so many parasites engorging at a war-torn limb. A sizable rank of townsfolk denounced him publicly. A pastorate as habitually blasphemous as his was insupportable. Lyte was again made to answer to Reverend Parry's reproof. And one night, to my horror, I entered the schoolroom after lessons to find Lyte alone with Superintendent Woodruff, both men grim-faced and stiff. They looked startled by my appearance.

I begged their pardon and turned to go out.

"No," said Lyte. "Stay, Witherow. You know Mr. Woodruff."

Standing awkwardly among the desks with his one fist at his hip, the superintendent had the look of a tall thing uprooted from someplace and brought here.

"Hello, sir."

"Hello, young man." He had a voice like the deep spill of a tonnage of rock. His face was as grooved as pine bark, and long.

The three of us stared in silence a minute.

"Well," Lyte said finally, "I'll not spare them my conviction, contentious as they are."

"I knew as much before I came, but it was still my duty to come. The town'll have its way, no matter my feelings on it."

"I understand," said Lyte. He placed one hand at his lectern as though to steady himself. "But I'm not for half-truths," he hissed.

"Of course not, son," said Woodruff. "You're a man of Christ and that's as He would have it, surely. I've not come to press you to doubt your own heart. I just speak for the folk of this town, who pay tax for this school and who have a say in it, whether we like it or not."

Lyte stared at me with the ashen look of one accused.

"I'm to be supervised," he said, "evaluated at my post. Tried for sedition against God, the company, and the children of Nortonville by the people who jump up in terror at my sermons."

His words seared through my diffidence and something violent sparked in me. Some obstinate will beyond our control had now bent against Lyte from an irreparable angle. It no longer concerned me, though it had started there, hadn't it? Hadn't it begun with me? I couldn't puzzle it out. But clearly it was now beyond anything I could fix even if I should muster the unthinkable will to confess. How had that happened? I turned to Woodruff and fumbled for words.

"But Mr. Lyte's a fine teacher—"

"Witherow," Lyte said, "there's no changing it. Shhh."

"But he's excellently fair and the kids mind him, sir!"

"I know, young man," said Woodruff. "You've a good teacher here. I can see it as you do. But there's a spirit for change in the town—"

I found myself stepping forward, militant, fronting the armless man.

"But your wife, sir!" I blurted. "Your wife and my mother—I know how they've been talking! I—"

"Quiet now!" boomed Woodruff. His great ropy hand fell on my shoulder with a silencing weight. "Quiet now." He squatted and looked me in the face. "We all three know it well enough, but it's beyond that, understand? The town'll have its way."

Lyte came near.

"Mr. Woodruff's right, Witherow. He's here only because now it's set, do you see?"

All at once the orange glare of the schoolroom lamps seemed edged and sharp, canceling the darkness with catastrophic brightness. I shook wildly then, my body locked up against some impalpable onslaught. Woodruff's awful tree-face was too much to bear. And that emptiness at his left side, where the unused sleeve was rolled, was a dread and sickening sight. I wanted to plunge my hand into that blunt spot, yank a new arm up from inside the severed joint, wanted to squeeze it and make him yelp—only not that ghastly nothingness there!

Lyte laid a hand on the superintendent's back. "Mr. Woodruff's an upright man, a good man. You shouldn't kick against his news. He wouldn't have come if it could be any different. This is just the course of things." He was glaring in his probing way.

I started to turn but he clutched my sleeve.

"Stay, Witherow. Stay."

He pulled me back.

The superintendent rose to his feet again, terrible in his height.

"Please stay as you are, Mr. Woodruff," said Lyte, much as he would speak to a student. He stepped behind me and steered me by the shoulders into the superintendent's shadow. "I've seen Asher this way before. I think you frighten him as I once did."

"Well, that's normal enough," said Woodruff, though he had knelt again at Lyte's request.

Lyte squared me in front of the armless man, anchored me there under the weight of his clutch. "No," he said. "Fear of this nature is too thick in this town."

His cold hand gripped mine and lifted it to the empty socket at the superintendent's shoulder. I gasped. But Lyte spread my fingers flat beneath his, against that knobby hump.

Woodruff was silent. He gazed blankly at the floor.

Shirt denim filled my palm, coarse and warm. Beneath that: the rounded shape of a cauterized thing. Soft flesh and jutting bone. Then Lyte's icy hand slid off and my thumb and fingers prodded. I watched them stirring there. They resembled the faintly lascivious limbs of some pumping insect. I remember the moment: I am making out the angle of that once nimble shoulder, kneading away at the history of a wound. Now Woodruff's craggy voice, the vibrations of it under my touch:

"I was in a team timbering a gangway down off the Karkin Tunnel," he says. "The boys had hoisted the collar against the ceiling and I was to work the leg in under it. Plenty of clearance at the joint. The beam was just wobbling in and would have to be wedged for a fit. I hugged the wood and shimmied it close to the wall."

He pauses. He seems to listen a moment to the tiny pressures of my fingers.

"But as the leg was coming to rest," he says, "the rock caved and the wall bulged against the post. It clinched the joint but it caught my arm too. The timber creaked a lot but held the rock fast."

His voice goes down upon the floor, like rock tailings pebbling over the wood.

"Me and the team talked a while. We were sure that cutting into the leg would snap it. The wall would cave, then the ceiling. I'd be smashed along with whoever sawed the timber. So since I couldn't twitch a finger anyway, we determined that my arm should come off. Someone went above to fetch a doctor. He refused to come below himself. He feared a cave-in. But he lent a clean saw to the team and told them how best to cut and said he'd be ready for me aboveground."

Under my fingers I find a thin little lip, two layers of flesh laid one upon the other. The seam where the wound was sewn. The tiny mouth so long closed upon that injury and its secrets.

"One of the boys, an old chum, aligned the saw in place and then

172

we snuffed the lamps and he and I stood face to face in that dark corner where wall met wood, screaming together while he worked away cutting as fast as he could and still be careful."

Woodruff's memory is stark and clear. He travels in it without bitterness. He is a tree, weathered, grown free of that.

"That was an everyday job, that timbering—so many hundreds of beams along every tunnel . . . Once I was loose and on my way to the surface, the team cut the hand free of the one side. Didn't want to do away with a piece of me without my consent, so they put the hand in a pail and brought it to the doctor. Later, when I was able, I took it out on the hillside by my house to bury it."

He lifts his eyes to my face.

"It's strange, son, to have some pieces of yourself die before others. Terrible strange . . . There's still a hunk of me down there in that tunnel. Knowing this, I never went back—though they told me, probably to console me, that I could be of some use with the one arm. No. Instead I put my sights to a school for this town. That was better work."

Woodruff fell silent, but still I pressed at the stump, thinking my way back to that now-vanished L of torso and arm. The superintendent's eyes strayed to the floor again, vacant under the touch, like the eyes of a dog.

Finally I dropped my hand and he rose to his towering height before me.

"I'll do my all," he murmured to Lyte. Then he lumbered to the schoolroom door and went out.

We listened to his going—the crunch of his long strides, away down the hill.

"He's a good man," Lyte said. "He won't let them run me out."

Standing beside Lyte in that familiar lamp-glow, I sensed the ardent surge of something alien in my limbs: a new and heavy sap.

173

I would forever after carry an awful knowledge of that big appendage, that brawny dismembered hand which lay for days in a battered pail, then finally got brought out to the knoll behind Mr. Woodruff's house. The dead hand lay entombed down there. I could just see it beneath the knoll, pressed with soil, the flesh slowly blending into earth. Huge, ungainly seed. I swore I heard it growing.

At night, lying in my bed, I imagined a crude claw-bush jutting knee-high and flowerless like some desert scrub. Imagined the grown tree itself, tall as a man, a desperate mitt grasping from the underworld at the air, fingers splayed out into misbegotten branches naked of leaf.

For a week or so after that visit from Woodruff, a delegate taxpayer was posted in the schoolroom. But Josiah Lyte proved to be in no way deviant, and since the superintendent demanded nothing less as grounds for formal admonition, the supervision had little effect.

Yet the begrudged will of the people managed a greater influence in the church.

6

B Y AUTUMN I WAS AT WORK DOWN IN THE ROOMS ON THE CLARK Vein. Father finally took me as a knobber at his side. I watched him wriggle on his belly up into a slanting pocket of wall till the darkness swallowed him, heard him chiseling away deep within. On my stomach I followed, eight inches between my neck and the ceiling. I shoved bushels of coal along iron sheets slick with whale oil.

Those small cavities, our workspaces, were braced with puncheon we cut on the spot to fit. Joel Aitken worked close by us, filling the cars and sizing lumber to father's specifications. The rooms from which the cavities ran were dark maws, usually just high enough to crawl in, with walls soft like cheeks. If you brushed those walls the earth fell away in little cascades, like saliva in a mouth.

Father was quiet as he worked. He whispered incoherently while he gouged at that darkness, as though he nurtured a fragile intercourse with the rock and shale and coal. Intermittently, he shouted to Joel, the two men speaking in terms I had yet to grasp.

Father tailored my initiation in bursts, little discontinuous explications coming week by week. I watched him pull his brass tag from the gridded board at the mouth of the shaft, then I found the box below his—*Witherow A.*—and fingered my tag free as he had done. Those honey-colored circles we stuck in our pockets—our identities, should the mine devour us that day. Bringing his candle to the upper wall in a room, father swung his pick there and a trail of sparks floated down.

"See that hardness," he said. "That's limestone—*bone,* you'll call it."

I labored for days with no more instruction, squirming up and down that deep passage. I learned to turn round and get the coal in front of me in a three-foot space. It seemed an impropriety, even a hazard, to speak much to father in those confines, absorbed as he was in his chip and murmur. Too much talk would crowd that space like another person, claustrophobic and blocking us in. So I worked in patience as my father's sparse lessons stretched themselves wide.

Those rooms were preternatural caverns of a kind—low earth-chapels, vaulted out of impregnable rock by dynamite. On a morning late in my first year of knobber work, father showed me how the brown-paper cartridges were set. By nebulous candlelight I watched him settle the bit of his hand-drill against the bone, fit the cylinder in, tamp it snug with dirt, withdraw the needle and inject the safety fuse.

We beat it down the tunnel while the fuse sizzled toward violence, crouched behind a shelf of wall and let the blast play out its thunder. When we came out into the dust and debris, large sheaves of bone still clung to the wall, cracked through but not yet giving. We worked at these by hand and pick to get clear to the next solid spot.

I can still get back to the particular moment: that tiny lapse in which the curtain of illusion falls and all history settles real. There's nothing between me and that morning. I am there again.

A wide mat of bone cracks under the bite of my pick to crumble at my feet, and there upon the wall—splayed against the rock—is a big gray frog. It sticks there a second before sliding free. When it drops, it leaves a clear mold of its form in the bone. It lies amidst the rubble on the floor, twitching. I bend and bear it up in my palm. It seems asleep. Through my callused fingers I feel that its body is dry, waxy and cold. I turn it over. Its white belly gleams, almost phosphorescent. In the sag of its thin foot is a soft, irregular throb, buoying the limb gently. I've seen frogs like this in the spring ponds that appear in our hills for a few weeks each year. But this one has been down here how long—locked up in this stone?

Behind me, father crawls close to peer over my shoulder.

"I'll be damned."

"See the foot," I say. "It moves."

Joel crawls near with an extra lamp. For a long time we huddle by that band of yellow light, studying the animal, its throbbing foot. This pulse is something we feel we know, even if we can't make sense of it. The incomplete burial of an age. Life sedimented in rock.

I kick a clear space amidst the debris and set the frog down on its four limp legs. We watch it silently, awaiting some bold flourish. We are like pilgrims over a relic, working hard to animate a thing with the sheer tenacity of our faith—to see blood, glistering wet again on a sliver from the cross. Maybe human beings are the unassuming birth-givers of God, the interpreters at the end of some long excretion. *Though we abandon the depths of the mountain / where no more gold is entrenched, / sometimes a river streams through the silence of stone, / and carries to light the thing we've sought. / Even when we're not desiring it, God ripens.*

At day's end we carry the frog to the surface. In talking of it with the crew boss, he suggests we have it analyzed by some San Francisco geologists who were down on the Little Vein making notes some weeks ago. So father and Joel and I walk to the postmaster's and entrust the creature, still pulsing, to a lot of parcel paper and a small wooden box, into which we drill several quick holes. We draft a letter and send the parcel off, inexplicably anxious at surrendering it.

> *Dear sirs,*
>
> *The animal herewith enclosed was discovered by the undersigned on the twelfth of October, 1873 in some newly blasted rock off the main gangway of the Clark Vein, Black Diamond Shaft, Mount Diablo Coal Fields, California. The creature was embedded snug in a layer of hard limestone some three-foot thick. At the hour we posted it, it was alive and moving very slightly, and if it should be delivered to you dead, you gentleman may judge for yourselves that it has not long been so. We respectfully request, in all good curiosity, a few words concerning your expert opinion on the frog's history. Should you humor us in this matter, it will be our pleasure to remain your admiring students,*
>
> *Joel Aitken*
> *David Witherow*
> *Asher Witherow*

We had set aside the imprinted layer of bone, and soon we decided to send that along as well; it would no doubt assist in the scientific determinations.

We received a reply in a letter labeled *San Francisco Academy of Sciences*. The frog had been safely delivered, followed shortly after by the layer of limestone. The two had been examined by scientific process and though the frog had arrived dead it was judged to be contemporaneous with the bone, which had formed in the Early Tertiary period some fifty million years ago, that epoch in which primates first appeared on earth. The frog had been sealed up in a strange sort of *suspended animation*—a phenomenon held by science to be inconceivable, given the doubtful nature of the few documented cases. The academy asked permission to keep the specimen and the rock for the sake of science and history, proposing that the animal would henceforth be catalogued as the "Black Diamond Frog."

So we left our ancient creature to science and went back to our daily grind, though for some months afterward we often wondered aloud on the impossibility of what we'd found.

"I suppose if it didn't have to move for anything, it wouldn't have reason to age," father would say. And though his comment came straight out of the blue, Joel and I would enter right into new speculations—sometimes logical, sometimes poetic.

That little frog has haunted me keenly since those days so long back. A tough, invisible thread ran down through those tables of rock, invulnerable to our pillage, though we blasted the walls to crumbs and shoveled them out. The world—its lives and many stories—became for me an ever-mounting rise of sediments. The great earth: a contoured repository. I plunged into it each day— choked on the stale, dense dust of it. Waded in the muck and shit of it. Somehow it was beautiful.

C⁓

COME 1874 OUR COAL STILL HELD STRONG AS LEADER OF THE SAN Francisco market, and that year our yield and profit reached its uttermost peak: 118,000 long tons of coal rode the rails out of Nortonville, exceeding the prior year by 14,000 tons. The Black Diamond Company paid its employees at this time in excess of $40,000 per month.

Still, the wave didn't crest unchecked. That October a violent fire roared at the works. Late one Sunday the people flooded the streets in pandemonium, the tall derrick flaming monstrously, terrible centerpiece to the destruction.

We assembled a massive bucket brigade, encircled the blaze and cut it off. But before we could put it down altogether it had gobbled up the main Black Diamond engine house and the hoisting apparatus was lost. The operators channeled water through the steam-valves in the derrick, dampening the heat enough that the framework at least was saved and the tower didn't fall—but still the huge thing was crippled.

Later, when three five-gallon kerosene cans were found amid the ash of the engine house, it became clear that the cause was arson. A quiet rancor and suspicion poured through the town for a while, contiguous to the stewing distrust of Josiah Lyte. But the works were roused again in what seemed a matter of days and the prosperity of the crowning year was not much overshadowed.

I sat some nights atop my slag heap, looking down at the gutted ghost of the engine house, then out through the moonlit air over Main Street, and in that scenery I first beheld the dark warp of transformation. I saw the old, old waters of the primordial Miwok sea pouring in, flooding our valley again, capping the ridges. Sky and water without edge. And that skeletal derrick, haggard and burnt, stood weirdly in the depths of the sea basin, jutting against silence like the ribs of a long-sunken ship. Everything got covered, uncovered, covered again. Only water and star remained all along.

I saw the warp in my father too, as his body grew leaner and his cough more regular—his laboring hours accreting slowly into a red savaging of his lungs. In the long, narrow coffins of earth he hacked roughly and spat in the corners, his cough blunted against black walls and dirt. Some of the coal that I pushed out left red streaks on my hands. The outer color of the inner struggle. The element of measure for erosion of a man.

Joel Aitken saw me once, rubbing the blood from my palms.

"He's got it in him now," he said seriously. "But there's nothing to fear. Your father's too able a man to be brought down by it."

I nodded and held up my hands. "He's got this much out of him at least." Then I spat the color off.

That year, as I continued growing, father's shrinking began to seem a natural contrast to my changing height. But then in the evenings whenever he smoked his pipe he fell to fits of coughing. Mother brought him an old kerchief to expel the brightness in, holding it to his mouth for him. She rinsed it and wrung the pinkness between her knuckles and I knew it was more than my growth that brought out his diminishment. Still, father remained agile and sturdy—and tough as a horse when he worked.

C━

ONE SPRING NIGHT I WAS UP ON THE CUMBERLAND RISE WITH Josiah Lyte, the grass high and moist, the bay leaves fragrant. We were threading the dim labyrinth of trees when we came out onto an open crest and saw a figure crouching in a meadow far below us. Lyte stopped.

"It's Sarah," he said.

We stood and watched her, curled over in the greenery, a dark humped shape. The moonlight sent a pale web of branchwork slanting over the meadow, amaranthine shadows across the grass, and the lady's black figure moved there in tiny throbbing motions, like a spider stirring softly in its net.

"She's planting," said Lyte. For a long moment he was silent, and then I thought I heard him sigh. Without turning, he said, "Is

there a new child in town?" The question spun quiet into the night
air, eerily timid, as if he directed it to some moth-like angel hovering before him.

I stood there mute. My body burned in the spring evening chill.
In the silhouetted trees at our backs an owl was mooning its song.
Sad spring nocturne.

Lyte turned and stared at me and I saw a fury in his eyes as I'd
never seen before. "Well? Is there a new child?"

"Yes. The Langdon baby." I was surprised he didn't know of it
already.

He turned back. "Ah, Sarah," he said, as if he thought she could
hear him. "She says the cottonwood seeds have children in them.
Says the seeds pull her into the hills, toward the planting place.
You should hear her talk about it, Witherow."

He gazed down the hill, motionless, as if bewitched. After a
moment or two the figure below us stood, sauntered across the
meadow, and disappeared under the mesh of tree canopies. Her
skirts bent a faint moonlit trail through the grass.

Finally Lyte's voice entered the air again like shadow. "You must
find it, you know. It's ten years full now, and you don't know where
it is, do you?"

"What?"

"Your cottonwood. It must be as thick as your neck now."

"No. I don't know. I was never told."

"So you must find it. It's pulling you already."

I had not felt it, or had not known I felt it, but I stood looking
down at the grass still glistering from Sarah's passing, and I knew
he was right.

"You'll know it," he said. "In the way you know your own hands
and legs."

"Yes."

"You must."

His voice had grown crisp, almost angry, as if he thought it somehow shameful—the need to speak to such a thing. A thing I should have known already.

I felt the weight of a promise upon me.

"I will."

Very promptly after that night, my cottonwood tree began to prickle in my limbs, magnetic like a fate, as if Lyte had initiated some potent longing, some restlessness I was helpless to ignore. I yielded to it, and soon I was moving toward the slender thing that shared my birth-night, my body tuned to the frequency of sap and twig and stem. I found myself walking alone under canopies and my feet were light and soundless, as in a dream. My shadow bent across the grass like a leaf's shadow.

For hours in the hills I would follow some inexplicable green instinct and some vegetable law seemed to echo back along my path, spurring me forward. I don't believe I've ever gone more wholeheartedly into the grip of a thing than in those days. It seemed a sudden answer to Woodruff's fiendish hand-tree rising nightly from the undersoil of dream. I couldn't say what it was that clutched me, but I see now, by the sadness that comes with remembering it, how very much it meant to be clutched.

On DAYS WHEN THE HEADACHE STRUCK—LIVID BLOOD THROBBING in my skull—I lay in the reduced light beneath my bed till evening. Then came the reprieve of darkness, when the monstrous pain slipped away as mysteriously as it had come and I rolled out and walked, fresh from my anguish, up the hills to find the mountain there against a wall of sky.

The mountain knew. It stood pure witness to everything: torments and trespasses alike, mine and all of Nortonville's. That immense knowing was a kind of backdrop to the yen of the sap flowing silent in my tree. I moved through groves of oak and buckeye, pine and aspen and laurel—the many trunks like a mob obscuring the one who called. I paused at young cottonwoods, listening. I ran bare hands over bare wood. I lay down over roots. But it was no simple thing—that finding.

One night I came dizzy from a grove of cottonwoods and crept downhill to sit atop my culm bank and gaze into the evening stillness above Main Street. My tree still threw its rings toward me and my heart was hammering, weirdly violent. I thought the pounding would fill all my limbs and send me flinging off through the dark. But I sat there very still, and after a time that high view nourished a new tranquillity within me. The silent town changed to my eyes. Storefront and house, railroad and window, all settled into the two-dimensional.

A bold figure bounded across the tableau. A girl in white, mounted on a horse, cantering into the yellow corridor of light at the livery stable. Her moving shape was embossed against the flatness. After the gleam of a moment, she vanished in the barn. I watched vague forms shifting in that shaft of light from the door, yellow on yellow.

In a minute the girl came out again, not so white now, and without the horse. She walked through the street shadows and I lost sight of her amongst the buildings. I felt I'd not seen her before. She was vivid and new.

That Sunday, early April, I met her again.

The Nortonville Oddfellows' yearly box social was held in the sunny north pasture that day. Fifteen tables were brought out from the Exchange Hotel and set up in a long row across the grass and thirty young girls in sun hats and gingham lined up shoulder to shoulder, each with a fancy dinner box displayed before her. A file of boys marched by in front, coaxed forward by their mothers, who stood watching under parasols. The Nortonville Brass Band played heartily on a stage of plank-wood laid over the grass.

I found Anna Flood clasping her hands at her back. On the table in front of her she'd set a large ebony box, stenciled with white-rimmed flowers. Her dark hair trailed down against her throat and she gathered it with a clawing motion again and again. In the sunlight she was waifish and small. She wore a plaited blouse, peach colored ruffle-work running across her flat breasts. Something tugged within me and my arms and legs tingled, as though she flowed with cottonwood sap. She extended a lean arm and hinged open the box.

"Fresh bread, still warm." Her fingers touched a lump of blue cloth and the scent rose to me. "Salt pork, oranges, olives, eggs soft-boiled, cider, a wedge of watermelon."

"I'll have it, thank you."

She gave a coy little smile, closed the lid and lifted the box to my hands. Then we strode along the length of the tables, the wide wood flowing between us, till the tables ended and she stepped round to wind her arm through mine.

"Where shall we dinner?" I said.

"This way."

Her arm yanked and she led me running across the pasture, toward where the valley narrowed and the creek sank low under clefts of earth. I let her guide me down among the live oaks and lau-rels. She laughed as if in mischief.

We found a shady place at the foot of an oak and spread out our dinner and sat back against a long, low branch. A few spotted heifers swaggered in the sunlight beyond the tree.

She unfolded a blue napkin and draped it across my lap.

"I saw you," I told her. "Just a few nights ago. Watched you ride into the livery. Where were you coming from?"

"The slough," she said.

Her fingers dug and tore at the yellow bread and it rent softly between her small hands. Steam flickered up. She had packed butter, which she began to spread for us now with a bone-handled knife.

"Why the slough?"

She shrugged. "I'd never been down there," she said. "To see the water. It's no Purgatoire but it was lovely. Then the sunset caught me up and I was terrifically late. Mother had a conniption fit."

"Have you always known how to ride?" I said.

She laid the bread in my lap. She tore hers with her teeth and spoke again with full mouth. "Yes. Haven't you?"

I blushed. Anna saw it and laughed. She had to press the back of her hand to her mouth, that the food wouldn't come flying out.

"I'm all wood-legged on a horse," I said. "And don't laugh."

"I'm sorry, it's just awfully funny. I remember when we first came to this creek and decided you weren't a coward."

I thought she might choke. Her face was maroon.

"I guess maybe I am," I said. "I guess that's that. Laugh if you want to."

She saw my injury and swallowed hard, the whimsy draining from her cheeks. "Oh no, it's cruel. I won't laugh."

She unwrapped the glistering pork and laid two strips between the remaining loaf.

"You're far and away my favorite coward, Asher Witherow."

She leaned swiftly and touched my cheek with a gentle kiss—I remember the effect of that gesture now. There was no need in her, just as there was no bitterness over our long estrangement. She was filled with choosing.

She brought out a tin canteen and two dainty glasses and poured us some bitter cider. "Asher Witherow," she intoned. "Such a sad little name. I guess you were bound to be afraid of something or other with a name like that. Guess it's not your fault."

She remembered the eggs. We held the moist things in our hands a while, chewing. The white stuff chunked off in soft jags that filled our mouths. Then we bit dark olives from our fingertips. Finally we gnawed our meat in silence, waving bees from the cider.

"Do you care for me kissing you?" Anna said. Her eyes were low as she asked it, and I thought I might answer her directly, but instead I told her how I'd dreaded her resentment.

She was ripping at the orange, stripping the softness bare and wetting her fingers. She made no answer as she tossed the scraps of rind in the grass around us, but neither did she ask my meaning. Then she broke the dripping thing open and handed half to me. She sat back and pulled the wedges free one at a time and put them in her mouth to suck.

"I knew you'd pick me today," she said, her mouth full and holding back the juice.

"Yes?"

"Yes. I suppose you knew the whole time too."

"I did. Yes."

We swallowed the last of the orange, then passed the triangle of watermelon between us. Its coolness faded on our warming tongues.

Anna came closer, her arm brushing mine. The heifers groaned and their thick hides quivered at flies. Grass separated from earth at the yank of their teeth. The orange rinds that lay in the sun began to darken and curl.

It seemed we'd both arrived someplace at last, seemed a great gulf had closed behind us now—yet I was haunted by the condition this homecoming required. I saw how I'd hardened, how rock-like

I'd become. Well, maybe Anna would unburden me of that. If anyone could do it, it was she.

She touched my hand. Our skin stuck and pulled softly where the streaks of juice had dried. Within me a thousand fibers tautened, training toward her.

"We shall cherish one another," she said.

Then we were silent.

And we did cherish each other, Anna and I—in new suddenness. The fresh immediacy of it was bewildering. Warm hands. The odor of breath and hair. Unbridled talk. It was like we could sense that our partnered hours together were already termed.

Within days we had begun confiding things to one another, things large and small alike, all the shameful things that had long lain silent within us, most every indiscriminate shred, confessions we passed back and forth like a compulsive yarn game. We could not quickly enough know one another's carried secrets. Anna told me she once spat in her mother's Bible in a fit of rage against God and parent. I told her I'd seen a man and a woman at love in a lodging house window and had not turned away.

She took to joining me at the culm bank by night. We looked at the stars when they shone, or else we gazed in quiet fixation over the town below us. She was a girl of the fewest fears I've ever known. It was an alarming thing, packaged in that smallness of hers. She had wrists and ankles like tinders.

Our dark commerce of shames was a libidinous kind of obsession. It troubled us with all the adduction of sex, which was not yet in us but which came nearer our bones by the day.

The disclosures were often terrible. She told me she'd spread chicken shit in her father's soup after a beating and had hoped he'd die of it. She'd seen an Indian man stabbed by three company thugs behind a Colorado hotel and had run away and never said a thing. I felt sure that one day soon I'd tell her how I killed Thomas Motion.

The rest of that spring and early summer were trance-like for me, gravitating between the pull of my cottonwood and the company of Anna. I felt a slow seepage at work, the juices of my being swelling out to the walls of my body. On lone nights, I haunted the trees, obsessed by the magnetism of sap. I felt myself nearing it.

From the culm bank one night we watched the weightless fur of cottonwood seed floating through strips of lamplight, thick as snowflakes in the air.

"I think mother'll die soon," Anna said. "She just gets worse and worse."

She was looking at her hands, webbing the fingers together, canopying the palms upward.

"Sometimes I think I'll just stir rat poison into her porridge. She seems to want to leave us so."

I asked her if she loved her mother.

"I don't know. I did once. But she's been sick so long. She's hardly in the world now. I think she sucked up all my love."

We sat quiet. A dimly illumined sky spanned above us.

"Tell me the things you love," I said.

She shook her head. "No. You first. And don't say your father. It should be things we don't already know."

I thought.

"I don't know," I said. "There's so much. Don't you have a lot too? Don't you think it's hard to say it all?"

"Don't say it then," she said. "Just show me."

"What?"

"Don't say a word. Just do something. Show me."

So I leaned against her slender body and her eyes fell closed as I kissed her. When I came away I saw the bluish lids palpitating as if in wild dream.

The day's gray smoke still hung in a net over the town, thinning. Now and then it gave a veiled glimmer to some stars. It made me think of one of Emerson's poems. Anna laid her head across my legs as I spoke the words.

"Our eyes are armed,
but we are strangers to the stars,
And strangers to the mystic beast and bird,
And strangers to the plant and to the mine."

Anna sighed. She sat up again and kissed me softly.

"We *shall* have to call you David after all," she said. "You remember that, don't you? I don't think it's too late yet."

We drew seed from each other's hair.

"This is cottonwood," I said, combing it from the soft darkness of her head. We watched it lift from my cupped hand and go trailing away.

Anna turned and opened her mouth to the breeze, closed her eyes as if against snow, let the downy seeds alight on her tongue.

⁓

I FELT THE WORLD WAS SWOLLEN WITH SEED THAT YEAR. IT SANG IN TUNE with the swelling in my own limbs: my body pulsing fuller, nearly twelve years old, bones lengthening under skin, strange sap rising daily. Lyte, with all his shrewdness, saw it in me at once.

"Every year we die somewhat, are born somewhat," he said. "The arc of our living is drawn over this cycle. This year will likely grapple with you, Witherow."

The grasses of our hills grew crisp and yellow. Sun beat down. Heated winds blew. I felt myself pressured flat under that sun, growing restive in those winds. Squirming against earth, a thing in metamorphosis. Everywhere the air was musky and sweet, redolent with sage.

I sought out my tree with a new wildness—a gut-force. Loin urge. I pulled the spade-shaped leaves from unsure cottonwoods. They lay cool and flat in my hands, but they seemed to hum, communicative. I roamed long shoulders of hills, wide meadows, moonlit yellow grass.

I felt charged to tell Anna of Thomas—it seemed some terrible disloyalty that I hadn't yet. With all our confessions, we'd taken up a perilous kind of game. Anna, laying open her secrets, had flung herself out into that danger, but I had held myself away from that, and the shame of it was growing by the day. I think I believed her to be the portal through which I might pass to enter my real confession. If Anna knew everything, couldn't anyone know? If she heard me tell it, what shame should I feel before anybody else? One evening, recalling that I'd never yet confessed my night-prowess, I told her I could see in darkness. It felt like the first step toward the bigger matter.

"Can you?" she said. "Are you a wizard?"

"No."

"Let's see it," she said, and she leapt down the steep face of the culm and dashed away.

I chased her through the litter of the company yard, scrambling over beams, hurtling wire and iron debris. She led me up the black crevice of the canyon through fretted limb and root. We scared night animals back into the brush. I pursued her clear to the ridge top and over the flat of dry grasses. I finally caught her at the base of a new rise. I touched the nape of her neck where her hair brushed cool. She halted, standing there under my touch, facing away.

The grassy earth slanted up before us. A few trees obscured the sky—shadow under shadow. I took my hand away, unsure of the motion to end our game. The summer wind hovered warm between us.

Anna turned, her face grave in the dimness. "So it's true then."

"Yes," I said, "and you can see too."

"Yes."

Her mouth flitted in a tiny smile and I thought: *Of course you can.* And if it had been in me then to speak it clearly, I would have said how right it was, given the verdancy of her girlhood and the sentience of all that growth around us, that she should simply see. That it should be effortless for her.

She reached for my hand and brought it up in hers and held it flat in the space between us, as though trying to read a leaf.

"I'm hot," she whispered.

She came nearer and pressed my hand to her midriff. Dry cotton pleats. The heat of her beneath. Her belly urged with breath and sank again.

I felt myself go electric and race right through her then—down her legs and into the ground like a bolt through a conductor. Then a jagged circuitry split the warm earth and my roots flashed bright in the soil.

I turned from her and stepped through darkness. I traced a long knuckle of root, as though walking a wire high in space. The grasses parted. Just outside a loose ring of old trees stood a young cottonwood, a few heads taller than me. Rough, light bark. Flat spades catching moonlight, glowing dully.

I drew near and closed my hand about the trunk. I felt I'd reached into a mirror to grip my own arm. Above me the leaves clattered softly. I lay down over the weave of roots. Knees of tree nudging my spine. Trunk rising through heart.

Anna lay down at my side, silent. I crooked my arm to stroke her hair, petted the blackness down against buoyant grasses. I felt her turn her head. Her lips at my neck. Breath.

Something of me unpent itself and entered the tree and climbed, sap in sap. Magnetism broke. The earth seemed to float, unfettered in the darkness.

"I bled yesterday," Anna said. Her voice touched my neck, spreading over my throat. "I think I must tell you because mama's past hearing now, and besides her there's only father."

She raised herself on one arm and lay half against me. I tasted her breath as her words grazed my face.

"Mama used to ask me often if it had happened yet, if blood had come. When I told her no, she got coarse. She knew she was sickening and I think she was waiting the day she could tell me what the blood meant. She thought it would frighten me. But I know what it means."

In the leaves above, I made out the trim figure of a night bird or a bat, motionless in the waving green. I half expected it to float down to us. Everywhere in that shadowy air, tendency was plain and readable. I too knew what Anna's blood meant.

I turned toward her. A little space opened between us as I rolled. Her arm lay along her slight hip and I reached for the wrist. It was stem-like and warm in the clasp of my fingers, the skin like oilcloth over the bone. Her lips parted with a gentle tearing sound.

Between us, a few cottonwood leaves lay weightless upon the blades of grass. I freed her wrist and picked up one of them and turned it by its stem, then tore it softly with my fingers. We listened to the rending fibers. An infinitesimal thread of dark juice rose to the break and glistened.

"This is my tree," I told her, "planted the night I was born."

Anna came close again. She urged me back down and lay against me.

"We mustn't tell anybody," she said.

"I think—" I said, "I think I learned to see just for this." And then it was plain as anything how I would say it to her. "I haven't told you of the way I learned—"

But Anna took my fingers in hers and led them to her lips and made them trace the fullness and moisture. I lost hold of the words, let them go freely like insignificant shavings of grass.

We lay long in silence. Then we walked home unspeaking.

ANNA'S MOTHER DIED THAT AUGUST, CONSUMPTIVE AND WITHERED. Her light coffin was borne to Rose Hill. I stood in the grass up on the Somersville Rise, waiting, while a few shadows moved in the lamplight between the cypress trees, amassing at the grave. Reverend Parry spoke the prescribed words. Then the party broke.

Anna walked slowly toward me up the hill. She wore a black dress with ungarnished sleeves and high collar. A dark shawl draped her head. She drew up to me and kissed my lips.

"Father's filling the grave now," she said. She shook the shawl from her hair, twisted it between her hands, tied it in a sash about her waist. Her face shone clear and she smiled weakly. "It's done with. Now whither?"

We walked down the hill into town, then along Main Street toward the works. The blackish dust of the road was stirring in small eddies. Anna turned her face to my shoulder and shut her eyes. At the wide porch of the lodging house someone sat in shadows talking—smattering of Italian and Welsh. The saloon was in an uproar, the golden window projections crowded with silhouettes. We passed through the shadows of buildings, inadvertent procession of two: funeral walk.

Main Street dropped away and Anna opened her eyes. On our right the fretwork of the rail trestle rose, the towering derrick behind it. We moved to the backside of our culm bank and climbed. Anna gripped my shirt as the looser slag slipped under our feet.

It was late in the month, nearly September. The night sky curved over us as we topped the bank. The air had been burnt clean by the heat of the day and it was sheeny with stars. To the north, the yearly meteor shower was blazing, white flame scorching in streaks, extinguishing fast. The night seemed to hiss. We sat beneath it. Anna's hand clutched at my arm like a claw.

I gazed toward the smokestack, the long rows of cars at rest along the trestle.

"Yesterday, I heard my father talking about all the wheat getting shipped from San Francisco. He said those wheat ships bring coal when they come back. Good coal, and lots of it. He thinks ours won't sell much longer."

"I don't care," Anna said.

"I'm sorry."

She spread my palm against hers and pulled softly at my fingers, angling them back and letting them fall.

"You're all I have in the world," she said, and the words seemed threaded with resentment and thankfulness, both. I was trying to get at which she might be feeling when she turned and pressed her hand at my shoulder. Sternly, she urged me down against the culm.

In my memory of that touch there is a vividness intense and frightful. Her hand is there, forceful and stiff, pressing just under my collarbone, and in a fluttering motion she spreads her skirts and sits astride me.

I see her dark form against the night sky. Her shadowed face is sullen and tense, adult-like. Then tears begin trailing slow, without a whimper. She falls forward over me, her mouth against my mouth—generous and hungry. My chest bursts under hers, the heart distended, raging.

Anna ebbs back along the length of me and sits up again, her thin legs still astraddle mine. She is without mass, skeletal and light. I want to take her hands and lead them down. But I wait and relax. Her cool fingers are tracing rings beneath my shirt. I fall to the trance of that circular motion.

Moments later, when she has grown fervid and torn back my belt and we are locked in a deep paroxysm of breath and heat, I feel the culm shifting, separating beneath me. The dull shards part at my shoulder blades. A furrow opens under my spine, drawing me down. With every press of her light body the pocket deepens. And I know now, with an aching sureness, that I cannot hold back my secret from her any longer. She is already flying out there amidst unstable things. I must join her there, must keep hold of her as we go, I cannot abandon her to that. But I cannot speak just now. I would have her drive me into the slag like a spike. I would have this black hillock of culm swallow us both as we are.

Anna sobs aloud. A white fire streams upward between us. It scores the night, then fades, and our skies darken again. When she takes my hand to help me sit up, the culm trails down behind me, filling the hollow with a shimmery sound. She weeps against me, her face hot and wet. My hands are buried black in her hair. Her body is a burning filament and she is incandescent. I am startled by all her definition.

{7}

I T IS HARD TO TELL NOW, AS I TRACE THE STEPS OF THE YEARS AGAIN,
just how the peculiar nature of each took shape. Does my
memory conflate and embellish, or is it that time was condens-
ing for me then, narrowing as it does when one's days steepen
toward the arc of life? At any rate, that year moved to its close in
elegiac fashion, by fading light. And then each following year
shrank a degree, time constricting.

In September 1875 father and I stood by the foot of the shaft at
end of day, awaiting our lift, and saw Cale Carver, the hoist-man, get
smashed under a falling car. The exchange of cars—loaded going up,
empty coming down—happened at an incredible rate, and Carver at-
tached and detached the steel hoisting ropes with expert grace. This
day, without warning, the cable parted and a loaded car that had risen
four hundred feet came down again. There was a thunderous crash,
the deafening rattle of coal, and Cale folded weirdly beneath the tonnage. It was strange and chilling to see: like some heinous optical illusion. In the split second as it happened, I pictured Carver sitting

beside me on the settle at the Exchange, talking of father's misgivings on the eve of my first shift underground, waving a cigar in his burly hand—yet here he was now, crimped instantly beneath a coal car, his huge body as unresisting as crumpling silk.

I remember father's roar: full-throated above the shaft noise. He scrambled over the wreckage, mounting coal and buckled car, wild to clear that disordered cairn. I stood by, transfixed, bewitched by the instantaneousness of that death, the futility of father's rage against it. Every new such shock frayed him markedly in those years. He let the black poison of shock spread in his limbs, gritting up his lungs death by death and day after day.

After several hours the wreckage was cleared, Cale Carver heaped up and brought out. I helped with the rubble. Father hacked and spat through the whole ordeal. That night mother could not coax him to bed. He went out coughing and drank himself free of it, staggered to work in the morning.

The following night Cale Carver went up in a box to Rose Hill. A large company sang him to the grave. Father stood swaying on his feet, his eyes shut. When he tried through all the fatigue to sing, he only vomited brown into his kerchief. He withdrew early and mother and I walked him home.

◈

JOSIAH LYTE, STILL BARRED FROM THE PULPIT, HAD STARTED GOING TRUant from church on Sundays. I think he knew he could not cast his brave ethics elsewhere, so he stayed to dig in against whatever dent he'd already made in the town's piousness, though the people still repudiated him. Then too he had the school. One Sunday I stole from the house early to share his truancy. We climbed to the

Cumberland Rise in an opaque red dawn. The mountain burned apocalyptic before us.

"Let the Pharisees sing to themselves," said Lyte. "Here is church enough for us, Witherow. That mountain's unsmirched—look at it! It is witness to everything like God is, sustains us like Christ, shall smash us like the Holy Spirit."

A wide nimbus of orange framed the slopes and began to burn the sky blue.

"Fitting that we the Christians should name it for the devil," he said. "God must be playing us for fools, we who stand the farthest from Christ's heart. We who abhor nature, as though God's lost control of it. Wasn't Christ abhorred in the same way?"

We followed the line of the mountain along the ridge. Then Lyte stopped and fixed his gaze down the eastward grade. He gripped my arm and bade me look. Fifty yards off, near the foot of a eucalyptus, a raven held a red squirrel pinned against a hunk of limestone. The bird's beak drilled roughly at the white fur on the squirrel's underside, and the squirrel gave out a gentle chirrup as a diamond of red gapped its belly, its tail worming fast. It was a kind of privatized ceremony, equally innocent on both sides—the murderous bird and the furry thing. The white limbs of the eucalyptus branched nakedly in the air.

Lyte and I crept away along the ridge, careful not to upset the sacrifice. Then he stopped and faced Diablo again.

"This mountain is such an altar for us, Witherow," he said. "Soon we'll be broken against its flanks. Soon, Witherow. As Christ was broken against the Father. Can we honor the test, as he did?"

Lyte's talk had grown harsh and feverish in his long interval away from the pulpit. I winced at that. And although he never confirmed it outright, I felt sure the blame was mine. He never spoke to me of my duty, as if he'd forgotten my complicity altogether—

though that was not it at all. I am astounded now to think of his patience, his fidelity. He tended some inexhaustible faith in my goodness, as if this vigil itself had become his life's work, but at times I saw how I ratcheted up his inscrutable rage at the world. I sensed the dark truth in his remark now, felt the awful teeth of it. Something was coming. We'd been holding out, Lyte and I and everybody, against it, and it wouldn't humor us much longer.

∼

O N AN OCTOBER NIGHT JUST A FEW WEEKS BEFORE MY BIRTHDAY, Anna lay with her head in my lap, atop the culm bank, black hair fanned out over legs and slag.

"I cannot cry," she said flatly.

"No?"

"No. And I can't remember crying."

"But must you cry?"

"Yes. I must. Of course." She sounded angry.

"But you can't make yourself cry, can you?"

"No . . ." Her left hand turned and scooped a mound of blackness. "But father cried endlessly. Like a girl. And he didn't even love my mother. How can he cry?"

"Maybe he did love her."

"No!" Her will was turbulent tonight, like a mad horse. "He did not."

"Maybe he loves her memory."

"No! I do. That's for me."

"Then that's real grief too—even if you don't cry."

Anna grew silent at this, as though the suggestion were settling and she should not disturb it. She rolled her head to the side and her narrow cheek lay plain from her hair.

"I did cry," she said, "once."

"Yes?"

"Yes. Once. The night she was buried. With you, here."

"Yes, I remember." A sharp heat flashed in my legs. It bolted up my spine to my scalp, an echo of that night's suddenness.

Without turning, Anna folded one arm upward and her fingers fed along my forearm and wrist, found my hand and squeezed it, pulled it closer to her breast.

"Your hand's warm," she said.

The evenings had cooled considerably. A vesper wind stirred tonight, purling over houses and grasses. Anna's fingers were chilled. Her words moved slow, like milk seeping from a mouth.

"I ought to tell you," she said, "that I know how it is. I mean that I haven't cried . . . that I haven't cried since that night."

I listened.

"Here, that night, all the empty space got filled up . . . Death left me hollow but something new came in."

I touched her hair, gazed over the lines of bone in her face. I moved numb in her nebulous words, trying to read the meaning. She seemed to know so deeply what she said. She was bright with knowing. I was dim against that.

"That new thing is inside of me," she said. "It's been filling me up." Her voice grew thread-like, spinning, feeding out into the October shadows. "You put a child in me."

My limbs fell slack. I tumbled back from my body and saw myself: my small feet touched the feet of a monstrous shadow. That shadow swelled hugely away from my little form—a feral, billowing force. It was alien to me, yet my body gave it shape.

Anna lay very still. Her jointy shape jutted against darkness. She pressed the back of my hand to her mouth and her words brushed warm across my knuckles.

"It must come out of me," she said. "I've still to cry."

"What?"

"It must come out of me."

I asked her meaning and she spelled it out for me. Then I saw nature mastered weirdly by man's hand, plied and twisted and shoved through a funnel. How did Anna know of this? She knew things it seemed forbidden to know.

"Soon?" I said.

"Yes."

We could not have spoken anything of the other way. The other way was inconceivable against our youthfulness, let alone against Anna's smallness, though we could not yet think of that danger, for all our naïveté.

I bent and kissed her with an energy harsh and inexplicable. And I thought I would tell her then the thing I'd kept from her so long—but at once I saw how far entrenched it was beneath all her confessions, her plainness, and now: how far beneath this new enormity that we shared.

"Soon," I said.

"Yes. We'll find help."

❧

THAT YEAR OUR PROFITS SLID STEEPLY—25,000 TONS SHY OF THE last year's yield. Underground, the men chattered over rumors that prices for better coal were dropping, that the wheat exchange was crowding us out, so much high-grade coal coming back from overseas on the wheat ships, that a whole new country of unworked anthracite beds lay up north in Washington Territory, just awaiting claimants.

Father spasmed and choked, lurching over the basin that mother kept out for him now. Despite the fortitude of his smile, his face grew pocked and haggard. He couldn't bear the draft as he perched naked in the washing barrel, but his chest collapsed inward like a punched hat and he lost himself to the sputtering in his throat. Mother heated the water to scalding, backed the barrel up to the oven, and scrubbed with new haste. Then father went straight to bed.

One such night, while mother skiffed the hard soap over my back, she said: "You'll be through school soon," as though the milestone called for some announcement. Her tufted hand spread water over my shoulders.

"Yes," I said, "but I like the learning. Mr. Lyte says I can keep attending and he'll adjust lessons to my place."

The corner of the soap lingered near my spine, digging softly. I heard her draw a breath. "That's peculiar, son. It won't do."

"No, ma'am?"

"No."

"But I'm a fine student."

"That's well enough without going on. It's imprudent for Mr. Lyte to persist with you. I can't approve."

"Well, you might speak to Mr. Lyte himself—"

"I wouldn't dare. Reverend Parry has put him down with reason. It's bad enough you're under him still at school, but a boy needs instruction and that couldn't be helped. I'll not stand by more than is necessary. You ought to know my feelings already, Asher."

"Mother—"

"It's peculiar, son. Every boy is done with school at your age. Josiah Lyte will not put you out of place."

She tilted the carafe and rinsed me clean in silence, then turned away to consult the stove.

I HAD STOPPED ATTENDING SUNDAY SERVICES. LYTE AND I SAUNTERED. Inevitably, I told him of Anna's condition.

"I've seen her in town," he said. "I called on her mother once, but Mr. Flood sent me off. She's a small girl."

"What can we do?"

"You must see Sarah Norton."

"Do you damn me for it?"

"No," he said. "I see how it has surprised you."

"It has done, yes."

He held one spiny hand up before me, clustering the fingers like an unopened blossom. "There are things in us that are larger than we can know. Life in us. Death in us. They hide huge in the small shells of our bodies."

Darkness drummed in my skull and in my chest. I stopped and stared at the ground. "It'll be a death," I said.

"Yes," said Lyte. "And a death all the more because it's unparticular. Because it has no body or name."

M OTHER SMARTED AT MY NEGLECT OF CHURCH. "You don't consider what it's like for me," she said. "Your father stays in bed on Sundays now, and you leave your mother to sit in church alone."

"I'm sorry, ma'am, I don't mean to shame you, but—"

"But what?"

I made a fist in my lap and said it: "But there's a spirit I must follow."

Mother blanched. "A spirit?"

"Yes, ma'am."

"Be wary what you follow, son. A proper spirit would have you in church with your mother. Where does this spirit take you?"

"Out under the sky," I said. "The Lord's sky. Up into the hills. Up to a view of the mountain."

"That's backward, son. Looking to the devil's hill when you ought to be in the house of God."

"But it's the Lord's mountain, mother—"

She stiffened and knifed one finger into the air. "Nothing with such a name," she said, "belongs to the Lord. Ah, I wish my vote had cast a greater weight to change that name some years ago. Better Coal Hill than Satan's Mount!"

"But they were Christians who named it in the first place," I said. "Mr. Lyte's told me so. I don't see the unholiness in it."

She had fetched father's basin from beside the bed and was about to rinse it fresh of its reddish water. Her voice tautened. "I ought to've known," she said. "You've been with Josiah Lyte these Sundays?"

"Yes, ma'am."

"So you defy me twice. Will you undo all the good I mean for you?"

"Mother, you don't understand—"

"I understand, Asher." Her hands splashed in the basin. "And I suppose you mean to keep up that wicked schooling bargain with Josiah Lyte despite me?"

"No, ma'am. But won't you see the value in it?"

The battle went out of her then, left her with a single deflating collapse of her shoulders. She sighed and her hands lay inert in the pink water.

"David," she said. "David." She turned her head toward father but could not have meant to wake him, for she was whispering. "Will our boy run wicked while you lie sick?"

Father slept heavily in the bed near the wall. He did not stir.

THE FOLLOWING EVENING, WHILE SHE SCRUBBED THE BLACK FROM MY hair, mother said she'd have Josiah Lyte for tea that night if he could manage it. I was to ask him at school.

I couldn't see her intent. I squirmed through the lessons and afterward I jabbered out the invitation. But Lyte was unruffled.

"Fine," he said. "I'll walk home with you."

We went together down the hill from the schoolhouse that night, quiet amidst the flood of noisy pupils.

Mother was tending to father when we came into the house. He had lately been in a deep rut of dogged work in the pits all day, hasty bath, perfunctory supper, and then bed rest straightaway, his sleep broken with fits that splashed the basin. But tonight he had roused himself to sit in the rocker. Mother had spread a quilt at his shoulders and a blanket at his lap and was bringing him a cup of porridge.

She said nothing as I brought Lyte in. She squatted to help father tuck his beard into his shirt. Till recently he'd speckled it nightly with dashes of supper and blood, both sputtering up as he ate, and mother had tired of rinsing it. He looked small with his beard napkined away like that. His torso lay plain and thin. He had the basin on a stand beside the chair.

I showed Lyte to a seat at the table.

Mother stepped to the stove. "I've water on for tea."

"I'll have some, thank you," said Lyte. "How are you, Mr. Witherow?"

Father held the porridge in his lap with both hands, like something precious. Steam climbed in scarves to his face, branching off the sides of his head. "Well enough, thank you," he said in a grumble as magnanimous as his hoarseness would permit. "Just coming through a choppy spell."

"Yes. Reverend Parry and I have kept you in our thoughts." Lyte gave an affirming nod. Then he turned again to mother, whose back was to us as she stood at the stove. "Well, Mrs. Witherow, you've a great many things to tend to. I wonder how you manage it as you do, or how any of our women manage."

Mother shrugged a bit and did not turn. "God gives us strength enough."

"Yes, that's sure. And then some."

Mother let the prattle subside. We three sat wordless a while. Father's fuzzing breath textured the silence. At last mother turned and set out the tea, then sat opposite Lyte at the table. Her eyes grazed mine as she sipped. With an unsteady clatter, she set down her cup. Her hand rose and hovered a second, then sank slow and soft to the table—palm to wood like a sheaf parting air before it settles.

"I must speak plainly, Mr. Lyte, or we'll all age in these chairs before anything is said. You must know my conviction on a number of points already—that it was I who moved to keep you from the pulpit and so on."

"Yes."

"Yes. Well, now I'd have you forfeit your interest—whatever it is—in my son. I don't care for your beliefs and I won't have you clouding Asher."

Lyte sat motionless, looking mother in the face, all hearing, as though he sensed there was more she wished to say. This seemed to unnerve her somewhat, to lengthen her argument and sharpen its edge.

"We've forbidden you to him already, Mr. Lyte, but he thinks it best to defy us, so he's left us to this—to tell you that you're not to let him speak to you."

"Do you mean to take him out of school?"

"No. He'll finish the year. But your instruction is to cease each night with the school bell. You will not feed him anything more than the lessons the other children get from you. And when the term is done, your association with him is over. There will be none of this private tutoring he's told me of."

Lyte gently saucered his cup and leaned forward. His voice was soft. "Mrs. Witherow, your son is a rare young man. He's apt to find a worthy place in the world and lessons are what he needs, beyond regular schooling. I do wish you'd consider—"

"You won't instruct me, Josiah Lyte, in what I should consider."

Lyte turned to father. "But Mr. Witherow, Reverend Parry told me, direct from you, that Asher was hardly fourteen months when he started talking—"

"Yes. That's right."

"And he went straight to full sentences too. Didn't he?"

"Yes, yes," said father, rippling into motion and inadvertently tipping the rocker back till he had to steady his porridge, "that's true. You remember that, Abicca."

"I didn't ask you here, Mr. Lyte," mother said, "for argument. My position is plain."

"I cannot guard it's careless of you—"

"I won't be counseled by one who calls himself a minister and lures young boys from church. You're to keep off my son!"

I broke in: "He doesn't lure me, mother."

"Be quiet, Asher!"

"Christ himself," said Lyte, "urged men to a temple better than a Pharisees' den, Mrs. Witherow."

"Don't tell me of Christ," mother snapped. "You know nothing of His perfection—bless His name—or you wouldn't sit here comparing yourself to Him."

"Ah, but Mrs. Witherow, I think he exhorts us to compare ourselves."

Mother's lips lay together in a dark slit. She drew a loud trembling breath through her nose, and behind that dark slit her mouth churned full with a silent backdraft of flame. Her right hand slid back and clutched the table as if she believed it were a hinged desk and she might open it to bring out the certificates of all her rage.

"How dare you," she muttered. "If you keep on my son, I'll have you driven from this town."

Lyte fell silent. He sat back. His shoulders lifted with a deep breath. He turned to me and I saw that his green eyes were clear and wounded, but a pale shadow of acceptance spread over his face. Between us the imminent took shape. He folded his hands before him.

"I cannot assent, ma'am."

Mother's chin ticked sideways. She glanced to father.

Lyte said: "If Asher speaks to me, I won't shrug him off. If he comes for lessons, I'll teach. If he needs the sky and not the rafters of the church on Sunday, I'll hold service with him, be it against your wishes or not."

Mother clenched her jaw. "You do such harm. The boy is so young against your bedeviling."

"Not so young," said Lyte. "The world is his already."

"Blasphemous."

"Not blasphemous, Mrs. Witherow. True. He has it in him to choose. His heart will lead him."

Mother bit her words from the tense air. "That's a sure road to sin, Josiah Lyte. The boy's heart is young. Confused."

"His heart is pure."

"And so he defies me?"

"If that's as his heart must have it, yes. I wish most *men's* hearts were as resolute as that."

My hand came up from my lap and fell across the tabletop. I felt no governance over it—I watched it. The fingers twitched on the wood. "Mother—"

"Shut your mouth, Asher." Her voice was nearly at a shout and she launched straightaway at that volume. "You, Josiah Lyte, have so far escaped your due on earth, but you'll meet it elsewhere. The Lord has taken that out of my hands—so be it."

"I beg your pardon, Mrs. Witherow. I thought God alone could hold me to account."

"Then you're sadly bedeviled, my boy. God gives jurisdiction on earth too. Of course it's plain you heed none of that."

"If you mean Reverend Parry, Mrs. Witherow, I can tell you he's held me from the pulpit just as you designed it."

Mother shoulders sank a little. She looked so dismayed I thought she nearly smiled. "You're not ignorant, are you, of all that's known about you?"

"Mother, Mr. Lyte's been mistook—"

Mother hushed me with a gusting noise. She was all atremble, her hands fisted up and shuddering. She spoke lowly, venomous. "You've blackened this town with your heathenry, Josiah Lyte. Anyone properly Christian can see it—you and Sarah Norton working your ugly charms."

Lyte touched his teacup gently, as if it were a strange and golden artifact. "I don't see," he said quietly, "what you mean to say, Mrs. Witherow."

Her face was blood-red now, the righteous fire ravaging there such that I swore her veins would split the skin that had so far held them under. "I mean by your devilry a boy burned to death and a second boy nearly suffered the same."

There came a rude noise from the stove which I took at first to be a roar of laughter, but then we all turned to see father pitched forward in the rocker, clutching the chair with both hands and vomiting red over the blanket that covered his legs. His bowl flew out and cracked loudly at the floor and the porridge went splatting. The table shook as mother bolted up and rushed to him.

"David! David, hush now, dear. It's all right, dear, hush."

She got his basin and held it steady beneath him as he hacked. She wrapped herself around his hunched figure, her head sided up against his as if to lend agency and focus to the rough expectoration.

Lyte and I sat dumbstruck.

Mother's body quivered in time with father's, and as he kept up that ragged lung-rending noise she spoke soft in his ear, stroking his hair quickly with one hand: "That's right, dear. There it comes. It's leaving you now, see? That's all."

Finally father bucked the rocker back again, gasped and wiped his beard with the back of his hand, and it appeared the fit was leaving him. Mother remained there embracing him. She looked up at the table.

"Here's the man," she said to Lyte, "who brought your foul work out of the earth."

And then, just then, as if it had been simple all along, I was on my feet and stepping fast across the puncheon floor to stand before my mother and father both, my two hands held apart in front of me, palm facing palm as if I were gripping something fragile in that space, something priceless and unseeable and slippery.

"It was mine," I said. "It was my foul work, mother. Mine, father."

My voice was going out of me, just streaming forth into the

room like some immense volume of water disembogued from the most unlikely vessel, and I was looking hard at my two hands afloat before me, watching the great care with which they hung there, and I thought that those hands in that gesture were making the words possible—that I mustn't move them or everything would spill and there would be no cleaning it up.

As I spoke I saw my parents' eyes, though I was not looking at their faces but at my hands—their faces upturned and apprehended, father still catching his breath, mother's cheeks fading from their scarlet tinge to turn sapped and white. And I saw Lyte seated at the family table behind me, saw the great wide loneliness parceled neatly in his willowy form, his body poised and filled from bottom to top with nothing but silence, nothing but a sad and passionate hearkening. I saw too the ghastly bird-figure of the altar boy Isaac Payne, flapping ablaze in the nightmare darkness high above my head. Saw the great derelict hand of D. S. Woodruff, the branch-thick fingers scrabbling in the midnight air as if the darkness were a great silk mantling everything and the hand strove to grip it for fear some second hand of equal measure would gather it up from the other side and draw it clean off the world.

I gave out the words and all the silence, so inexpressibly huge for so long, became a tame and delicate thing flowing weightless on the thrumming noise of the words. And I saw they were just words, had always been just words, though they had hidden deep and dissembled themselves in such a monumental bulk. I spoke and spoke and then I had said it all and I fell mute and in the settling silence I watched my quivering hands sink again. They dropped dumb and motiveless at my sides.

Mother's closed mouth looked full of something. I thought she might cough or sob. I saw suddenly how my words weighed more to her than I could have known, how much she would bear because of them. Her hands twitched and fumbled, the right one rattling atop father's shoulders, the left one setting the bloodied basin to sloshing. I took the basin from her and set it by and she rose to her feet in a jolting way, clasping her red-flecked hands at her belly. She stared at the legs of the sawbuck table. She stared at the saucers she'd set out for us. Her hands writhed together, as if quashing one impossible thought after another. She seemed to enfigure the silence in the house, standing there gazing from her two defeated eyes. We all hovered in her silence. She looked at Lyte and said: "You've known this?"

Lyte said nothing.

"You've both kept this, haven't you, Asher?"

But she didn't seem to expect an answer. She turned and we all watched her lumber stiff to the stove. She stood there with her back to us, touched the black iron gently, lifted her fingers away, touched it again, as if it were a beast that required some gentle taming. The voice had gone out of her.

"David," she rasped. "David, make them go now, will you? Both of them."

Lyte stood. "I'll leave you."

I got up and followed him to the door.

Outside, a blustery wind brought dust against the houses. Oak leaves twitched tangled in the grass. The door scratched closed behind us and our boots scraped on the porch. The sounds seemed foreign and expulsive. We stood on the dirt footpath among the houses.

"I've done it, haven't I?" I said.

"You have," said Lyte. He dug his hands into his coat pockets and stood there looking at me. A tiny cyclone of dirt coiled upward around his legs.

"It's bad for her though, isn't it?"

Lyte didn't answer. He moved his mouth as if rolling some scalding liquor on his tongue.

"I hadn't thought how bad it would be for her. I—" My words broke off as I saw the wicked triteness of saying such a thing to Josiah Lyte of all people. "Why did you leave it to me?" I said. "All this time, and you just left it to me."

"You must tell her about Anna now," he said. "She thinks you a toddler still."

"Does she? Why?"

"It's hard for a mother. Her body shared your smallness once. Her body remembers that. She can't feel you as you are now. She doesn't know yet what's in you. Perhaps that's why this happened. So she'll see what's in you."

I was silent. Deep in my limbs, something radiant rippled up. I felt it expanding outward into the valley's darkness.

"Anyway," said Lyte, "you mustn't harbor secrets now. You must tell her soon."

I TOLD HER THE FOLLOWING NIGHT WHILE SHE BATHED ME, AS FATHER lay asleep before supper.

Her hands fell still on my shoulders. I felt the bare ridges of my bone and skin rising against her large palms, the soft settling weight of her exhaustion.

The water lapped the wooden rim between my knees, sloshed back, resolved into stillness. I stared at the floor and waited a gesture, giving her the silence. She must have gazed long at me under her hands—just looking.

I bristled with gooseflesh.

At last one hand left my shoulder and the blunt fingers entered my hair, clawed lightly along my head a moment. Then both hands left me and I heard mother step away. I gathered the towel and moved near the stove.

Mother stood at the window by the door, looking out. In the glass her face shone blank against the blackness, her eyes large and clement, as I had never seen them.

I pulled on my clothes. The shirt stuck to a swath of soap at my back.

"She's small," said mother as though to herself. "So small."

She turned her head and the curvature of her cheek came into the light. A few strands of hair lay flat against her temple. Her bone-white hair comb gleamed.

"She cannot have it, Ash."

"Ma'am?"

"It will break her in two." Her hand played upward and fell upon her hair, collecting it gently. It looked like an unconscious gesture, a thought made motion. She came from the window and stood before me.

"What shall be done?" she asked. She seemed like a little girl.

"Mr. Lyte will speak to Mrs. Norton for us."

She remained motionless, oddly torpid, and her opaline eyes did not leave my face. I thought I saw a perspicacious light come into that look, a gloaming ray.

"Yes," she said. "Sarah Norton. It must be soon."

"Yes."

"We mustn't tell your father."

"Yes, ma'am."

"I'll come. I'll be there. She'll be frightened."

"Yes, ma'am. She has no mother, you know."

"I'll come."

L YTE CALLED ON SARAH NORTON. IT WAS ARRANGED THAT WE'D GO to her house one school night that week. So on a Wednesday evening Lyte and I met Anna in the darkness at the foot of School Hill. She wore a heavy woolen cape, but stood shivering as we approached her.

"My good Miss Flood," said Lyte.

"Josiah Lyte," I told Anna. I touched her arm, slight as a butter knife beneath the wool.

Lyte stepped near to her and drew his hand along her hair, softly. "You're afraid," he said. "That's nothing strange. Don't worry. Here, take my hand."

"I think the child must know," she quavered. "I think I can feel it weeping in me. All day the sadness has clouded my belly."

"Shh," said Lyte, "don't worry."

Near the rail trestle we met mother coming briskly from the house, dark shawl round her shoulders, deep-brimmed bonnet shadowing her face. She moved with a stealing quickness, as though her whole frame were tensed in a whisper.

"I've just got father down," she said, then went straight to Anna's side. "Dear girl."

One white-gloved hand parted the woolen cape and vanished, flattening at Anna's abdomen, the skirt fluttering inward just neighbor to the hipbone. It seemed an old maternal custom, a primeval gesture above propriety, and Anna appeared to relax beneath the assuring touch.

We walked out under the trestle and along the rail bank, quickly. Mother and Lyte held the girl's hands, Anna gliding in a kind of delicate suspension between them.

Sarah Norton's house stood on the last slope below the Somersville Rise, just north of the road to church, a two-story place with a gabled porch. A round white lamp glowed like a moon in the window as we approached. Mrs. Norton appeared in the doorway, a dark shape, imposing and man-like. She brought us into a dim, carpeted parlor and we all sat down in a row on a brocaded sofa, Anna still flanked by my mother and Lyte.

A low fire burned in the hearth before us. This and the mild lamp near the window shed a minuscule light over the room. Our shadows lunged drunkenly on the wall. Somewhere an unseen clock sounded. The obliqueness was congenial, softening our pent turmoil as we sat.

"My dear Mrs. Witherow," said Sarah, "I must say I didn't expect you."

Mother stiffened and clutched at her shawl. "Well, at best I've a hand for holding."

But Sarah had trundled through a door at the side of the room. It squeaked three or four times on sprung hinges, then she returned bearing a kettle and teacup on a finished cherry tray. She set the tray on the little end table at my elbow, hefted her dress and knelt before Anna. A clinical silence settled over the room.

Sarah cuffed Anna's wrists, pushing up the sleeves to circumscribe the slenderness, the way one tries the handle of an axe before a purchase. Then her big hands floated up and doffed the cloak from Anna's shoulders and gripped the sloping rails of the collarbone, feeling outward to the upper arms, then down to the elbows. Anna sat rigid beneath the hands, her lean face close to Sarah's, shrunken before that fullness.

We all watched the silent inquest in a kind of stupor. A tart alcoholic odor rose from the tray beside me. At last Sarah sat back on her heels and looked at Anna sternly.

"How old are you child, thirteen?"

217

"Yes, ma'am."

"Mm. Just ripe. And it's you, Mr. Witherow, that's got into her."
It was a statement, empty of question or decree.

"Yes, ma'am."

"Well, if she were older or bigger there might be a question,"
Sarah said to me, "but she has no choice now, you understand."

"Yes, ma'am."

"We understand," said Anna, timorous. "We've come expecting
it." Her thin fingers crawled and curled into the grip of mother's
hand beside her. Mother looked stony.

Sarah stood up. She took the cup and saucer from the tray and
gave it to Anna. "Drink this. If it's too harsh, I've some hot water.
But drink all of it."

Anna sipped.

Sarah stood by in half-light. Her snub nose looked smashed in
those shadows. She wore a midnight dress, billowed at the shoulders, black stripes running vertical. Her long hair was bundled and
pinned. She waited while Anna grimaced at the cup, gulped the
serum down, tipped it to her lips again.

"I'll make ready," Sarah said at last. "Do call when you've finished."
She went out again through a door beside the mantel.

"Is it absinthe?" asked Lyte.

"Something like," said Anna.

We were quiet while the cup clinked in the saucer. All our dread
seemed parceled up in Anna. I felt dread move from me to her,
black intimacy of the inevitable.

Mother leaned. "You needn't have come, Mr. Lyte."

It was a thing to say to break the dread. It came out coldly.

"Of course not," said Lyte. "I wished to come. I can say a prayer
for the infant at least. I'm not sure any practicing minister would
have come, and I think it needful."

Mother pursed her lips. She stared ahead for a time. Finally she said: "It's needful, yes. That's kind of you."

"I'm glad you've come, all three of you," said Anna. "It's troubling, you know."

Mother pressed her hand. "It shall be, dear. It shall be. But you're in good care. Mrs. Norton delivered me. Her hands are sure."

Anna winced. It was an effort to give a reassured smile, I think. She set the cup down. "That's the last of it. I'm done. Shall we tell her I'm done now?"

Lyte rose to fetch Mrs. Norton. I took the saucer and set it back on the tray. Anna's hand dragged over the sofa and clamped my trouser leg.

This night is bleak in my memory, like an ineluctable stabbing with some blunt and heated thing. Red light. The pall of unintelligible circumstance. Dispassionate tang of absinthe, wormwood. There is something insidious in these inanimate elements. Odor and light. Saucer and tray. Their complicity infuriates. It would be madness to blame objects. Still, these *things* draw the memory's focus, and they nauseate and repulse.

I could hardly have understood the meaning of that night: its *repercussive* meaning—though I knew the objective, recognized the intent. Our bodies had stepped over without us, Anna and I. The rest of us had not been given passage. This night was our passage, I guess. Then came the moment that Anna rose from the sofa, escorted from the room by my mother and Sarah Norton. I can still watch her getting up. She stands dizzy, one hand floating away from her body as though the floor is tilting under her feet. Mother steadies her. Then Anna looks down and straightens her skirt, sighs softly as though catching her breath, and turns stepping with the women across the parlor—not walking, but stepping, for it seems to be not a single motion, but a series of a thousand tiny ones. And each little motion is terribly serious. *Nearby is that dominion named life. You shall recognize it by its intensity.*

They closed the door. Lyte and I sat alone in the parlor with our coats still on.

I cannot know what I thought in that quietness. It seems a weight stamps down on the memory to squash that which is formidable and lived only once. Perhaps I felt a disassembling of all that I had assumed cohesive: something cut off by that interposed door—the distinction of women by an untraversable thread, all their inveterate secrets somehow terrible.

More than this, I think that house must have seemed a haunted place, that parlor bedeviled by something invisible. Really, the room was a kind of antechamber to life—a big shed for things unliving, lives torn short of birth. There must be such a place, where all that is unlived is shored away.

I got up and stepped to the hearth. On the mantelpiece were scattered a number of little artifacts, bits of walnut and rock and crude-looking shards of bone. I touched the pieces lightly. The fire warmed my front, and though the women's door was directly beside me, I could hear only crackling flames.

Lyte came and stood at my side. "Indian things," he said. "Sarah's found all these in our hills."

He lifted a yellow sheaf of bone in his knuckly fingers, a flat piece no longer than my hand. A shoulder blade maybe, or a hipbone.

"It's a saw," he said. He turned it broad wise and pointed out the serrated edge, tiny saw-teeth. "It's from deer. They used it to trim the tule for their boats."

He picked up a thin pencil-like thing. It curved ever so slightly in his fingers, and as he turned it I glimpsed the tiny holes drilled up and down it.

"A flute," said Lyte. "From bird bone."

There was also a small handheld broom made of soapbrush. A large obsidian arrowhead. A silvery abalone shell disc with holes punched up the center—a pendant, Lyte said.

I took a little half-spherical thing between finger and thumb and turned it over. A cracked walnut with black resin dried across its top, bits of abalone shell stuck into the resin.

"Those are dice," said Lyte.

I placed it in my open palm and it rolled softly between the curves of my hand. Lyte took it and held it for a long moment, staring. At last he set it back on the mantel.

"It won't be long now," he said.

"No? That quickly?"

"Yes. We should pray."

We went to the sofa again and Lyte folded his hands. He looked up to the ceiling floating in shadow. His voice was grave. We wanted only, he told the God above us, to learn how deep and high and wide the single word of Christ could run: *Love*. Love awaited our expansion—that we might embody it as only Christ had done. It was by a hard gesture of love that we sent this unknown infant from its mother. Let the child dissolve now, completely and wholly, back into the infinite cloud of Love from which everything came— to become Love again, undifferentiated. Let the mother feel the crush of Love in all its fullness, supplanting her loss and ripening in her anew.

I listened to the words floating up against the silence, the clock. Not a sound from behind that impenetrable door. Every person, in some way, represents the world, Lyte had told me. And he prayed to that now—that the unliving child might embody for us the quintessential trajectory of all mankind: a dissolution in nonbeing and Love. I felt his prayer was chiseling the vision clear, delineating it so perfectly that it seemed made into immediate truth. I learned from Lyte then the real nature of prayer: to elucidate from chaos that which *is*, which *must be*.

He fell silent. We sat without speaking. The night halted and limped in that parlor.

At last the door came open and the two women ushered Anna out between them. She walked on her own, though rather unsteadily, looking pale. Sarah and my mother kept to either side of her, as if expecting her to fall. It was terrible to me that Anna could get up and walk, emptied as she was. She crossed the oriental rug to stand before me, red-eyed and drowsy in the face. She squinted in the dying firelight. The wormwood still wafted from her.

"It's best she get home directly," said Mrs. Norton.

Mother gathered Anna's cape from the sofa and flung it round the girl's shoulders. Mrs. Norton was thanked in a murmurous way by Josiah Lyte, then by my mother. We all went out the door together.

"Keep out of the sun, my girl," said Sarah. "That rue is hard on the eyes. I'll be round to see you in the morning."

Then she stood on the raised porch, looking after us.

ASH

1

WELL INTO THE SPRING, ANNA WAS TROUBLED BY AN INCESsant dream.

"It woke me early this morning," she told me more than once, while we sat at the culm bank together by night. "I dreamt I had already woke, for a wetness at my pillow and in my hair. When I sat up and lit the lamp I saw redness down the front of me, soaking my chemise. I stood up and turned around and there I was—I had stepped right out of my body and I could see myself still sitting there on the bed with blood rubbed all over my face and mouth. I tried to turn away, to leave myself there, but I only stumbled on something—bones. There were bones all over the floor. Little soft bones, still wet, like they just came out of a tiny body. Then I woke up, and it felt like something had fallen on top of me. That must have been me, falling back into myself. To wake myself."

I didn't know what to say to her. I felt she told the dream not to me so much as to herself, or in a gesture of contrition to something within herself. For a time, she was a haunted thing, still hollowing, hollowing. And though I'd told mother and father both already, I could not let go of my secret about Thomas Motion—not to Anna. I knew now I'd betrayed her in this, but I'd lived that once already with mother and father. The revelation had cast a murky under-color to the life of our small family. We moved in the tincture of it, like the stern-faced ghosts of some old daguerreotype. I couldn't bear to let such a thing happen with Anna too. I remembered her quiet hope of flight from Nortonville, her talk of freedom once her mother passed on. She'd said we would go together, she and I—to San Francisco or someplace. But she never talked of that anymore. Something had excised that hope, and now not only the hope but the very possibility seemed absent, and Anna had forgotten. How do such things so quietly vanish? I sensed I was responsible, yet how could I remind her of that which had left her, let alone restore it to her?

B Y EARLY SUMMER FATHER'S HEALTH ROUSED AGAIN, ALMOST AS SUD-denly as it had failed him some time before. He appeared to have expelled most of the ruinous stuff—all those basins that mother splashed pink into the dirt off the porch.

"It was not consumption," father said conclusively now, uttering the word that had seemed forbidden while he was sick. Still, he re-mained thin as the illness had made him, never really taking back his old form. And when he spat, the issue was often red, flaked black. But he took again to visiting the Exchange Hotel each night, infrequently at first, and at last with the old regularity—and now mother did not object.

Mother took on a new manner of relinquishment during this time, railing less, insisting less, and after that evening's visit to

Sarah Norton's home, she gave up all her staunch objections to Josiah Lyte. This new mildness was peculiar in one such as her—she who had thriven most in her pietistic furor. I felt she'd been struck shy all of a sudden, and I knew I was somehow to blame. Of course father's good turn of health undoubtedly eased her, but I still cannot know whether she was deeply paralyzed by some nebulous shame, or whether some startled impotence had stolen her will. Whatever, there was something melancholy about her—like a piece of her had been shorn away, or she had died in part. She just stepped back from the world and all sorts of passion or grievance streamed through her fingers.

The Nortonville Seminary's commencement was held late that June in the Good Templars' Hall and there, in one staid and public gesture, mother gave out a last burst of will. The place was packed to bursting, for we shared the ceremony with the day-school kids from New York Landing. Mr. Woodruff was present, presiding silently from a seat at the front. Josiah Lyte floated cagily about the place. Mr. Evans and Mr. Thomas each gave a stolid oration, then led all the pupils in a selection of songs sung heartily and gratingly, and finally, with the dispensation of the last certificate the ritual drew to a close and my official schooling was finished. But before the crowd could rise and set to streaming from the hall, there sounded a voice, loud and solemn, entreating the attention of everyone present. I looked to find mother on her feet in a row of seats at the rear of that assembly.

She declared that she had "some words to say," and then she stood there looking grayly into the middle distance while the crowd rumbled quiet, hundreds of heads swiveling round to get a gander at the speaker.

I heard the buzzing circuitry of whispers. *It's Abicca Witherow.*

Who? Abicca Witherow. Soon the only noise was the pregnant squeaking of chairs, and every one of us hung bated on mother's slow-forming words.

She wore her flowered cap, her hair parceled neatly up off her nape, and her two strong hands were gleaming in doilied Sunday gloves. Father sat beside her, bent forward in his chair and eyeing the floor as if praying.

Mother took a long breath before all those blinking eyes, then her chin rose sharply and she looked at me where I stood on the risers up front, and she said in an even voice that the folks of Nortonville had been awfully bothered for a great while over the wretched fate of a little breaker boy. She said she knew the event did not lie deep in the people's memory—it was fresh in the heads and hearts of everyone, though it had happened some time ago. She heaved another breath, as if the thick hush of the crowd were a weight filching the wind from her body.

"Thomas Motion," she said, "has become a name for all justice and goodness that's met neglect in this town." She paused and listened to her words settling hard and sharp. "But it's important to say—to make plain now—that there've been mistakes."

She touched her hands together, fingertips to fingertips: tiny pyramidal form.

"Unseemly and terrible mistakes—and, as most of you know surely enough, if there've been mistakes then I've been at the front of them."

Her eyes slipped over the silent heads. She looked leftward briefly, then halted and grazed the other way till she'd locked on Josiah Lyte. He was standing back against the side wall, packed in a cluster of people three or four deep.

"There's a young minister in this town—a young teacher—who's borne the brunt of all my error, but he was never to blame.

The reason for Thomas Motion's end sits much closer to my own hearth and home."

She stood there a minute. Her eyes rolled back and riveted at some spot near the ceiling. I felt all the impending mass of what she would say now. I saw that she wouldn't look at me as she said it, and this fired a sudden anguish in me, a pain such as I had never imagined I'd bear.

"My boy Asher, who's commencing from this school today, was a friend and playmate to Thomas Motion."

I wished she would look at me.

"He was there with Thomas when he burned in the tunnel that night. A frightful accident. The mistake of two boys at play."

A slow, mortified wave rolled through the crowd. Each row gave off a murmurous noise. Still mother stood there pale before them all, her voice ringing shrill and loud above the commotion. The blame, she said, lay no more with her son than with Josiah Lyte, and it was she, if anyone, who ought to bear what blame was due.

Then quickly I was stepping down from the riser, shouldering through the schoolkids in front of me, skimming floorward through the congested air in a kind of controlled fall, and I found myself standing leg-locked at the foot of the platform with both arms raised stiff, calling out above the growing din.

"It's true," I shouted. "It's true. But mother didn't know. For a long time only I knew it. I'm to blame."

At once I saw my voice pitching upward, as if some enormous hand had just tipped that hall like a tea-jar. The words drove up headlong through all the hard glue of some connate gravity which I had sworn indestructible, which I had never yet exploded—but now look: that gravity was papery as air—one could burst through that and take up some new sense of weight.

I watched countless eyes shifting toward me, the crowd falling quiet again as if sucked fast of its voice. All those gazes hardened glassy and cold. They appeared to await some further confession, but there was nothing more to declare, so I stood silent and bore their relentless looking. I felt that was my duty then, to bear their looking so mother needn't.

"That's all," she said from her standing place, and at last she fixed me with her eyes as she sat down again.

A granite silence coated the crowd, and the people of Nortonville hardly moved. Every face looked stony in that loaded hall. Despite the people's wordless ire and all the spurn in that dread quiet of theirs, I felt confederated with them before something inarguable. All together we marked the bare fact which stood sobering and senseless at the end of a long mistake.

I had no way of recognizing it then, but as I remember the look of that grave assembly now, I see that all the subsequent collapse was latent there already. We would find no remedy for the consternation that had brewed in Nortonville over several years. Some long wave had been slapped up and we were all standing at the midpoint of that accumulating force. The wave could not roll back, despite whatever pronouncements we might make against it. I think mother may have known all this already. Maybe her willful gesture in that hall was a vain cry into the thunder of some unstoppable thing. The last recourse we're ever given is expression, however futile that seems. A cry, a choke, a clenching of fists.

I remember walking home with my parents that night—the slow, subdued motions mother's body made, the placid shuffle of her skirts. All three of us were silent till we came into the house. Then father said: "We mustn't worry now, you know."

"No," said mother. "That's not for us. It's finished."

"Nothing more we can do."

"No."

"Now it's back to things as usual."

"Yes, of course. The sun comes to the hill, doesn't it, David?"

"That it does," he said. And he stood with the door still open at his side, all the summer blackness burning deep out there above the houses.

Mother hunched over the sideboard, pouring oil into a lamp. There seemed some wholeness of devotion in that posture of hers, as if all her silence unspooled into that act. Father and I stared with her at the liquid thread glistering softly in the dark.

⌒

THAT SUMMER I WENT STRAIGHT INTO PRIVATE LESSONS WITH JOSIAH Lyte, meeting him by dusk. Mother made no objection.

In July our town was rattled again, this time savagely.

Down on the Black Diamond gangway an explosion went up, asphyxiating nine men and then scorching their bodies beyond recognition. Five other men suffered debilitating injuries, but came above ground blinking.

It happened late in the day, about three o'clock—an ordinary blast caught some sulfur gas and touched off a store of powder, which then launched a flood of black damp all through the area, blighting every particle of air with unbreathable grit. I was up on the Clayton Tunnel with father when we felt the tremors at the floor. We might have thought it an earthquake but for the distinct discharge underneath us and then the contained rumble of the fire. It is a terribly conspicuous thing—that teething growl of flame as it chomps at the walls. I remember it like the dark belly of earth breached wide, magma shuddering out in a scream. Roar of labor. Strange how we can so surely know the sound of our earth rending.

Men swept thick along the tunnel toward the lifts. Father

yanked me out of the breast with him, dragged me into the current of miners, up to the shaft.

At the surface a crowd had already started swarming, boiling mad with question and rumor, waves of evacuees pouring through the mass and swelling it.

Our earth expelled man after man. Each came up identical to the last one—rubbed black from brow to toe and making motions that might have accorded with some bizarre procession: baring his bright teeth and squinting awfully at the light, lifting one hand to shield his eyes, snapping his head this way and that, then falling in among the crowd, idle before that throat of the shaft.

For all the shock, the multitude eventually grew quiet. A great dread sank over us like a quilt. We stood round as if in vigil, sudden strangers to that indiscriminate crust underfoot.

Women began to appear among the men, frantic at the news. Mother found us in the throng, harried and grinding her teeth even as she embraced us. She had never trusted the earth. She kissed father harshly on the mouth and coughed out a number of jolting tears. She was bright and lithe against our blackness.

At half after four the dead were brought up, one and then another for an hour or so—the severely injured stirring amidst them. The crowd gave out a horrid keen. The bodies were laid by, black and brittle as winter leaves, the misshapen mouths spilling dust. The kin converged like scavenger birds.

Mother took us home and washed us and the temperate water was a guilty pleasure on our skin. As the grime sloughed off us in the midday window light, our wan bodies seemed to rise from shadow. Perching naked, father looked boy-like in his sadness. I felt the sorrow too. It closed heavy around me like a cumbersome shuck. It surprised me how I could inhabit it—man-like as it was.

Mother dished soup for us, and bread, and we ate mutely.

Outside, the sun had not gone down yet. In the tiny moments when we lost hold of the day's wreckage, everything had the feeling of a holiday. Then we remembered and felt shame and endured the hard privilege of our relief.

Mother poured us tea and sat with us. She read from the Psalms: "*Thou carriest them away as with a flood; they are as a sleep: they are like grass which groweth up. In the morning it flourisheth and groweth up, in the evening it is cut down and withereth. For all our days are passed away in thy wrath: we spend our years as a tale that is told.*"

That evening she packed a large parcel of bread and fruit and pork to take to the Mutual Aid Society at the Congregational church. As she stood in the door with her arms full, father said: "You sure you must go?" Since the commencement night, he'd been wary that she not put herself in the way of more contempt.

Mother nodded. "I've got to see what can be done, haven't I?"

She instructed us to rest and left us alone together.

Father walked to the fireplace and spat.

I sat in the rocker for a time, stuck in place beneath the heavy indolence in that house. That indolence seemed a needful thing, but an indulgence too.

Father went to the washstand and cleaned his face, patted the towel to his cheeks and brow. He stared long into the little mirror, poured more water and washed again, pressing the towel to his eyes—a tired, repetitive motion. Then he lay down, full-clothed, and turned from me and wept. I saw that he'd been weeping the whole time he washed. I went to the bed and lay down behind him, close against him. His body shook under my arms. I held my father.

The next day the mines were closed. Most of the townsfolk gathered at Rose Hill—a big crowd spreading across the yellow graveyard grass, striped by the long cypress shadows.

Reverend Parry stood by the row of coffins, sweating madly in his robes. He spoke a long Welsh prayer for the dead. All the company groaned and wept. We sang while the coffins were let down, tossed wildflowers into the graves. Then all the people parted, moving back up the Somersville Rise toward Nortonville.

Father gripped my hand. "Come, Ash."

I walked with him to the graves, where a number of men lingered with shovels. We all took off our coats and set to work without a word. Flat scrape of metal. Soft padding of dirt onto wood. The noiseless dead, anchored in earth again.

WITHIN A MONTH OR SO, AS IF IN ACCORDANCE WITH SOME AIMLESS mordant charade, Josiah Lyte was serving again as an associate pastor to Reverend Parry. Mother's abandoned campaign allowed for his reinstatement without much rancor. But still there remained a strong, low-boiling sentiment against him in town.

Mother herself now sat placidly in the pew as Lyte administered communion. Her spirit continued to grow hushed that year. Her old habits fell away week by week, the stout suddenness in her limbs easing off. How quickly and urgently the spirit can transmute. It's still shocking to me that I should have learned this from my mother: she whom I had thought would never moderate—her mold had been so hard. But this new translation lent her a quiet luminance, like a girl. There was a sunken kind of beauty in it, and it seems a terrific shame that this of all things should have lent force to the bitter wind then shifting to front her.

That year the yield from our mines fell another 20,000 tons.

2

IN 1877 A FREAKISH UPROAR SHOOK NORTONVILLE. THE SUPERSTITIOUS amplitude was of such force that it tremored right to every doorstep, and each grisly detail of the occurrence entered the bank of common knowledge.

Two lads were out by the creek, playing with a revolver, when one shot the other in the head. The shooter, James Davey, a boy not seven years old, came sprinting among the houses for help. John Guy, hardly six himself, was found moments later, lying in the sun and bleeding quickly from the head and both ears. He was heaped up and carried to the Guy household, where the bleeding was stanched. Dr. McPhee came over from Somersville at once.

The bullet sat couched snugly behind the ear, just short of the cerebellum. The doctor refused to get it out: it would kill the boy, he said, and at the moment John Guy was lying there, blinking brightly, fully cognizant of all the discussion around him. Dr. McPhee bent down and asked him, *Don't you suffer, boy?* And John Guy's little face went gray with a disfiguring fear. *Why should I suffer?* he screamed, and tried to bolt from the bed so that his father had to restrain him. Over the next several days, Dr. McPhee called in physicians from Martinez and Concord and even Oakland. None would venture extracting the bullet.

So John Guy was deemed untreatable and permitted to romp about the town as if in perfect health. But still the gun work gapped his skull with a dark little wound like a mouth, and the folks of Nortonville found it an unnerving sight. In exasperation, Mr. and Mrs. Guy summoned Sarah Norton. She boiled elderberry root and caked a rude poultice over the cavity. But though the wound was plastered, the townsfolk seized upon Sarah Norton's part in the ordeal. Much was voiced about a "damaged innocence" in the town, and soon the rumors flew malicious—of devilry and the overthrow of death's dominion by séance and other dark practices. Eventually, Mr. and Mrs. Guy were compelled to keep their boy at home.

But in everything there is a seed of something else, or as Lyte put it then: "Nature never fails to embody its teachings for us. That boy is a forerunner—the very figure of this town." Indeed, the people of Nortonville could not look at little John Guy but they saw doom walking, death in the figure of a boy—the plain arrival of all they dreaded.

THAT SAME YEAR SAW THE INFLUX OF A NEW WORKINGFOLK IN NORtonville—Chinese laborers, a band of twenty or so, come from work on the cross-country railroad, already experts in blackpowder blasting and eager for employ at the mines.

They spoke a jagged, pidgin English, hardly decipherable, and of course not a word of Welsh or Italian, so they kept mostly to their own little insular community, setting up homes in meager lean-tos out past the houses, at the valley's mouth.

When necessity brought the Chinaman to the mercantile, the butcher, or the postmaster, he was set apart by a pregnant hush and a gallery of sour looks from the townsfolk, past whom he walked in his quick-footed way. The state was rife with economic trouble, and those folks faced a rampant bigotry because of it. Since the '60s—that decade in which Leland Stanford named them "the dregs of Asia"—state law had levied heavy taxes against the Chinese fishermen throughout California, and their situation would only worsen in the following years with the institution of other anti-Chinese legislation of the kind. But by God, they worked hard.

I recall their little figures standing in a cluster at the shaftmouth each morning. They looked so unlike us in their coveralls, which had never been sewn with the Chinaman in mind. They wore the trouser-legs rolled in thick piles over the boot-tops, and the sleeves of the shirts—being too long also—were cut straight off high on the wrist. From beneath their caps the thin black pigtail hung down along their backs nearly to the waist. They chattered to each other in their lively way, every man speaking at once it seemed, until the cage came up and they split off for the day's work.

Everything they did appeared lively: that fast, bird-like talk; the reflex of their legs in walking, bending, crawling; arms in gesturing, shoveling. At day's end they came bounding out of the lift and flounced home to their tents together, resuming that morning's cacophonous talk.

They were sprightly figures among all the weary British and Italians who slouched to the saloons. They favored pale lukewarm tea over the workman's night whiskey, and drank it avidly throughout the day, tipping the stuff from tiny cups no bigger than the palm of your hand. Their indefatigable nature made them all the more suspect to the townsfolk. Only their eyes moved slowly, perusing everything by their liquid darkness.

It's known today that their people first came to California in large numbers among the early Spanish armaments—that it was they who designed and built the great galleons from ages of ancestral sea-wisdom. In Manila, where the ships were made, the Chinese were baptized under the Spanish church and given Spanish names and they came to be known as *Chinos.* They set out soldiering on the new ocean routes, and with the Conquistadors they were the first to drive the ploughshares of European settlement here. Unthinkable: the massive circles of history—that it should be "celestials" with Spanish names who came exploring the Indian realms. And there they were in Nortonville now—perhaps their forefathers had been among General DeAnza's expeditionary force when it passed through that same valley back in 1776.

"They're Buddhists," Lyte told me one night.

We sat up on the Cumberland Rise above their encampment. Their fires flickered red below. Now and then a small shape moved past the flames.

"This world is illusion. They don't stake much on it. They don't lose themselves to its toil or pain."

He told me of the Buddha, how he had left his home as a young man. I saw the Buddha in the forest. I saw him at the Bo Tree, expressionless and poised. Love and Death beset him, at war against his meditation—but thunder and red-hot coals could not fluster him, and it all turned to flowers and ointments raining softly on his head and shoulders. Then Desire set upon him, but this too he repelled without stirring from meditation. He touched the earth with his fingers and the earth shuddered and roared till Desire wilted before his greatness. That night he came to know all the lives he had lived, acquired divine knowing, and saw the chain of causation revealed—that which animates all things. At dawn, enlightenment was his.

"Life is suffering, but needn't be," said Lyte. "There are sure ways free of that and you're not to take secondhand truths."

He sat cross-legged in the grass, gazing down into that darkness. Even from far below, the strands of firelight touched his face.

"It's like the flicker of a lamp," he told me. "The impermanence of everything. One can take leave of it all. Then mechanical experience becomes *true* experience. Then illusion slides back like the glass in a lamp."

We were silent a while. Moonlight played dimly in a sheet of cloud.

The voices of the Chinese trailed up through the air toward us. The smoke rose from their fires in tapering streams. A night animal rustled in the chaparral. It all passed in and out of our senses, everywhere ephemeral.

"Christ took leave of that pattern of suffering," said Lyte. He talked in a musing voice, as though the thoughts were just occurring to him. "Christ broke the pattern just as the Buddha did—opening to pure experience. Christ and the Buddha are both figures of possibility, one and the same."

Lyte's words were level and clear: evanescent things passing through the darkness.

Later in the year the town rose up against those Chinese.

One morning in August, Jim Winslow, miner from the Little Vein, stormed down the gangway with pick held crosswise at his breast and ducked into our room to stammer out the news that was flying through the ranks. "They're going under for a fraction of regular pay. Those chinks'll dig us right out if we don't cut them off where they are!" Every man was going asurface, he said, to make plain to the company that it wouldn't be stood for.

So we stopped our work and came out to the gangway, which was already aflood with indignant men.

The Chinese were rounded up from the pits and sent to the surface.

By late morning the company yard was thronged with angry miners and the works were at a standstill. A committee of union spokesmen went straightaway to the operator's office and made clear the workers' stance. Then followed the inevitable bureaucratic intercourse between the operators and their superiors, but within an hour or two all of the Chinese laborers were unceremoniously dismissed.

Some of the rowdier company boys fired up some ugly discord: spitting, ethnic forswearing and such—as the Chinese were ushered off the grounds. Then we all went directly back to work.

The Chinese uprooted their little encampments and most were gone by nightfall.

3

Anna and I visited my cottonwood tree again. It stood taller now, its limbs broader, its trunk thickened and hard. We sat down before it and its roots jabbed through the earth beneath us.

Together with the rest of Nortonville, Anna had learned at last the truth of Thomas Motion's demise, as though she were worthy of no more than to be lumped into the general crowd (though God knows she was a whole world for me). She had yet said nothing of all that. But I thought I must atone for it now and I tried to say all I felt. It was a miserable plea, though I did not beg her forgiveness overtly. She listened till I had finished and then she said simply: "My poor dear. You carried it for so long. You must have suffered for that."

There was no blame in her. She thought only of me. It pained me to see how simple it would have been—how much I had impoverished myself by resisting to confess it to her.

That night I told her of the Buddha and the Bo Tree, that life was more than the suffering most people knew, that everything we saw would just die or dry up or fall away, that we could let ourselves disappear and could become everything that all of this around us was just trying to be. She listened, touching my hand as I spoke, looking up through the dark air to the unlit leaves.

"That must be true," she said, as if to herself. "I think I knew it already. I think my child taught me that when it left my body so silently, innocently."

This is the last I can remember of Anna Flood, whom I loved in a way more bottomless than seems possible, and whose love is in me still, though I am old. It's essentially cruel that memory should end with her on this night for me, for I think I told her then the things my Greek poet puts in this way: *We run. We know that we are running to die, but we cannot stop. We run.*

⌒〜

ONE NIGHT THAT JUNE I CAME INTO THE HOUSE AND WAS ALARMED to find my parents' bodies locked together in a weird and maladroit configuration. Mother sat in the rocker looking impassive and gray in the cheeks, her shoulders squared up against the backing rails, her hands buried deep in father's hair. He was on his knees before her in a posture of wild supplication, his arms encircling her waist, his face shoved hard into the skirts at her lap. He was weeping with a muffled ferocity.

I froze beside the door. "Mother?"

"Ah, Asher," she said. Her voice was as gray and indifferent as her face.

Father did not cease from his fit. I think he hardly noticed me.

"Is it all right?" I said. I took one step toward them and stopped.

"Of course," she said. "Yes, dear. Of course it's all right."

Her hands moved languidly in father's hair as in the fur of a dog.

"But what's happened?"

"Father knows now," she said. "That's all. No secrets anymore. The people have learned everything. Now your father knows too."

I said nothing. The slack skin beneath her jaw pleated softly as she looked down on father all disheveled between her knees, the way a tired mother will look blankly upon her caterwauling infant. She studied her sluggish hands in his hair. Her mouth squirmed. She appeared to be forming words that would convey the meaning of father's mania. At last she said: "There are so many eyes in this town, so many ears. Nothing goes unrecorded."

She leaned the rocker forward, withdrew both her hands from father's hair, and spread them flat and wide along his back, stroking in great circles. Father's sobs jolted out like a high and cracking cough.

"They all know now what happened that night," she said. "At Sarah Norton's house. Martha Griggs saw us. She kept silent about it all this time. But now everybody knows."

She curled over and laid her cheek to father's shoulder blades, as if attending to the quiet beat of his heart amidst the raving. He seemed to get closed up inside her doubled form. Her eyes grayed toward the stove and she sighed and spoke softly with an air of aimless speculation, like a girl dreamily naming all that she'll acquire when she comes of age: *a house, a husband, a garden, a stove, three strong boys . . .*

My lungs hardened with a shock of wind. I sucked at the thick house air, felt my every tendon drawn stiff in immediate pity.

"Oh, father," I said.

But I couldn't go to him. I couldn't move. She had him there. I could see he wanted only that: to jam his gnarled face into her skirts. It was all the comfort that could come to him.

"I've shamed us now," said mother. She spoke so soft I think she meant it only for father. A little phlegm rattled in her throat and she didn't bother to clear it. "They'll damn me for it," she said. Her hands fluttered lightly, patting father's back with a gentleness incommensurate to his grief. She murmured to him—little absurd phrases over and over again.

"Mother, I—"

But there was nothing to say. I stood there listening to his heartache.

꒰

THREE DAYS LATER A FIRE RAGED THROUGH OUR TOWN, RAVAGING most the buildings along Main Street, reducing the hotel, the barber, Sharp's Saloon, Swartz's Saloon, Senderman's store, Mrs. Engler's cobblery and Noakes's Butchery to black skeletal beams.

Shortly after 1:00 in the morning, it flashed up in Noakes's Butchery. The flames stormed into the grasses of the Somersville Rise, fanning toward the sky. To the west the blaze fed along a trail of grass into the company yard and ignited the big culm bank.

Father and I ran out at all the welter of alarm. We raced in our nightshifts to join the rallying bucket brigade. We arrested the fire on the eastern side before it poured down toward Somersville. In the meantime, someone fed some dynamite to the inferno along Main Street, blowing the cobblery sky high to cut off the blaze there. So we watched it burn itself out, heat growing darker in its own devouring mouth. The culm bank too we left to smolder—the slag would shift and smother the flame.

At the cut of dawn, when the culm finally gave way and extinguished itself, Anna's body rolled out amidst the ashy rubble. She lay half-uncovered where the bank was eaten away. Since she was not badly charred, it appeared that the flame had surprised her atop the bank, then the slag had shifted and taken her under.

Somebody dragged her out and laid her by, steaming and thin in the morning sun. Her father was summoned to collect her. A watchman draped a canvas over the gaunt form. She was shapeless under that, amid the cinders.

I stood off from her and saw Mr. Flood come jogging up, looking haggard. He bent to lift the canvas, slumped to his knees, jumped up again cursing and kicked at the embers, then fell to silent weeping.

Father found me standing agaze there. He stood wordless beside me on the burnt earth, and for a long moment we watched the father crumpled over his girl. The weary men of the bucket brigade passed back and forth between us and that wretched pair.

Finally Mr. Flood lifted the light body and took it away.

Father murmured: "Now she's gone, isn't she?"

I turned to see him gazing at the culm bank.

"Scarcely a week ago I learned all she was and now—"

He broke off and stared down at the blackened front of his nightshift, like some unfledged sleepwalker just coming to.

Anna was buried as quietly as her mother had been a few years before—and laid in the same grave too, the letters of her name etched simply into the backside of Mrs. Flood's headstone. Neither I nor my mother or father could attend the funeral, not so soon after Anna's ordeal had come to the public light, though we ought to have bucked propriety and gone anyway. They buried something irreplaceable for all three of us when they buried that small girl up there. She went underground empty, a vessel that might in some more sensible order of things have been filled with all the inexpressible spirit of our hope, our love.

We never heard from Mr. Flood. He had always been lotted among the benignly uncouth of Nortonville, and no doubt there was little purchase for him in the stir of moral reproof then surrounding mother and all of us. He moved into Scammon's lodging house, which the fire had spared.

⁓

FOURTEEN BUILDINGS WERE LOST THAT JUNE NIGHT. $30,000 IN PROPerty, uninsured, which amounted to better than half of our yearly profits at the time.

For weeks we leaned heavily on Somersville, feeding ourselves from their stores while fresh lumber came up from New York Landing and was nailed into place along Main Street. Father and I helped in the evenings while the summer light lasted, and on Sundays, retimbering the world we knew.

Some nights, in the late star-thick air, after the light had gone down on our rebuilding, I climbed the disfigured culm bank to look out over the ruins of Main Street: members of burnt wood and wall jutting roofless below like the gray postures of the dead. It all looked somehow perverse, a delicate balancing of sticks, taken very seriously.

I held an egg of coal in my hand and thought of Anna and of the bright bewilderment she'd caused me, as if bewilderment were a thing she always trained behind her like a scent. I thought of silence and of the many events that could bring one to shame. The terrific impropriety of my restraint before Anna, it seemed to me now, may well have accounted for her early death. I'd held myself away from her. I had. There was no making it right. I had let our scale tip to an imperiling angle, never offering the counterweight of my withheld confession, and she had gone sliding off into a void, abandoned to the unreckonable power of her own dark confessions. Maybe I could have saved her. And maybe, had she held my secret fast between us, and by holding it sanctioned it somehow—maybe then I could have spoken earlier of all of it—everything that in reality I guarded till there was no saving anything anymore.

I opened and closed my fingers on the egg of coal. Watched the tiny specks coming off on my skin, glittery like tiny stars. I thought of star and night sky. I thought of sea reflecting it all. Then swamp. Then the monstrous thrust of the mountain. Then fire. Soon sea again. And in the interval: the ring of man's hammer. The tiny thunder of his cartridge underground.

I felt the slag heap beneath me, the valley spreading north, the foothills on all sides: that landscape like the muscled back of some great beast at rest.

I wandered home late. In my palm the coal had left its shape in shadow.

4

Mother got sick. It was an ailment far stricter than the frequent headache. She seemed surprised something could be worse than that. She stared up at us from the sickness with a startled look. She couldn't tell us anything of the pain—where it burned or ached or throbbed, whether it was in her head or breast or limbs. She just went to the bed and lay down, submitting entirely.

For a week father and I attended her however we could. We rubbed her ankles and feet and arms, brought her cold compresses, then hot, spooned porridge and soup into her flaccid mouth. Dr. McPhee came to our house. He measured her pulse, asked her to breathe deeply, peered down her throat, pried each of her eyes between finger and thumb, and prodded her stomach, her larynx, her skull with both his inquisitive hands.

"No fever," he said. "The heart's normal. Skin's not wet or dry. Eyes are clear. No swelling anywhere that I can detect. She doesn't tremor or ache." He told us to keep feeding her, to let her rest. As near as he could make out, it was a kind of exhaustion—and yet the body was not overly fatigued.

She managed to tell father and me, in a desiccated whisper, that she thought it best to be left alone to the infirmity, that we should not rearrange our days on her account. We obliged her in this, since it was her one absolute request and her disorder was so cryptic that only she could know what was needful. Within a week she was up again and working at the stove and ready with our baths when we came home from hanging the lumber on Main Street, though now she moved slowly and with a new kind of weightlessness, as if underwater. This lasted two or three days.

Actually, the inexorable fading was now at full tilt within her—whether in her blood or marrow or flesh. She seemed to admit it to herself, going to bed early every night, even sleeping through church on Sundays. Soon she had taken again to lying in all day. Father arranged for our dinners to be packed by Mrs. Aitken. Dr. McPhee came again. This time he drew father aside.

"There's something within her, that's sure. Though I can't name it, it seems the very thing I see in the old folk before they leave us. The body just dwindles. The life drains and drains. Strange in someone so young, but there it is. I think you must know that it's out of our hands."

Within the week mother died, whispering, blanched by her unnamable end.

We held a wake in our little house. The townsfolk sloughed their disfavor and most of mother's former lady friends came by, and of course father's chums from the works, who had never turned on us. Josiah Lyte came too. He shook father's hand in a sober way.

We had a tintypist in from Martinez, a corpulent man who stood father and me up next to the coffin, angled our chins precisely with his pudgy hands, tugged our collars straight. We posed, rigid and silent and afraid to blink while the blinding flash bulb burst. Our eyes swimming with silver light, we watched the photographer's tin shears slicing apart the two half-plate images.

Father's copy has since disappeared. I've kept mine all this time, though the paper holder was long ago misplaced and the thin plate is tarnished from its long seclusion in drawers. It's a chocolate-tinted image of the rustic type which were all the rage in that day. The three figures in it are pale forms, like people made of thin-worn paper. Father, long-bearded as always, stands at mother's feet, his hair oiled, one hand resting awkwardly on the lip of the casket. He looks smaller than I remember him. His face was never as diminutive and blank as that posture makes it here.

I stand at mother's head, just shy of fourteen years old, nearly equal to father in height. With my frozen glance, I look prim and disinterested. Between us, mother's body runs long. Her dormant face is just as I remember it, the profile of cheek not yet fallowed by death.

I look at this and can only wonder what father and I wondered then, without ever saying it. What is it that destroys?—that yellows the pages of untouched books, of drawered-up photographs? What invisible maw digests me and my kin?

When I go to the mirror now, I stare into a furrowed face, a mask corrugated by some slow attrition I cannot understand, though the process is a part of me. I have named it *age, time, entropy,* but all those terms are insufficient. It is unnamable.

We buried mother. Father was silent the whole day long, sweating in the August heat.

In the following weeks we returned to our all-day work at the pits and at the reconstruction of Main Street. Mrs. Aitken continued to pack our dinner pails and had us for supper once a week. Father and I accustomed ourselves to bathing each other every night: the two of us alternately naked in our motherless house, scrubbing the blackness off. We cooked suppers of pork and dry beans. Often we dined at the boarding house. It was an awkward time, taciturn and hollow.

Though mother was gone and though her own enmity against Josiah Lyte had been publicly relinquished, her old drive against him began to sprout with new purpose in a faction of congregants appalled at his ungodly doings. So he had no involvement in the breaker boy's burning, but he *had* presided at the Flood girl's devilish operation that night in Sarah Norton's house.

In the meantime, though, with the public censure having lately been directed at Abicca Witherow, Reverend Parry had found a sufficient abatement of the hostility against his young minister and had invited him to the pulpit again with full confidence. So that Christmas Lyte preached his first sermon in a number of years—a short, blazing speech.

This was the fourth Sunday of Advent. I remember the way he gripped the lectern like a battlement. He cast an implacable glare over the congregation and stood motionless in a long, dogged silence. He appeared to be fixing his weight there, entrenching himself before an ominous vanguard.

The churchgoers grew grave and still.

Then Lyte spoke. His stare never wavered. He didn't consult his notes. He simply discharged his tamped-up heart.

He began with an Advent prayer, beseeching God to distill our consciences by His presence each day, that when Christ arrived He should find us ready to welcome Him. He gaveled a fist at the lectern and declared that each of us, at bottom, quailed from Christ and dreaded His arrival on Christmas day.

"Christ's yearly rebirth comes to us all like a harrowing shadow,"

Lyte said. "As it lengthens, we shrink and pray we'll become invisible. If for a single moment we looked plainly at ourselves we'd see how Christ, who means to enlarge us by His coming, finds us shriveled and closed and saying meekly: *My smallness is god enough for me.*"

A current of shock ran through the pews, but Lyte held fast and raised his voice.

"The true figure of Christ," he said, "is a symbol of the promise in every man and woman—that every man and woman may struggle to embody the world as Christ did—that the world might find deliverance, in some way, through each one of us."

The congregation seemed to gasp and choke, as though the church were filling up with dust. Lyte squared his shoulders and stood taller.

"This is the challenge we shirk," he said. "This is the call the Christians have yet to answer. Instead of rising up and taking the world within them, they glut themselves on Sunday sweets and the sugary words of ministers who assure them that Christ's work was finished with his sacrifice at Calvary."

He gulped in silence a moment, seeming to put down some great ember that rose hot in his throat.

"But Christ's work only began at Calvary," he said. "We all are Christ's work. It lives with us, just as Christ lives through us. We must save Him. Will we be Christ, as God intended it? Or will we keep Him down for the sake of our precious fear? I say we ought not only to pray that Christ find welcome in us, but that we not block His work any further by this shriveling kowtow that we call worship. That we rise to our own cross as He would have it, and not fall sterile at the foot of His!"

This unsettled the people beyond all decorum. A number of men rose to their feet and bellowed.

But Lyte was finished. He stepped back from the pulpit with a tranquil smile, walked up the long middle aisle through all the uproar, and disappeared out the doors at the back, leaving a flummoxed Reverend Parry to sedate the crowd.

The squall of Lyte's sermon quickly broke through the walls of the church to ensnarl and provoke even those few who thought little of religion. By Monday afternoon a prodigious force had risen to condemn him and that evening the outrage, now both righteous and civic, came to a head at the door of the school, the mob swarming the hill, chanting and shaking fists. Josiah Lyte, heretical in the pulpit, could not be principled in the classroom. He would unmoor the children just as he meant to subvert the church.

Superintendent Woodruff lumbered up the hill and steered the crowd after him into the main room of the schoolhouse. An impulsive assembly was held among the desks. Reverend Parry was summoned.

But Josiah Lyte was not there. He was wandering up in the darkness above the Cumberland Rise. I was with him.

"They'll oust me now," he said. A bluish light burned in his cheeks and brow, blue veins radiating under opaque skin. I think it was an equanimity in him, raying from someplace secretive and deep. But his serenity appeared perverse to me then.

"They're calling you blasphemous," I said. "They say you spit on Christ's holiness."

"No matter, Witherow," he murmured. "There is no more blasphemy."

"What?"

We came out of the trees into moonlight. Lyte stopped and took me by the shoulders, his breath trailing sideways from his mouth. The grasses bent about our legs as he looked hard into my eyes.

"You have understood me," he said.

"Yes."

"That is enough."

"Then why did you preach to them in the first place?"

He drew back and his eyes glazed in thought. For a moment he looked at the sky, black, silvery with moon.

"Because it was all I could do," he said, "because it seemed I must. Because something had to happen—and now it has."

My dread began melting off. A comfort, black though it was, spread through me and smoothed down the turmoil. I stepped forward and clutched Lyte's wrist. He stood still in the moonish light, staring down at my gripping hand as though mystified. His slack mouth hung dark like a lesion.

⁓

THE WILL OF THE PEOPLE WON THROUGH. JOSIAH LYTE WAS DEPOSED from the pulpit and from his position at the Nortonville School and exiled from town. Early on Christmas day he rode the Black Diamond passenger car out of the valley, bundled up in woolen coat and mittens and bearing a single trunk of belongings.

I've had no word of him these seventy-two years. By now he's dead, probably. But in all this time, whenever I've thought of him, my mind has placed him in India, somewhere among the gentle people of that country. There was nothing and is nothing in a nation like ours for someone as religious as he. Some years ago, at some bank of the great Ganges River, a good funeral pyre was built for him, no doubt.

That week in Nortonville I conducted my own ceremony of a kind. I hung a notice at the postmaster's and at the church of a public service to be held for the minister Josiah Lyte at Rose Hill burying ground, December 27. When the night came, I was alone in the graveyard.

I dug a shallow hole at a bald spot of earth amidst the head-stones. I lit three eggs of coal and dropped them in and watched them burn. Then I read from the Psalms, aloud, my voice lone among the dead.

"I will sing of mercy and of judgment: unto thee, Oh Lord, will I sing. I will behave myself wisely in a perfect way. Oh when wilt thou come unto me? Mine eyes shall be upon the faithful of the land, that they may dwell with me: he that walketh in a perfect way, he shall serve me."

While my words trailed into darkness, I saw a figure coming through the stones. Soon father moved into the glow. He greeted me softly and stood with hands clasped before him.

I handed him the red volume of Emerson, bade him read the passage I'd marked. He studied the page a moment, tilting it to the light, then drew himself up and the words spread through the stones under those trees, edged soft by father's Welsh cadence:

"Show me the sublime presence of the highest spiritual cause lurking, as always it does lurk, in these suburbs and extremities of nature; let me see every trifle bristling with the polarity that ranges it instantly on an eternal law; and the shop, the plough, the ledger referred to the like cause by which light undulates and poets sing;—and the world lies no longer a dull miscellany and lumber-room, but has form and order; there is no trifle, there is no puzzle, but one design unites and animates the farthest pinnacle and the lowest trench."

I bent and fisted up a clump of earth and threw it over the flame. Father and I stood silent as the dust and smoke mingled and rose.

I don't know what the ceremony meant, don't know if I somehow buried Josiah Lyte that night. But an honor was due and I tried to pay it. And more than that: there was the beginning of something. An inception.

5

WE FINISHED OUR WORK ON MAIN STREET. AT LAST THE scars of fire were erased. But despite the fresh lumber and paint and the resurrection of commerce, something was dying in Nortonville. Profits continued to slide. In the dark pits by day we all felt a salient sucking in our limbs, as though the earth were a mouth that would sap us, drawing the futile labor out of sinew and muscle.

At night I stood at father's naked back, pouring the tepid water and watching the line of murk flow down from his nape. He told me a foreman had broached a company secret to him. Pierre Cornwall, president of the Black Diamond Company, had sent a man to the Washington Territory to scout the coal reserves. If the emissary were to send back promising coal samples, Cornwall would dispatch a mineral specialist.

"There won't be much to float us here," father said, "if the deposits up north are rich as they say."

A pall was over him. It haunted his countenance and his voice.

It had come with mother's death and had not rescinded since. It was the pale shadow of unstable things, the anemic hue of roots torn up.

⌒

IN OCTOBER 1879 THE SOUL OF NORTONVILLE PERISHED ON A DARK hillside facing west toward the mountain. A buggy broke free of its skittish horse and the soul tumbled out, was thrown to the ground and impaled on a spoke from the fractured wheel, killed suddenly in the figure of old Sarah Norton, who lay pinned to the earth, her heart punctured.

Death arrives this way in all things. There is a dying and a dying and all the time it's held at bay—then comes a sudden stop. Whether person or animal or empire, nothing and no one enjoys immunity from the antediluvian ritual.

Granny Norton had hired a mean horse to pull her over the Cumberland Rise to Clayton to call on a sick woman there. Many God-fearing folks, though never indecorous about it, were no doubt glad to be free of her at last. But there's no denying that through Sarah Norton, be she witch or pagan, some essential undercurrent had coursed in Nortonville. All the people mouthed their pious qualms by day, but never would one of them forbear to fly to her in the quiet of some desperate night, begging an Indian cure or importuning her presence at a wife's delivery. With Sarah Norton's untidy end a specter was loosed in Nortonville, a disembodied wraith that skulked in the town, slouching through doorways, brushing everything with the soft chalk of death.

Her legend has since been inflated with all the flares of a ghost story. It's often told how a great storm awoke in Nortonville while her body was carried to the church. Knifing thunderbolts sent the animals and livestock running pell-mell through the streets, till the townsfolk flooded from the funeral to contain them. The second attempt at a ceremony precipitated an equally raucous storm, and this time the supernormal intercession was not lost upon the townsfolk—so Sarah Norton was finally buried without a funeral, conscribed to haunt the valley for generations hence.

I've heard this legend so many times that I can only capitulate to its account. At any rate, if a funeral happened, it has since slipped from my memory. It seems myth will finally assert itself in this way—superseding the dull and incidental reality of things because it speaks more entirely to the essence of an event.

In those years I felt that something had gutted the town, as we gutted our black chambers of earth, and that the town, the earth, all of it, was standing by some accidental persistence, just waiting to crumple. This was despite the fullness of Nortonville's population, which had shrunk, but was still substantial; despite the regular progression of our mines, which had slowed, but were fully operative; despite all the superficial upkeep.

I think I sensed the influx of an evolutionary wind like that which had rippled the old swamps before our mountain rose. It was some ancient force in nature, reasserting itself—the turning of an omnipotent wheel. Beneath that, we were clay.

I saw our hard-built world eroding, flaking, swaying to fall. It is uncanny: to be so young and to see the days turn bloodless and skeletal. But the outward will convey the inward, ruthlessly, until the outward at last surrenders to collapse. Then the earth reclaims by weed, by wind, by water—and all those things that appeared absolute are shown to be no more than the toys with which the earth has humored her transients. —How can I say it clearly now? How make plain these hard rhythms to those who are young in life? I am dumb to tell of it; so shall you be too.

~

I N 1881 THERE WAS A MURDER IN NORTONVILLE—A DEADLY DISPUTE over wages paid to some new Italian laborers. Word got around that they were cutting coal for lower pay—trying to worm in under the Welsh majority—and one night, in a tussle outside the lodging house, the Italian worker Lorenzo Barreri took a sure blow to the head with a big stone. The killers fled and he fell face down in the street. Bigotry flamed up and havoc woke in the pits—but I'll not tell much of that. Ugliness and calumny. The raving of a moribund town.

By 1883 the long fingers of the decay had spread like saprogenic tendrils into every house. The Black Diamond Company had purchased a sizable tract of the coal country in Washington. The operators left promptly after, and water soon began collecting in the lower works, rising toward the Clayton Tunnel. The workmen complained, but the owners would not try to expel it. The gangway mules were brought out of the underground stables and spurred into the lift cages and sent floating up the shaft. They pranced in constrictive circles on the rattling platform, their tall ears shorn blunt by years of low ceiling. At the blue light of the surface half of them went mad, frothing and snapping free of the harness to pound round and round with rolling eyes till finally they buckled dead at the gun of the mule driver. The carcasses lay with their long cheeks to the earth and bony legs splayed out, sacks of knob and bulge for the slavering turd flies, till they could be sawn up and taken away.

~

I 'LL BE HEADING NORTH WITHIN THE WEEK," FATHER SAID TO ME ONE muggy night, while his rough hands worked the grime from my neck. "Will you come?"

At my knees, brown water lapped and streaked—the day's residue pulling in trails down flesh and hair.

Father doused my shoulders. "Done," he said.

I rose and stepped out of the barrel, displacing a long stain of water over the floor. Father had turned to the washstand. He scooped some water into his mouth and went to the basin by the stove, swishing his cheeks. He stood bare-chested in trousers, his eyes at the floor as he worked his jaw.

I let the rinse slide off me, awaiting the dripping chill under that night's swelter. Father spat, patted his beard with a towel, then handed the towel to me. I bent to dry my legs.

His question still stood in the torrid air, carved into that stagnant heat as into a cake of soap. He leaned at the stove while I pulled on my trousers. Then he came and stood before me and his look was raw and close. He seemed in some way powerless.

I saw how slight and worn he'd become. The skin of his freckled arms sagged from the bone like narrow sleeves, shoulders grading steeply toward the elbows. Behind his beard I could make out his slumped chest, deflated under the wired breastbone—the folding inward of his form.

He laid his fingers at my sternum, gingerly, as one might try the flex of tree bark. I recalled Thomas Motion's fierce knuckles at that spot years before. Father's eyes rested there while he spoke.

"You'll not come, I know."

"No, sir."

He took in a full breath and nodded. His hand lifted away again. "You are able, boy."

"Yes, sir."

He went to the barrel, bent and dragged it over the puncheon to the door, embraced it and tipped it over the porch. Water shushed into the dirt and grass. Then he came in again and touched the table, drawing fingers over the grain.

"Will you stay?" he asked.

"Not long."

"And when you go, whither?"

"I don't know."

It was all fronting me then—the blankness of it. Resignation. Possibility.

"I'll need word of you time to time," said father.

"Yes, sir."

Again he stared plainly at me. For a minute his mouth distended itself, something rising to his tongue. His fingers hovered up off the table, closed in a loose fist, then sank again, knuckles to wood— contending gesture.

"I am *this* now," he said. "All my hours have made me *this*."

It was an admission, an atonement of some sort, and the expression of it appeared to unburden him. He fell silent after that. We dressed to dine at the boarding house.

In a day or two father had gone. All that I remember of him consists of how I knew him in Nortonville. He died up north in 1890, crushed under a caved ceiling of coal.

{6}

THAT SUMMER WAS DRY AND CRACKING, WHILE THE GRASSES bleached under incessant sun and the mines limped hopeless with a handful of wretched miners.

I did not go underground again after father left, but tended my days alone in the familiar hills, walking and gazing long upon Mount Diablo. I fed myself with what food remained in my empty house. I bought some fare at obscenely low cost from the failing stores on Main Street. I wandered the bare grids of earth where houses had been taken up, watched the sluggish traffic of those few who had chosen to linger, heard single voices carrying hundreds of feet through the valley. The old village, newly altered, echoed back my aloneness.

Nights were peculiar, sleeping companionless in that cavernous little house. I lay in my boyhood bed, encircled by the pregnant stillness of objects: rocker, table, washstand, kettle. Those things are the mundane props that evince life—and I had taken them for granted during all those years when they gave their daily testimonies. They had been mastered by movement, use, placement, replacement—the commerce of will and thought constantly demonstrating that which is otherwise so subtle and indemonstrable. But now that they were static they became crowding, malevolent. Inanimateness throbbed and droned and ruptured the familiarity of the things, and I saw that they were no longer amiable or serviceable. They reclaimed themselves and became strange to me, even hateful—that they should go on without me, alien and lifeless. This antipathy runs through all of the physical world: brute indifference to our mutability.

That summer I could not have understood why I loitered in Nortonville. But I believe I can see some reason for it now: everywhere, nature was taking back its aspect. Everywhere, man was sliding off. Russian thistle sprouted down Main Street. The refuse of fences lay tangled in grasses. Skunks roosted in empty houses. Jars, forks, bits of colored glass, tin cups, broken brick lay strewn, half-covered in dirt, the *disjecta membra* of a race and an age. A neglected wheel rotted from its hoop, the bent rim rusting red in the sun. Everything was elemental again, subdued to its properties alone, disburdened of use. And I was witness to the inevitable reassertion, reclamation over and above human ambitions, alliances, endeavors, successes, pains, amusements, convictions of importance.

I've heard of a mythic coal village in China, a country township which was abandoned after an ungovernable fire woke in the pits, blazing rampant underground for an area of some fifteen or twenty miles. That village remains abandoned today because the fire still roars. The houses, stables, stores, all stand vacant on that thin crust of earth above the inferno. Geologists say the place will not be livable for another hundred years at least, because the fire is expected to burn that long, gnawing at that immense store of coal.

One can go there and walk among the buildings. It's an unremarkable ghost town—faded and paint-flaked and quiet, even serene—spilling across two or three wild hills. They say you wouldn't suspect that directly beneath you the earth is embroiled in a livid storm of flame, that the crust could give way where you stand and there would be no chance for you, that your earth is an indiscriminate, unembattled thing that does not keep to your law or abide by your sense of scale.

When I went away from Nortonville after those final weeks, I had a potent sense of something like this, though I could not have spoken to it then. Before leaving, I felt that I'd gone out of the town already—ejected somehow. Though all the trappings of the life I knew remained in place in that little house, it was clear I'd gone out of those things. The town too had gone out of the valley, though edifice and façade still stood along Main Street. By extension, I think I could see how that valley would one day go out of that place, as the two ridges were leveled by climate, or brought lunging together by a geologic convulsion, or sent wandering as a chasm slit the crust, or inundated by sea again. Yes, all things pass, shift, lose themselves in the memory of the earth. We already know it to be true: we've known it for millennia. Still, this etiology floods back to us in story after story, pounding the shores of our collective mind.

And yet as I walked from Nortonville up the Somersville Rise and stood alone on that ridge to look down again before going, I think I was struck by an incredible sense of permanence.

I think I saw the valley below as it would be one day: nothing but sliver and nail left of the buildings, a whole history covered in thistle and dirt, the landscape altered almost indistinguishably. And I see now what I understood in a wordless way back then: that it was a place and would always be a place, however mutable. That I would always be in that place for having been there once.

I think maybe this is my plight as an ephemeral creature. In all my temporality, I shed a kind of inexplicable residue at every moment, a substance I would know on looking back despite any alteration, for it's as elemental as nature herself. *Diagenesis* is the term the geologists use. It describes the process of sedimentation—the slow transformation of residue to rock. So my Nortonville is a faint ribbon-like stratum in the multilayered rock. So shall I be. In the meantime, of course, I'm given memory.

I was twenty years old that day I left the Black Diamond Coal Fields. Nortonville was dismantled by weed, tree, grass, and vandal. I have since grown old.

EARTH

SPRING, 1950

MY GREAT-GRANDSON IS TEN. I JUDGE THAT MATURE ENOUGH to take him down into the valley below the old Rose Hill miners' cemetery. His father drives us into the hills and waits in the car while the two of us ramble out into the open greenery.

There are trees everywhere in this basin—cottonwoods and live oaks—and now, in the spring, the meadow is teeming with wildflowers.

We blunder through the high grass and the brambles, making a path for ourselves. We're headed toward the narrow rocky canyon on the western side, up which we'll climb to the mine mouth that I've promised is there, despite the boy's incredulity.

He's impatient at my slowness. I'm still quite limber—and fairly gutsy too—but am nothing to his agility. He'll just have to suffer his eagerness. Only I know the way.

Near the base of the canyon, a big heap of dark rock and dirt swells upward out of the grass. Around it, all the high greenery is stained gray. This seems to surprise the boy—that this tall thing should stand here in this field as it does. He stares at it a while, walking half way around it, climbing up on the slant of it, only to slip in the loose rock and come up all grayed himself. Then he remembers our purpose and goads me to lead him onward.

We range up into the canyon and the thick tree-canopy closes over us. There is the shadow of a path here, amid all the brush and low limbs. I lead him slowly along it. My great-grandson clutches my sleeve now, a bit mystified, maybe, by my progress through what seems to him impenetrable vegetation. He does not complain about my pace anymore. He's just quiet now.

But by the time we've breasted the bank of hill and the mine mouth is clear to him in the hump of earth ahead, he has loosed me again to go running in front. He stands at the dark portal, gazing in, trying to penetrate the blackness. A cool wind rises from inside, fluttering his hair.

I remind him of the flashlights we've brought and he digs excitedly in his knapsack. *Click, click:* we wave the white beams into the adit. The floor near the entrance is covered with leaves. The walls are braced with posts like sawn telephone poles. He turns to me as if unsure whether it is safe. I edge him forward ahead of me.

"Slow now," I say, "don't get ahead of my light." My voice is strange to me in that enclosure, ribbed and croaky.

The boy goes forward, leading me. He's guiding me through his own discovery. This empty adit is his somehow: his imagination already owns it. Not a soul has explored this place as he does now. At his age there is no history, only discovery—fresh, momentary scenes all his own. I won't disrupt that for him. I'll let him lead me.

At the last edge of daylight the boy turns, afraid of the overwhelming darkness farther down. He looks back at me, feigning impatience at my slow following, secretly hoping I won't speak to the fear I see in him.

Still, he gives me his hand to hold tight before that darkness engulfs us.

ACKNOWLEDGMENTS

Foremost, I wish to proclaim my bottomless love for my wife, Katie, who has believed and has made so much possible. For their loving support, I wish to thank the Cunningham family, as well as the entire Alonso and Harvey bunch north and south. Prodigious thanks to Virginia McCarthy, Mary Anne Ferrigan, and Vonnie Cunningham, whose smile shines in my memory. For years of friendship and encouragement, I am grateful to Dan and Jack Small, Jacob Lilja, and Paul DeNola. Thank you to Roy Hagar for early inspiration and instruction, Jill Harcke for constant ebullience and loan of books, Julie Burton for comments on the manuscript in its formative stages, and Cassandra Braun at the *Contra Costa Times*. I thank my agent Judy Heiblum, for her belief, magnanimity, and literary savvy. I'm equally grateful to Sally Wofford-Girand for ideas and support, and I thank all the folks at Brick House who offered their expertise and opinions. Tremendous thanks to Greg Michalson for his readerly enthusiasm and editorial insights. Immense gratitude to Fred Ramey and Caitlin Hamilton. My sincere appreciation to Betty Maffei at the Contra Costa Historical Society for her graciousness in sharing her abundant knowledge of local history as well as her own memories of the Black Diamond region in its later years.

It is important to emphasize that *The Green Age of Asher Witherow* is a work of fiction. Though I've drawn on selected facts from a real era in the history of Contra Costa County, the portraits of characters are fictitious and many details have been manipulated or subordinated in the interest of story or language. Those seeking a regional history would do best to consult the sources mentioned below. The actual Black Diamond Mines are located just south of Antioch, California, are an East Bay Parks regional preserve, and may be visited year-round for hiking. To learn more, visit the East Bay Parks online: www.ebparks.org. Mount Diablo (3,849 feet) is a state park, open year-round to visitors and seasonally to campers.

Many sources were useful to me while writing this novel, chiefly these: *History of Coal Mining in the Mount Diablo Region 1859–1885,* a masters thesis by Margaret Ballard, 1931 (Bancroft Library of the University of California, Berkeley); *The Move of Miners from Nortonville, California to Black Diamond, Washington Territory, 1885,* a senior honors thesis by Jacqueline Byer Dial, 1980 (Contra Costa Central Library); *Coal Mines of the Western Coast of the U.S.* by W. A. Goodyear, 1877; *Mount Diablo Coal Mine Railroads* by B. H. Ward (The Western Railroader, San Mateo, CA, 1972); *A History of Mount Diablo,* a timeline prepared by Seth Adams of Save Mount Diablo (Mount Diablo Review, Fall 2002); the Bay Miwok Exhibit at Diablo Valley College Museum, September 2003; *The East Bay Out* by Malcolm Margolin (Heyday Books, Berkeley, CA, 1988); *Growing up in Coal Country* by Susan Campbell Bartoletti (Houghton Mifflin, 1996); *Coal People: Life in Southern Colorado's Company Towns, 1890–1930* by Rick J. Clyne (Colorado Historical Society, 1999); *The Welsh in America: Letters from the Immigrants* edited by Alan Conway (University of Minnesota Press, 1961); *A Way of Work and a Way of Life; Coal Mining in Thurber, Texas, 1888–1926* by Marilyn D. Rhinehart (Texas A&M University Press, 1992); *Fusang: The Chinese Who Built America* by Stan Steiner (Harper Colophon Books, 1980); *Ovid's Metamorphoses: The Arthur Golding Translation of 1567* edited by John Frederick Nims (Paul Dry Books, 2000).

Some material in this novel is based on information gleaned from articles printed in the *Contra Costa Gazette* and *Antioch Ledger* during the coal-mining era, and for this I utilized the extensive newspaper archives at the Contra Costa Central Library in Pleasant Hill, CA. Thomas and Asher's encounter with the pigs is based on a remembrance of Nortonville by Ellis Griffith, as reported in the *Pittsburg Post-Dispatch* in April 1941.

My line in BONE, beginning "There must be such a place," is a reference to Rainer Maria Rilke's "The Book of Hours," and its particular parlance is inspired by the fine translation of that title, *Rilke's Book of Hours: Love Poems to God* by Anita Barrows and Joanna Macy (Riverhead Books, 1996).

Elsewhere I've used two direct quotes from Rilke's original text: "Though we abandon the depths," and "Nearby is that dominion named life," translations my own.

The Greek poet first mentioned at the beginning of BLOOD is Nikos Kazantzakis, and all references to him derive from his book *The Saviors of God, Spiritual Exercises* (translated by Kimon Friar; Simon & Schuster, 1960) including the conceit of the heart's "sheer bluff" toward the end of BLOOD.